CHAPTER ONE

London, 1881

"Tell me what you want, darling." Victoria pressed hot kisses against his chest, scooting lower and lower with those pouty red lips of hers until her hand cupped his sac and her tongue danced teasingly over his abdomen and toward his half-stiff cock.

Nick Riley wasn't generally a man to complain about being in such a position. "I have some errands to attend to this morning," he said as he fisted his hand in the fall of Victoria's blonde tresses.

When she rotated her tongue around the head of his cock, all his good intentions and morning obligations went out the window. Anything that needed taking care of could be done after that pretty little mouth of hers got his cock off.

Cat-like green eyes stared up at him, all innocent—though that was the last thing Victoria could be called. His hand tangled in her hair, angling her head back. That didn't stop her from flicking out her tongue once more.

Refusing her would be like looking the gift horse in the mouth. While they'd agreed to end their affair last night, that hadn't stopped her from seducing him right back into her bed. Not that he'd tried very hard to dissuade her, so he was just as much at fault for their current position.

And what a perfect position this was.

"Victoria," he growled as her head lowered once again to the prominent protrusion standing very ready between them.

She didn't hesitate to take in the full length of him, practically fucking him with that sweet mouth of hers. His hips thrust off the bed as her mouth drew on him. God, she felt good. She continued to swirl her tongue around him until the first bit of semen emitted from the tip. Sucking that into her mouth, she released him with a pop before she crawled up his body. Her breasts swayed enticingly as her hard nipples stirred the hair on his chest, begging him to say yes.

"I'm just making certain you start the day on the right foot, Nicky. You cannot very well go around with a massive bulge in your trousers. What should the delicate misses think to see you in such a state?" As she spoke, her hand curled around his shaft and stroked it from the base up. "We did agree on an amicable parting, and I find our position perfectly...*amicable.*"

Nick sat up with Victoria poised above him, her legs straddling his hips. The tip of his cock brushed against the damp curls between her thighs. He clasped her waist, stopping her from lowering. There was no way he was getting out of this bed without feeling the tight clasp of her sheath at least once more, but he would be the one in control.

Flipping her onto her back, he slammed into her welcome heat. Her legs curled around his back, her heels digging into

DESIRE ME NOW

TIFFANY CLARE

AVONIMPULSE

An Imprint of HarperCollinsPublishers

Excerpt from *Desire Me More* copyright © 2015 by Tiffany Clare.
Excerpt from *Bad for Me* copyright © 2015 by Codi Gary.
Excerpt from *Wild With You* copyright © 2015 by Sara Jane Stone.
Excerpt from *The Devilish Mr. Danvers* copyright © 2015 by Vivienne Lorret.
Excerpt from *Need Me* copyright © 2015 by Tessa Bailey.

EPub Edition MAY 2015 ISBN: 9780062380432

Print Edition ISBN: 9780062380425

AM 10 9 8 7 6 5 4 3 2

To my sister from another mister.
I couldn't have done this without our
crazy-mad brainstorming sessions.
Love you!

his ass as he took her hard, pounding into her with a ferocity that didn't ebb as her nails bit into his arms, and she screamed his name until her voice was hoarse.

He pumped into her so hard they almost tipped right over the edge of the bed by the time he had emptied himself inside her sweet little cunt. He stayed inside her until she milked every last drop out of him.

Sucking her bottom lip into his mouth, he pulled out and flopped them both back on the bed, with her draped over his chest. They stayed that way long enough to get their breathing under control.

"That didn't feel like you were done with me, Nick." Victoria slipped out of his arms and the bed to retrieve the blue silk robe draped over a chair. Cinching the robe tight around her waist, she stared back at him, expecting him to respond. "I'll draw you a bath before you leave," she said, with just enough annoyance in her voice that he nearly told her to come back to bed.

Instead, he gave her a curt nod as she stood in front of him, her arms crossed over her middle. "Will you stay long enough for breakfast?"

Threading his fingers behind his head, he looked at her. The drape of her robe skimmed off one shoulder, revealing the creamy expanse of her right breast but covering her ruby red nipple from view. There was no sense hiding just where his eyes lingered as he answered her. "Yes."

"After five years, you're just going to walk away from what we have?"

"You knew this wasn't permanent," he said, wishing the damnable material would slip right off her shoulder to give him the view he craved. When she only shrugged, he continued. "What we have is nothing more than a convenience."

"I fail to see anything wrong with that," she replied.

"Everything, for a woman who needs to keep up a pristine reputation for practical and business reasons."

As a prominent businesswoman and successful shopkeeper, Victoria had to remain above reproach if she were to gain the things she craved most…which only a week ago she had said was marriage.

That simply wasn't something that Nick could offer.

She walked away in a huff, throwing the double doors open to the adjoining plunge bath. The rush of water drowned out the silence of the room, and tendrils of steam drifted into the bedchamber, laced with the light scent of rose oil.

"Your bath is ready," Victoria said as she walked back into the bedchamber and sat at her dressing table to brush her hair.

Nick padded across the floor until he stood behind Victoria. Settling his hand on her shoulders, he leaned down and pressed his lips to the top of her head. Even now, his cock stirred as though not sated by their morning interlude.

"You will find someone who can give you the things you want, Vic."

"I don't want a man in my life who will dictate my actions."

He wasn't up for a fight. "Then find someone better than that."

She sighed as she set down the silver brush and slid the slipper chair out from beneath the dressing table. He didn't fail to note that her nipples were pebbled into two perfect peaks beneath her robe. They might be finished with their affair today, but that didn't mean they couldn't feast before he left.

"And what about you?" She tilted her head back to look up at him.

He shrugged and headed into the bathing room. Men like him didn't settle down with a family. His nature was too dark for that kind of life, his past too fucking brutal.

"I'm busy enough without that kind of entanglement," he answered.

Victoria let out a mirthless laugh as she followed behind him. "Seems like a contradictory standard. Because I'm a woman, I should marry and start a family, and you, being a successful businessman, should bury yourself in your work. What of my shop? My employees? Should I hand those over into the care of a husband?"

Once he stepped into the porcelain tub, he turned to her with a frown. "You're more than capable of running things yourself and having the family you told me you wanted."

She merely shook her head and pulled up a wooden chair to the tub. Grabbing a sea sponge that overfilled her hands, she motioned for him to sit with his back to her. She didn't touch the scars that covered most of his back; she just squeezed a hot stream of water over his shoulders and arms.

"So we're to break off our arrangement *amicably*." She dipped the sponge into the water next to his hip. Her hair falling forward stuck to his shoulders. "What will you do when you want to keep your mind off the things that keep you up at night?" Hot water trickled over his chest as she squeezed the sponge again.

"I will manage."

"I don't believe you can truly stay away," she said, soaping up his shoulders, her slender fingers kneading into his tense muscles. "We need each other, even if it's not for the right reasons."

"That is probably the best reason to end our affair."

"I know you better than anyone else."

He couldn't refute that claim, which was to say Vic knew more about him than the average man, aside from Huxley, who could never be described as average.

This topic was not up for debate. He'd made up his mind. Finished talking, he turned and curled his arm around her waist to tug her into the tub. Water sloshed over the edge and splashed on the tiled floor.

She grumbled about her silk robe, but she didn't struggle to get away.

His mouth hovered above hers as he stared into her sultry green eyes. Sometimes he wished he could be the man she needed. For now, they could each be what the other craved in the moment.

"This does not change anything," he said.

"You're an ass," she replied, a second before he slammed his mouth against hers and settled her knees around him. As her fingers threaded through his hair, he plunged into her once again.

CHAPTER TWO

The last thing Amelia Somerset could recall with any clarity was dinner, followed by the hot tea her employer had insisted she drink. The events after that were hazy at best, so she thought hard about the last thing she remembered as her mind slowly awoke.

She'd been enjoying a hearty serving of beef stew in the kitchen quarters with the rest of the household staff when her employer, Sir Ian Hemming, had called her up to his study for his nightly update on his sons' studies.

Sir Ian was a stern man with a strong—if somewhat frightful—bearing. She always stood to attention when in his presence for fear of reprimand on something as small as her posture. She kept her head down and remained diligent in all her duties so he would never have reason to fault her, as he did so many others.

Now...

Now Sir Ian's breath was hot against her ear as he spoke. "Just a dream, Miss Grant. Sleep easy; I shall take care of you."

What did he mean? Was she having a dream?

With her fists clenched tightly against his chest, she lifted her arms with all her might to push him away. But her arms were trapped. She shoved harder, struggling to be free, even though she wasn't quite sure from what she needed to be freed. She blinked back the tiredness that assailed her. When her surroundings finally came into focus, the reality of her situation grew sickeningly clear.

"What have you done to me?" her voice croaked. Her mouth was so dry that her tongue stuck to the sides, making it difficult to talk. Her arms were a dead weight, though that didn't stop her from trying to push him off her.

"Shhh, dovey. Let me take care of you," he said, his finger pressed against her lips. "Relax. I can make it better."

She turned her head away from the heat of his stale breath. Even that proved too hard to do. Her head spun and throbbed with the continued motion, but when she turned away, there was sudden clarity to her situation: She was lying on her lumpy bed with Sir Ian stretched out over her, covering half of her body with his own.

How was he even in her room when she didn't remember getting here on her own?

Her lips trembled in fear and disgust. A cool breeze brushed over her legs where her drawers had been unfastened and pushed out of the way. Sir Ian squeezed her upper thigh with his rough hand, and the pain he caused helped to snap her out of her groggy state, giving her the strength she needed to fight back.

Jabbing her elbow into his cheek, she tried to roll out from under him, but her skirts were trapped beneath his bulk, and her body was sluggish and uncooperative, despite her mind growing more alert by the second.

When he shifted himself between her thighs, she opened her mouth to scream. Sir Ian's hand slapped down, muffling the sound.

"You would not want to wake up the boys, Miss Grant. You be a good girl and hush up."

She bit him as hard as she could, tasting blood as he ripped his hand away. She spat it out, not wanting the foul taste in her mouth.

His hiss of pain wasn't as satisfying as she had hoped. It only angered him further, for he reared his arm back and smacked her hard across her cheek. The force of his blow knocked her head to the side, leaving her dazed and her ears ringing.

Bringing up one knee, she twisted and pushed it between them, trying to squirm out from under him with renewed desperation. His hand tangled in her hair, and he yanked her head back so hard that her neck cracked. She stilled immediately, though nothing could stop the whimpers of fear and pain that slipped past her lips.

He leaned over her helpless form, instilling his dominance, his upper hand. The stench of his whisky-laced breath nauseated her, and her stomach roiled in protest.

"Please," she begged, hating herself for the despair in her voice. But this couldn't be happening to her again.

"Stop your wriggling," he said roughly, his hand tightening in her hair. His other hand squeezed painfully at her breast, causing her to cry out.

She shoved harder against his weight. Sobs tore unwillingly from her throat, and fat tears fell down her face. She didn't want to cry. Sobs amounted to weakness. And weak was the last thing she wanted to be. She had not escaped her past only to surrender to another kind of vile, unacceptable future. She wanted to scream, but her voice was lost to the hopelessness of the moment.

Finally freeing one hand, she scratched the exposed skin above his shirt as hard as she could. The enraged shout that came from him was just loud enough to let others know he was in the staff quarters. She wasn't so naïve as to believe anyone would come to her rescue, as they hadn't already, but the ruckus they surely made might be enough to stop him. At least for tonight.

Sir Ian hauled himself off of her, his body vibrating with a violence that had her cowering.

Show no weakness, she told herself over and over again.

Show. No. Weakness.

Amelia scrambled up and pressed her back hard against the wall to anchor herself. She clenched her hands into fists, prepared to defend herself from further attack.

Be strong.

Sir Ian swiped his hand across his neck where her nails had scored three angry furrows into his pale flesh. She took pride in knowing that a necktie would not easily hide the evidence of her struggle, and it was that thought alone that had her chin jutting forward defiantly and her fists rising marginally.

He looked like a wild man—nostrils flaring like a horse after a hard race, hair disheveled around his face, eyes pinpricked and focused on her.

If she stayed in this house another night, she knew she would pay for her actions. He cracked his knuckles as he flexed his hands. When he tilted his head to the side to give his neck the same sickening pop, she flinched. He continued to stare at her as he wiped the blood from his hand on a handkerchief and dabbed at the nail tracks of blood on his neck.

Amelia didn't move and didn't dare break contact with his emotionless blue eyes.

To her surprise, he turned away, shutting the door softly behind him, as though no one knew he was in her room to begin with.

She exhaled in a rush and slumped forward in relief. Legs numb and shaking, she stretched them out in front of her, letting the pins-and-needles sensation fade.

She needed to get out of this house—and fast. Sliding out of the bed, trying to make as little noise as possible, she knelt on the cold plank floor and pulled out the sack she'd stowed under the bed. Retrieving what clothes she had, she rolled them up tight and stuffed them into the bag.

At the washbasin, she gathered the last bit of soap she'd taken from her home in Berwick and the silver brush that had been her mother's. She had no other possessions, except a small oil painting of her parents in a broken silver locket, given to her on her tenth birthday and torn from her neck during one of her brother's rages on her eighteenth birthday.

Pulling up a loose floorboard, she retrieved her drawstring reticule with the money she'd stolen from her brother. It wasn't a lot of money, but it had been enough to get her to London and pay for lodgings for a month, if she had needed that long to find a job. The money would be put to good use now.

She packed only what she'd come with, as she didn't want her employer accusing her of thievery. Hopefully, if she left quietly,

Sir Ian wouldn't pursue her, as she knew something of the determination of men when they were denied what they wanted.

With her sack tied and slung over one shoulder and her shawl and mantle over her dress to keep her possessions safe, she tiptoed down the servants' stairs and escaped out the back gate near the stable house. The cool air bit at her cheeks, so she quickened her stride, hoping that would keep her warm.

Once she was on the main streets, Amelia kept her head down so no one would see the tears flooding her eyes. It hit her suddenly that she'd left behind her last hope for a decent job.

Had she known how abhorrent her employer was, she'd have turned down the opportunity to teach his children. Sir Ian hadn't wanted a proper governess for his young boys; he'd wanted a mistress living under his own roof. A woman he could visit in the cover of night, when his ill, bedridden wife was none the wiser.

She covered her mouth with her lace-gloved hand, feeling sick to her stomach. All she could do now was go back to the agency that had placed her and hope to find new employment.

Where would she go if they turned her away?

She picked up her stride, even though she'd developed a stitch in her side that made breathing difficult. She had only been in London for three weeks. Not enough time to make friends or learn her way around. She didn't even know where she could find decent, safe lodgings. She supposed there was enough money to put herself on a train and go back home to her brother.

No. Never that.

She refused to lower herself to that type of desperation. She would find another job. In fact, she would demand a new placement from the agency. She was well educated and the daughter of a once-prominent earl, which made her valuable and an asset for any job requiring someone intelligent and capable.

The only problem was that she'd told no one in London of her true identity.

Someone jostled her shoulder, spinning her from the path she walked.

"Pardon, ma'am," he said, grasping her under the arm to right her footing.

Before she could turn and offer her gratitude, he was just another bobbing hat on the street. Reaching for her reticule to pull out her handkerchief, she came up empty-handed.

"That thief!" she shouted, then slapped her hand over her mouth.

Those around her called up the alarm. She pointed in the direction she was sure the thief had gone, but there wasn't a suspicious soul to be seen.

Amelia started pushing through the crowded street, apologizing along the way when she knocked into a few pedestrians. She grew frantic and inhaled in great gulps, trying to get air into her lungs and to keep at bay the panic that was threatening to rob her of her ability to think rationally.

Eventually, her feet slowed as the cramping in her side worsened. She could barely see beyond the tears falling from her eyes. Her face was damp, and she had nothing to wipe it clean except the sleeve of her day dress. She was unfit to go to the agency, but what other choice did she have?

Despair robbed her of the last of her breath, and she was forced to stop her pursuit.

Bracing one arm against an old stone building, she breathed in and out until she was calm. The last of her tears had dried on her face and made her cheeks stiff.

She should give up, crawl back to her brother, and beg for his eternal forgiveness. There were few viable choices left to her. She couldn't stay out in the streets. Awful things happened to women who had no place to go. Things far worse than what she had escaped, though in a moment of clarity, she might refute that statement.

Walking around to the side of the building where she'd stopped, she threw up the dinner she'd eaten the previous night. Feeling dizzy and unwell, she drew on the last of her courage, straightened her shoulders, and somehow found the strength to continue walking.

She needed to find new employment and accommodations without delay. The agency had been a room full of women; they would understand the situation she'd found herself in. They would help her.

Light-headed, she walked toward Fleet Street where the agency was tucked neatly behind a printing house. While the day had started rather dreary and dull in so many senses, the odd peek of sunshine cut through the coal-heavy air and pressed against her face. The sun warming her skin gave her a glimmer of optimism.

When the sun disappeared behind the clouds again, she focused on her surroundings and caught sight of a group of urchins, recognizing the tallest of the bunch immediately.

"You little swindler. Give me back what is mine," she cried out loud and clear.

The boy, who had been counting the contents in her reticule, pocketed her money and took off at a full run. His pace was quick and light-footed, and she was sure he took one step to her three, though she still tried to catch up to him.

Shaken, with a cramp in her side and the dizzy feeling growing worse through her body, Amelia refused to give in. When the urchin dodged across a street heavy with traffic, she knew there was no time for hesitation. She needed that money back.

Before she made it halfway across the road, the urchin was lost among the carts. Tears welled in her eyes again, blurring her vision. Someone yelled for her to get off the road; someone else emphasized his point with obscenities she didn't fully comprehend.

Though nearly to the other side, she didn't move quite fast enough for the two-seat open carriage clipping down the street much more swiftly than the other carts.

"Move, you bloody fool," the driver bellowed.

His speeding horses, black as pitch, headed toward her like the devil on her heels. She hiked up her skirts and ran but tripped over the stone curb and tumbled hard to her knees, twisting her foot on the way down. The pain of the impact caused black spots to dot across her vision. As she tried to gain her footing, she collapsed back onto her bruised, pained knees and cried.

A strong arm supported her under her elbow and hauled her to her feet, but it was apparent to them both that she couldn't stand on her own. When the stranger knelt before her, all she saw was his tall beaver hat as he put one arm around her back and shoulders and the other under her legs.

That was all the warning he gave before he lifted her into his arms and walked up the lawn as if she weighed nothing.

"Thank you," she said weakly, her heated face pressed into his finely made wool jacket. His cologne was subtle and masculine with undertones of amber and citrus. She inhaled the scent deeper, wanting that comforting smell to wrap around her, wishing it would let her forget just how her day had unfolded.

Instead of releasing her when they were away from the road, he continued walking up the slight incline of the grassy field. A flush washed over her face as she stuttered for words of admonishment that anyone might see this gentleman carrying a poor, injured woman in his arms. She didn't actually want him to put her down, but common decency demanded it of her.

Gazing at the face under his well-made top hat stopped any further protestations. She dropped her gaze and stared at his striped necktie tucked neatly into a charcoal vest.

"You need not carry me. I can find my way," she said, but her request lacked any conviction.

The sun shone through the clouds once more, shining directly in her eyes and allowing her to pull away from the power that radiated from his gaze.

His short, close-clipped beard emphasized the strong line of his jaw. Black hair fanned out a little under his hat, longer than fashionable, but suiting to the rough edge this man carried.

She could tell that his mouth, though pinched, was full, the bow on top well defined. The type of lips young ladies tittered and wrote poems about.

"I just witnessed you hike up your skirts well past your shins to run across one of the busiest streets in London." His voice was gruff, with a sensual quality that warmed her right to the very core.

Just as she thought her blush couldn't get worse, she felt her ears burning from the blunt observation of what he'd witnessed.

Amelia cleared her throat, realizing she'd been staring at him too long. "I am sorry you had to witness that."

He settled her down on a slated wood bench under the shade of an ancient burled oak tree. "It's arguable that you did that in a careful manner," he said.

The gentleman removed his leather gloves, set them on the bench beside her, and went down on his knees to stretch out her foot to look at the injury she'd done herself.

She tucked her feet under the bench, away from his searching hands. They were in the open, and anyone could see his familiarity. "I only need to rest a minute. I wish I could repay you for your troubles, but I have nothing of value…"

When he looked at her—really looked at her—she was struck speechless by the sincerity of his regard. His eyes were gray like flint and as hard as steel. *Unusual and beautiful*, she thought. But it wasn't the color that had her at a loss for words. It was the intensity behind his gaze that made her feel that she was the only person in the world he was focused on; almost like nothing but the two of them existed on this tiny patch of grass in the middle of the bustling city.

This perfect man before her, who clearly didn't have to worry about putting a roof over his head or bread on the table, held a maelstrom of emotions in his cool, assessing gaze. She trusted what she saw in his eyes, trusted a man for the first time in she didn't know how long.

She wanted to reach toward his face but grasped the edge of the bench tightly instead.

Just how dire her situation was hit her so hard, she swayed where she sat. Her money was gone, her only picture of her parents taken with it.

And then she cried.

She didn't mean to. She didn't even think she had the energy left for such an outpouring. But she couldn't stop now that the dam had broken on her emotions. Histrionics didn't seem to put her rescuer off, because he only huffed a helpless breath and waited for her to calm herself, which she tried to do in great gulping breaths.

"Let me get you to a doctor." His voice was deep and commanding. He would never have to raise his voice to draw the attention of those around him. It was the kind of voice to which one was naturally drawn, and it stirred something deep inside her.

She shook her head at his offer.

She needed to loosen whatever spell he had over her.

She felt the command of his stare but did not turn her face up to his again.

"Let me see you to a doctor to ensure it is nothing more than a turned ankle," he offered, his voice full of sincerity.

She shook her head again. She tried to explain about the agency, but none of what she said came out coherently, and her tears fell harder.

Before she could attempt saying anything more, her rescuer lifted her in his arms once again and strode toward the street.

Chapter Three

Bloody women. Why did they have to cry?

Nick called a carriage over to the curb, the inconsolable woman tucked tightly against his chest. Her sobs calmed only slightly after what felt like forever. He couldn't complain about holding on to her, though; she had curves in all the right places, and his hand squeezed a little tighter than needed around her ribs. He was an ass, but she felt good in his arms.

He was almost reluctant to slide her into the seat but must needs...

Had this woman not had an uncanny resemblance to someone he'd known a long time ago, he might not have been so quick to cart her back to his home. He'd seen her by chance as he walked through the park. Then, she'd dashed through the traffic, giving him pause and causing him to think that she was headed in his direction. His heart had practically fallen out of his chest when she'd stumbled into the path of a moving carriage. And before he knew it, he was hauling her to her feet, looking her over for injury.

With a knock at the side of the carriage, the horse pulled forward, easing into the busy street with well-practiced precision. Soon, they were clipping at a pace in stride with the rest of the carriages and carts. The inside of the cab smelled musty, with a faint trace of tobacco smoke, and while the odor didn't bother him, the woman across from him wrinkled her nose. He opened the window a smidgen to allow fresh air in.

Twisting around on the worn leather seat, she looked out the window, wiping the tears away from her swollen eyes. Even while she cried, she was pretty.

"Allow me to introduce myself." He took off his hat and tipped it toward her. "Nicholas Riley, though everyone calls me Nick."

"Miss Som—" When her voice caught on another sob, he handed her a handkerchief from his vest pocket. Her fingers brushed against his. It took everything he had in him not to hold on and pull her over to the bench he sat on.

"Thank you." She blew her nose. "Miss Grant. Amelia Grant."

"Well, it's a pleasure, though I would have preferred introductions under better circumstances. I will have my physician assess your injury when we are back at my townhouse."

"You're far too kind and need not go to the trouble." When she looked at him, he could tell she was out of her element, lost. A look he was familiar with. "I have an appointment I cannot be late for. You may drop me off wherever is convenient for you so I can be on my way."

Tenacious. He did love that quality in a woman.

But he would not give her what she wanted. When he'd inspected her in the park, he had also noticed how delicate she was. She was half a foot shorter than he was, which made her taller than average for a woman. But her frame was slight, beneath the ill-fitting plain dress she wore.

"Your accent is not typical of a Londoner," he said, knowing full well he was ignoring her request.

Wisps of her hair that had escaped the tight chignon at the base of her hat revealed the color as a sun-kissed brown. A becoming color next to her fair skin tone, though the bruise on her cheek stood out in stark contrast.

"I lived in northern England most of my life." She tucked the stray tendril of hair behind her ear.

"How did a country girl end up in London instead of married with a brood of her own?"

Miss Grant didn't seem taken aback by his blunt question and kept her stormy blue eyes steady on him, though he did notice her curling and twisting the handkerchief between her fingers. Did he make her nervous?

"You are rather direct, Mr. Riley."

"A forward approach tends to garner truer words," he said honestly.

"When my father died, there wasn't much left of his estate. There are few marriages open to a woman of gentle breeding when there are no coffers to cushion the failing estates across England. And there are even fewer jobs available for a young woman. I came here to teach." She screwed up her nose. "Which seemed logical at the time, considering my education."

Made sense to him. "How long have you been in London?"

"Nearly a month."

When they hit a rut in the road, Miss Grant let out a sound filled with pain as the motion jarred her bad foot. Nick wanted to haul her into his arms and comfort her. That would only frighten her, he realized, so he settled for the next best thing, because, dammit, he wanted to touch her.

"Here," Nick said, hiking up her skirts before she realized his intention.

Panicked, she tried to push his hands away, which only confirmed the source of the bruise darkening by the minute on her cheek. He ground his teeth together. The bastard who had done that would pay dearly.

He gentled his voice, not wanting to frighten her any further. "You need to elevate your foot. To alleviate the swelling."

Pressing himself against the far right of the carriage, he motioned to the vacated side of his seat, hoping she'd humor him in raising her foot herself; otherwise, he'd have to insist.

"The carriage is enough to satisfy any momentary pain I'm feeling." The defiance in her voice only added to the strong vibrancy of her character. He wasn't a man who often gave in to emotion—it revealed weaknesses to those around him—but he wanted to smile at her stubbornness.

He *liked* Miss Grant. Perhaps more than he should have, considering how little he knew about her.

This time when he lowered his hands, he didn't try to lift the soiled hem of her skirts out of the way. He grasped her booted foot, raised it carefully, and perched it on the bench next to his thigh. The motion forced her to focus on balancing herself instead of pushing him away.

"We should arrive at my house shortly."

"I was telling the truth about my appointment."

"And what could be more important than seeing to your well-being? I can send a note along if you tell me where you were headed."

She pinched her lips together, contemplating her answer. "To an employment agency."

"Your teaching job did not work out?" He searched her eyes, knowing full well that the bruise could only have come from her last job.

She looked away from him, confirming his suspicions. His hands curled into fists so tight that his knuckles cracked on one hand. When Miss Grant flinched, he forced himself to relax.

Finally, they pulled up to the front of his townhouse. Opening the door, he stepped out of the carriage and tossed the fare up to the driver. Reaching inside, he gathered Miss Grant in his arms. He told himself it was because she shouldn't walk, but he knew damn well it was because he needed to feel her in his arms again.

As he approached the stairs, his man of all affairs, Huxley, opened the front door. If he was astonished to see a woman in Nick's arms, Huxley didn't give it away with any sort of facial expression; it was as if it were business as usual.

Many might guess Huxley to be in his midthirties, judging from the lack of wrinkles on his clean-shaven, pock-marked face, but Nick knew the man was close to fifty. Huxley was discreet and never gave an opinion when outside of Nick's company. Though he doubled as Nick's valet, they had a much darker, intertwined past, one that had first overlapped some fifteen years ago. Huxley's loyalty was unwavering, and Nick trusted him implicitly.

"Huxley," he said as the door closed behind him. "This is Miss Amelia Grant. Conveniently, I found her on my way home, and she is in need of employment. She will be our new secretary. Would you call my physician to the house? By appearances, she has sprained her ankle but the doctor will need to confirm."

Some might question Nick's sanity for taking a woman on for such a task, but his mind was made on the matter. Nick held tighter to his prize when Amelia wiggled to be put down. Walking past Huxley, who left to do Nick's bidding with no more than a grunt, Nick headed toward the parlor.

He approached the oversized yellow-and-pink floral-patterned sofa; he was reluctant to release her, but he ceded to better judgment and set her down as carefully as possible. She pressed her back to the farthest cushion from him and stared at him with furrowed brows.

"I cannot be your secretary, Mr. Riley."

"Oh, but you will be. It's a generous offer, and I have no ulterior motives." Which was a lie, but the one thing he wouldn't do was hurt her. He motioned toward her cheek. "You will not find that kind of treatment in this household."

She touched it fleetingly before tucking her hand away and sitting up straighter to face him, though she fiddled with a crease at the front of her dress.

While the dress had seen better days, it was well-made and only tattered and stained around the edges. He wanted to see her in silk and taffeta, not the stormy gray material that draped her unbecomingly.

"We never agreed to terms," she said.

"If you think I offer this generosity to every woman who falls in my path, you are mistaken. The offer was not for your sole benefit; I am in need of a secretary. My paperwork has been in shambles for months, and the applicants who have come to me were nothing but buffoons. I see you, Miss Grant, and I see an honest woman."

She blushed, the red a becoming color on her cheeks. "I have no experience in being a secretary."

Perhaps not, but she was in need of a protector. Needing to see if there was any other damage to her, he freed the pin that held her hat in place. She tucked loose bits of her hair back into the chignon. The bruise darkening her cheek and the cut under her lip were the only visible signs of a recent struggle. He silently vowed to find the man responsible.

"Can you write correspondences and organize invitations and responses?" he asked.

She nodded.

"Huxley, the man we passed in the hallway, will settle you in and explain anything you need to know about my affairs."

"Is he leaving the position?" she asked.

"Huxley's time is better used elsewhere."

"Why would you want to hire me without references?"

A valid question. He couldn't tell her that from the moment he saw her, he knew that he had to have her. There was that and the fact that he had a penchant for bringing in strays. Though he didn't think she'd appreciate either answer. "I will obtain the references you submitted for your last job. I assume you were placed through Everett's agency for young women."

Her eyes narrowed suspiciously. "How could you possibly know that?"

"That is the closest agency in the area where we came upon each other." It had also once been his agency, before he'd handed the reins over to one of his mother's friends.

She lowered her gaze and stared at her lap with a defeated slouch curving her shoulders. He wanted to wrap his arms around her, tell her that the bruise on her cheek was a thing of the past, and that he would never harm her. If there was one thing he could promise her, it was that she would be safe in his household.

But would she be safe from him?

He wanted her with a fierceness that crossed the line of decency.

He would scrutinize both those thoughts later.

Amelia hated to admit anything to her perfect stranger, but he'd find out sooner or later. And if he was willing to give her a chance at a job, how could she not be honest? "The agency may not provide references, as I left my last job without notice."

"Leave it to me to sort out the finer details, Miss Grant."

Before she could refuse him again, Huxley entered the room, announcing, "The doctor will arrive within the half hour."

Mr. Riley nodded his thanks and retrieved a tasseled velvet stool from under the window. "Once we're finished with the doctor, Huxley, I should like you to show Miss Grant where she'll be working—a tour of the house will have to wait until she is steady on her feet. She also will require a key to my study."

If Huxley thought his employer insane for allowing a woman they knew nothing about to handle Mr. Riley's day-to-day affairs, he said nothing. She wondered if they would discuss the matter when she wasn't privy to the conversation.

"Miss"—Huxley addressed her with a curt tip of his head—"You'll want refreshments, so I'll locate Joshua." Without further ado, Huxley left the room. Focusing on Mr. Riley's intent stare, Amelia wasn't sure how she felt about being alone with him.

Mr. Riley placed the stool in front of her. Before he could assist, she lifted her leg and settled her skirts around her so she wasn't revealing anything but the edge of her short leather boot. He took a seat across from her and slung his arm over the back of the ivory-colored Louis chair. She flitted her gaze away from his, unable to stand up to the scrutiny behind those assessing grays.

"Aside from teaching children, what other skills do you possess?" he asked.

She studied him for a few moments before answering. "How can you even consider taking on someone who, up until now, has been more or less an encumbrance?"

"It is possible we view a burden as two separate things."

"I doubt my skills would be useful to you. While I know how to run a household, put menus together for dinner parties, and teach children a number of topics that include the rudiments of mathematics, biology, geography, Latin, dance, and piano, I haven't the slightest idea what would be required of a secretary."

"Women often downplay the true extent of their abilities. Running a household is not as easy a task as you would have me believe. I know this for fact, as I struggled through it with Huxley for a number of years until we hired Marney, the housekeeper."

Her mouth opened to argue her point, but a man carrying a large brown leather bag rushed into the room.

"Mr. Riley," the newcomer said, slightly out of breath. "Huxley sent for me. He said it was urgent."

Mr. Riley stood, motioning toward Amelia. "Miss Grant has taken a fall and twisted her ankle."

The doctor knelt next to the stool her foot was perched upon. "May I?" he asked, motioning toward her booted foot.

She nodded and curled her fingers around the piped edge of the sofa. The doctor hesitated as he searched through his accouterments, pulling out scissors and then deciding against them. Instead, he unlaced her boot, careful not to move her foot in the process.

Sucking in a pained breath, Amelia couldn't help but wince as her boot was tugged off. The pinch of pain lasted only a moment.

Mr. Riley took a step toward her, as if he would stop the doctor. She watched Mr. Riley cautiously. What was he about? This time, she intentionally tried to catch his gaze, but before she could garner his attention, he turned and strode out of the room.

Amelia breathed easier the moment Mr. Riley left her in the care of the doctor. Something about Mr. Riley's presence made her feel things she'd never felt before—foreign things that had her blushing as images of him holding her close in his arms flashed across her mind. She'd been raised a lady and had respected that upbringing. What she felt for this man crossed every boundary of propriety that her father had instilled in her.

With a shaky breath that had nothing to do with the swelling pain in her ankle and everything to do with Mr. Riley, she looked at the doctor, needing to focus on something else.

Anything else.

She guessed the doctor's age was around forty. His face was clean shaven and his black suit decently pressed. There were crow's feet at the corners of his eyes, as though he often found reason for laughter. The kindness she saw there put her at ease in her strange new surroundings.

The room was grander than any in her childhood home—the ceilings had to be twenty feet high, making the room bright and airy. Above each of the lead-paned windows, decorative stained glass was fashioned into the shape of a fan. The walls were papered with a deep burgundy damask, and the furniture—two sofas and a chair in her seating section—were a mix of ivory chintz and floral patterns to balance the dark walls and wood trim. It was a richly appointed room. Every detail looked carefully selected, and nothing looked neglected, not even the curtains. In the house where she'd grown up, the curtains had been filled with holes from moths over the years.

"It does not appear as though anything is broken," the doctor said, drawing her attention away from her surroundings and back to his kind brown eyes. "May I ask how you hurt it?"

She bit her lip. It was embarrassing to admit what happened, so she opted for a much shorter version of the truth.

"In my haste to cross a busy street this morning, I managed to trip over the curb separating the lane and the park. My ankle twisted when I fell."

He looked at her silently, assessing her injuries. She knew her lip had a split at one corner; she felt the constant sting, especially when she talked. Mr. Riley had confirmed that Sir Ian was successful in bruising her where he had struck her.

"You will need to stay off your foot for a few days, preferably a week if you can spare the time."

She needed to work, not laze about like an indulgent cat. "Is there not a salve I can use to heal it quicker? What if I wrap it so I can better support my weight?"

"I'm afraid neither will be sufficient. You need rest to bring down the swelling, and time will heal the rest."

She looked away from the doctor, her vision blurring. She hated the tears that filled her eyes at her predicament. She was stronger than this. "I'm not in a position to do any such thing," she said, hearing the break in her voice.

"You most certainly are." Mr. Riley spoke from the door, startling her. The tone of his voice was commanding and brooked no argument. "You will sit at a desk to deal with my correspondence over the next week, if that's how long it takes to heal."

"I could..." She wasn't sure what she could do. And this was not a conversation or argument for the kind doctor to hear. She would deal with Mr. Riley in due time. She ducked her head. "Thank you for coming to see me on such short notice, Doctor. I am grateful for your services."

"I am always available when Mr. Riley calls." He packed up his bag, stood, and bowed to Amelia. His smile was warm as he placed his hat on his head. "Call for me again if it worsens, though I think you're in good hands now."

She nodded, not sure how to respond to the doctor's assurance of Mr. Riley's character.

Mr. Riley spoke with the doctor before he left. They were too quiet for Amelia to overhear what they discussed before the doctor shook Mr. Riley's hand and left.

Silence descended upon the room when she was left alone with her rescuer. She understood cruelty, unkindness. She understood the demands of men bent on humiliating her. Any of those things she could easily skirt around and make an escape for the nearest exit. But Mr. Riley bewildered her on so many levels that she was at a loss in determining her next step. He was kind, and he seemed genuinely interested in helping her.

Still, she couldn't help but wonder: *Why me?*

CHAPTER FOUR

There was an awkward moment of silence as Amelia stared at Mr. Riley. She wished she knew what he was about. Wished she could grasp the fundamental nuances of his character so she could understand his determination to hire her as his secretary. What could she possibly offer him that an experienced secretary could not? Right now, she had no references for her character or ability. Touching her tongue to the tender part of her split lip, she assumed her appearance suggested that her background was dubious at best. That wasn't to say she couldn't learn exactly what the role entailed, but she had not escaped the clasp of one devil to find herself in another kind of hell.

Mr. Riley revealed something in his hand as he walked toward her. She eyed him suspiciously. He handed her a small glass pot with an amber-colored salve inside. Kneeling in front of her, he scooped some of the salve onto his fingers and reached for her face. When she flinched from his outstretched hand, he said, "It will help lighten the bruise that's setting in on your cheek."

"Yes, of course," she replied and held still for his ministrations. She felt suddenly shy and vulnerable. Those were weaknesses she needed to guard against. She must remain strong.

Mr. Riley's fingers were warm and callused, and he was methodical but gentle in applying the strong-smelling concoction.

"You said you were released from your duties," he said offhandedly. "Might I ask whom you worked for?" There was a hint of danger to his question.

"It does not matter." She never wanted to think of Sir Ian again, or what he'd almost done.

The look in Mr. Riley's eyes said he definitely thought it mattered, but he didn't ask again.

Amelia leaned over to put her boot back on. Embarrassment had her ducking her face in a poor attempt to hide the bruise. She couldn't stay in this house, and she had to find a way to pay Mr. Riley for the doctor's visit.

"What do you think you're doing?" His question was sharp, almost angry.

"I am beyond grateful for your kindness, but I cannot be an imposition to you further. I have to go back to the employment agency before they close at the lunch hour."

"There is no need. I have sent them a note to advise them of your new situation."

Her fingers frozen midtie on her laces, Amelia opened her mouth to protest but then closed it again. What could she say? He was domineering and had no right to make any such decision for her. Yet…yet he'd been there for her when she needed help most. And she hated to admit it, but she was indebted to him, as she had no means to pay him back for his assistance or for the doctor's services.

Amelia blinked against the tears forming in her eyes. She didn't like this feeling of helplessness. She hated that she had no control over her situation. "Why are you being so kind when you don't know if I am even capable of the task?"

"It is interesting that we met, when we both require something of the other."

"That is not explanation enough. I have already told you that I do not know the first thing about being a secretary."

She saw nothing but kindness radiating from his eyes. And she wanted to trust him on this, because he seemed concerned about her welfare, if his insistence that she stay was proof of that. But she wasn't sure she could trust him.

"We will have to educate each other along the way," he said, "as I haven't any idea what I require yet from someone whose sole purpose is served as a secretary. Huxley is my man of all affairs, but some of his tasks need to be alleviated. I have entertained the idea of a secretary for some months and I believe you'll be perfect for the job. You can start with my neglected correspondence and learn how to keep my schedule."

"I—"

He shook his head. "No more objections. I will have a warm lunch brought up to chase away the morning chill and then turn you over to Huxley to review some of your duties."

Amelia pinched her lips tightly together and stared at Mr. Riley. He was so sure of himself, so sure she'd do exactly as he bid. But what right did she have to refuse the very thing that would save her from a far worse fate than working for this man? And she hated to admit that his concern for her being warm and well fed broke through the careful guard she had erected when around men.

Then something occurred to her. Something she should have thought of sooner. What if he wanted the same thing that Sir Ian had wanted? Her heart lurched painfully in her chest with that realization. Something in her expression must have given away her thoughts, because Mr. Riley's focus on her was as sharp and intense as ever. He reached for the bruise on her cheek, where he'd rubbed in the salve moments go. His touch was light, and she wanted to turn her cheek into his palm.

That wasn't right. She shook off the thought.

"You have no reason to fear me, Amelia." The use of her Christian name caused a flutter of butterflies in her stomach. She took a shaky breath and pulled away from the comfort of his touch.

"I believe you," she admitted, meeting his penetrating gaze, knowing that none of this felt right. Why did she believe him? Was it because she was at the end of her tolerance for bad luck today?

"Lunch will be served in here," he announced before standing and leaving her abruptly. Had he left so quickly so she couldn't refuse his offer again?

Taking a steadying breath, Amelia pushed to her feet and made a tentative step with her injured foot. The pain that shot up her calf was nearly debilitating, but she soldiered on, refusing to give in. And it was the pain in her ankle that decided her course. She had no money; her face was bruised, making her unfit to be under public scrutiny; and she hated to admit, but until she could walk without feeling like she'd throw up, she was stuck in the care of Mr. Riley.

If there was one thing to come of the day thus far, it was that Miss Grant would be more trouble than he might be willing to handle at present. Well, not precisely. It was more a matter that she caused him a great deal of moral grief.

He wanted her. But part of that wanting was to protect her from the look of weariness that clouded her eyes. He knew that look, had seen it in his own mother's eyes. Not willing to delve too far into his past, Nick busied himself with reviewing the ledgers of his shipping company.

Someone, somewhere, was dipping his fingers where he had no right. And while Nick might consider himself a fair employer, he supposed there were always those who wanted more than their entitled share. Studying the ledger Huxley had prepared over the last six months, the wool weights from origin to final docking in London were anywhere from 10 to 20 percent off. So where in hell were the items being fenced?

He leaned back in his chair, no longer needing the evidence in front of him. He'd been right all along. His business partner and friend, Landon, had been the one to notice, since the wool was coming from his farm in northern Scotland.

Huxley joined him in his study, perching himself on the arm of the leather chair facing Nick's desk. "We going to weed out the accomplices?" he asked.

"Yes but carefully. This affects our partners too, not just my shares in the sales."

"I have my eyes on the wharfinger. The man always had an untrustworthy face."

"Even if it is him, we need to know where he's selling the goods before we have him charged with theft."

Huxley crossed his arms over his chest and gave Nick a level stare. "On to other topics, then. Miss Grant's a scrap of a woman. Could use a few good meals to fill her out some."

Huxley was fishing for information. And damned if Nick had answers. He couldn't explain why he'd offered her a job; he'd just known he didn't want to let her go.

"That should not be a problem once Joshua sets eyes on her." Nick flipped through his appointment calendar, not wanting to discuss Miss Grant with anyone. It was bad enough he couldn't stop thinking about her.

"You're going to pluck her off the street when you know nothing about her? Take her under your roof, when she could steal off with half the house's silver come morning?"

Nick almost chuckled at the absurdity of the comment. "I'm not concerned she will steal off with anything."

Except perhaps his sanity. Women never held sway over him, yet Miss Grant did just that with her air of innocence and her stubborn manner. Without doubt, the best thing he could do to preserve that innocence would be to set her free. But to what fate? He could protect her while she was in his house and ensure that the mark on her cheek was a thing of the past. Really, he was unwilling to share her with the rest of the world.

"She is not up for debate, Huxley. She will remain as my secretary."

Huxley stood and jammed his hands into his pockets. "What do you want me to show her?"

"Any and all the tasks you don't have time for. You can start with the invitations and the appointment book. Make sure she's familiar with my business associates. When she is better able to walk, she will attend meetings with me."

Huxley gave one succinct nod and turned to leave Nick's study without further objection.

Nick sure as hell hoped he knew what he was doing by offering a position to Miss Grant.

Sitting at his desk, he penned a note to the employment agency, which he had lied about in order to keep Miss Grant here. He let the agency know that he had stolen one Amelia Grant into his employ. In closing, he requested a list of the houses she had previously served in. They'd think he was interested in recommendations, but really, he wanted to sort out who had dared to raise a hand against her.

Trusting Huxley would settle in his new secretary, he left his letter with the kitchen boy for delivery. Pulling on his coat and straightening his cuffs, he left through the back exit of the house so he was less tempted to stop in on Miss Grant.

Amelia made it to the window seat just as Mr. Huxley came into the room with a tray. Setting the silver dish on a side table close to her, he scrutinized her from head to toe. His gaze was not possessive, like Mr. Riley's; she had the feeling he was measuring her ability and worth.

"I'll show you to the study once you've eaten," Huxley said.

Instead of leaving her with the tray of food—eggs, sausages, and potatoes—he watched her eat from where he leaned against the doorframe. His bearing was intimidating, his size compact but sturdy. His face was pockmarked, and he wore a permanent scowl that had her shifting constantly in her seat.

She picked at her food, unable to stomach anything when Huxley was staring at her so coldly, giving her the impression that he disliked and didn't precisely trust the newcomer in his house. Not that she could blame him for such a notion. She still wasn't quite sure how she felt about being here but had resigned herself to staying for at least a few days.

"If you would be so kind as to sit with me, I will eat much faster and let you get on with your duties," she suggested, hoping he might let his guard down a little so she could gain his trust at the very least. If her last job had taught her anything, it was that she needed to make more friends. Had she done so, maybe…

She closed the door on the *what ifs*. It was in the past. She was safe now…wasn't she?

"I'll wait here, if you don't mind."

She placed her napkin on the table and turned toward Huxley. "I do mind, in fact. I feel as though you're waiting for me to falter. Or to make a mistake I cannot possibly know I'm making. It is not so hard to guess that you like my presence here as much as you would like a toothache."

Instead of the scowl she expected, her comment seemed to earn her a smile. What a strange man Mr. Huxley was.

"You can tell a lot by the way someone eats," he said, but he walked into the room and sat on the sofa she'd vacated after the doctor's visit, which was close enough to acceptance for her.

Placing her napkin back in her lap, she continued to eat. "How exactly would one make out a person's character by the way she eats?"

"I can tell you've never had to fend for yourself, even though, by the looks of you, you're a few meals short of content. Though I suspect there was never a missed meal not so long ago and at a proper table."

Amelia swallowed her half-chewed eggs and set the fork down on the side of the plate. "You can tell this, how?"

Huxley crossed his arms over his chest and leaned back into the sofa. He gave nothing away in his expression. Was he trying to intimidate her? If he was, it wasn't working. She raised her eyebrows with indifference.

"Grew up in a small house with seven brothers," he went on. "Nothing like fighting over a ration of one loaf of bread meant to last a week, sometimes two."

"I see." She looked back at her dish, lifted it, and held it out to Huxley. He grabbed a sausage and chomped into it with exaggerated vigor and a smile that held no laughter.

She cut a piece of the sausage for herself and nibbled it delicately. "You are right about the proper table. But it was a poor table, and there was not always enough to go around."

There was no harm in revealing that much to this man. She would have to work with him, and they might as well get along so their days were enjoyable. She finished the remainder of her meal—even though it was far too much food—because she didn't want Huxley to find her wasteful.

Once finished, they walked slowly to the study, and he showed her the appointment book and where the mail and invitations were stored. Mr. Riley was nowhere in sight. They didn't look at the appointments in any great length but went over the engagements that would keep Mr. Riley away from the house for a few days. Huxley had her write out a list of tasks she would be responsible for in the coming days.

"Does it worry you that I'm here without references, Mr. Huxley?"

"It's just Huxley." He gave her a long look that dared her to be formal again. "As long as I don't find you stealing off with the silver or trying to climb into Mr. Riley's bed to further your position, I think we'll get on just fine."

She opened her mouth and closed it. Shock didn't even describe how she felt, and her face flamed at the insinuation. Did he think her that type of woman?

Not sure what to say, she cleared her throat and changed the topic. "How many businesses does Mr. Riley own?"

"Never enough, by his estimation."

"That is not really an answer."

"S'pose it is not." Still, he didn't elaborate.

"How does Mr. Riley generally spend his time, day to day?"

"Out and about, here and there. Once you get a handle on his schedule you'll have a better understanding of his business ventures."

Amelia spent the day familiarizing herself with names: peers, merchants, and business owners—all those who shared interests with Mr. Riley.

It was impossible to get a good sense of what exactly he did, as his business ventures varied. He owned a bank and a theatre outright. He owned large lots of land. Some were located next to the docks and used for storage and warehouses; others held residents in the east end of the city. He owned shares in shipping companies and railroads. It was as though he were amassing as much wealth as he possibly could.

Curious about so many things, Amelia couldn't stay quiet forever. "Mr. Riley has interests everywhere. Has he always been a businessman with so many tastes?"

"Not always," was all Huxley said.

Not quite satisfied with his response, she pushed for more information. "How long have you known him?"

"Since he was nothing more than a scrap of a boy. If you want more answers, you should ask him your questions directly."

Because it was her first night, and Huxley insisted on her learning more about her new job, they didn't go down to the dining hall. Instead, Huxley left her for a quarter hour and returned with two steaming bowls of lamb stew with hunks of bread, which they enjoyed in silence.

There were a thousand and one questions going through Amelia's mind about Mr. Riley, and she vowed to find the answer to each and every one of them. But her questions could wait for another day.

It was hard to believe that she'd found a position so easily, and she would remain vigilant while completing her duties. It all seemed too easy, though.

While she was thankful to have a roof over her head and a bed to sleep in for the night, she would wait for the other shoe to drop.

CHAPTER FIVE

Amelia woke bright and early the next morning, so she could limp her way around the house without someone at her elbow, guiding the way. She wanted to see it with her own eyes, learn every nuance, and discover everything beautiful and everything hidden and ugly about the house.

Sleep hadn't come easily, despite her being exhausted from all that had happened. And while she hadn't seen Mr. Riley again last evening, her curious imagination had invented a hundred different impressions of him through the long night, none of which she wanted to rehash, for most made her blush furiously. And why should she think any of those things about him? He could still be the wolf wearing sheepskin to hide his true nature.

Yesterday, she'd been far too drained after dinner to do more than sit at the secretary desk, read through the appointment book, and review one of the many stacks of invitations that had been tossed into piles as high as the length of her arm. Huxley had remained with her, so she couldn't snoop around the study to see what secrets her new employer might be hiding.

All she had learned about Mr. Riley was that he was a very busy man and that he received more invitations to gatherings than was possible for one person to attend. After two hours of reviewing invitations and penning responses last evening, she realized Mr. Riley hadn't been lying about his need for a secretary.

Exploring the second floor of suites, she found two beautifully appointed drawing rooms, one very masculine, with dark mahogany paneling three-quarters of the way up the wall. The furniture was overly large, and the sofas were hunter green in color, with a mix of brocade and velvet in the other furnishings and textiles. It was an inviting room in which she could easily imagine sitting with a book and enjoying a hot cup of tea.

The sunroom on the second floor was a wall of windows, the upper half stained glass that depicted all things nautical: a ship with a full amber-colored mast blowing in the wind, a raging storm done in shades of blues and grays, a seabird soaring high in a crystal blue sky. The furniture in this room was buttercup-yellow chintz. There was a nook with chairs near the windows, making this room a part-time breakfast area for immediate family, she guessed.

The last drawing room on the second floor faced the back garden of the house and carriage house. The windows were at least fifteen feet high, and heavy curtains made of the most delicate golden velvet draped around them, inviting the viewer to look outside, as though it were a landscape of art.

While the back garden wasn't large, there was a stone terrace at least ten feet deep, set against the main floor. It was big enough for a rose arbor, a pair of stone benches for two, and an angel-topped fountain. The sight took her breath away.

The burgundy backdrop of furniture was less inviting than the green drawing room but so much more tranquil with the scenery below.

Once she could tear her eyes away from the sight, she took the stairs slowly to the main floor, hating every pained step along the way. Although she'd been up for less than an hour, she'd already overtaxed herself.

She headed directly to the study, as she was somewhat familiar with that room and because she had the key tucked into her bodice. Sliding walnut doors at one end led to a large library. She'd only glimpsed what was inside yesterday and was desperate to explore it more thoroughly today.

Her gasp of surprise couldn't be held at bay when she opened the doors. Tall blond shelves filled the walls from floor to ceiling. Each shelf was filled with row upon row of books, and she thought it would probably take a week to sort through all the titles.

The terrace she'd seen from the second floor was off this room. And what a sight it made. She wondered what the house said about its owner, other than the fact that he loved beautiful things. And he must like to read, to have so many books in his possession.

Pained as her ankle might be, she couldn't stop herself from walking past the shelves and running her fingers over the spines of the books. They were sorted by author and then by genre. She even found a whole collection of Jane Austen, though the spines were in pristine shape, so she thought Mr. Riley had not read those. Oh yes, she could get lost in this room and planned to do so the moment she was given spare time.

Everything she'd seen in the house only confirmed her theory that Mr. Riley was a very wealthy man. She would know the answer to that soon enough, if she was to handle all his affairs.

With her foot and ankle throbbing like a hive of angry bees, Amelia knew she would have to explore the rest of the house another time.

Turning away from the terrace, the last thing she expected to do was to walk right into her employer.

Quickly stumbling back a step, she stammered out an apology and said in a rush, "I'm sorry."

He caught her by the elbow. "We really must stop meeting this way."

Was that humor she heard in his voice? It unsettled her and had her stuttering for excuses at being caught wandering through the house.

"I promise I'm not usually so clumsy, just a bit unsteady since yesterday. I didn't know when it was appropriate for me to come down, so I started my day as soon as I was up."

"You should not be walking without support. I don't want you to injure yourself further."

Even today, his voice did strange things to her. It made her feel things no decent woman should ever feel. It made her want…but want what? She reminded herself that his kindness could be a façade she had yet to crack through.

"I would have taken you around the house," he said, almost as if it was an apology.

She didn't miss the note of intimacy in his comment. And while his admission and the underlying innuendo should have her running from the house, she found herself intrigued.

What in the world was wrong with her? Her imaginings from last night were what was wrong with her. She'd sketched a picture of this man in her mind that was too perfect and without flaws. Everyone had flaws.

She decided right then and there that she couldn't trust herself in his presence. Her imagination had run wild with this man's character, and she couldn't help but paint him as some sort of hero, not only for rescuing her but also for giving her the things she desperately needed right now—a safe place, a job...a chance.

With self-preservation finally at the forefront of her thoughts, she managed to take an uneven step away from him. The misstep shot a heavy dose of pain up her leg, and it felt like her stomach was in her throat with the sudden correction in her balance. But Mr. Riley grasped her arm firmly. Instead of toppling back, she was crushed along the length of his body.

With her hands wrapped around his strong forearms, she let him steady her long enough that her head stopped spinning. His thumbs brushed back and forth over the inside of her wrist, letting her focus on the intimacy of his touch instead of the pain radiating from her ankle.

His nearness did strange things to her, things that made her want to step closer instead of away from him, to be touched everywhere as familiarly as he stroked her wrist. She shook her head and dropped her arms to her sides. She needed to get a better grasp on her emotions, her desires.

She reminded herself that she knew nothing about this man. And these were not the types of thoughts she should have of her employer—and an attraction of any kind was entirely out of the question.

When his gaze probed so far as to make her feel as if he were sifting through her secrets, she lowered her gaze. She didn't know why, but she liked the fluttery sensation she felt in her stomach when he was near. That was the last thing she should feel, she reminded herself for the umpteenth time. Mr. Riley could cut her loose just as fast as he'd tied her to his household.

Not willing to meet his gaze again, she focused on the cloth buttons lining the front of his maroon waistcoat. That did not help her imagination in the least, as she wondered if the material on the buttons was soft or coarse, which led her to wonder if his body would be as firm as it looked too.

"My apologies," she said again.

What else was there to say? *I'm sorry I'm a buffoon, Mr. Riley, but it appears to be a general state for me whenever you are in the room.* That simply wouldn't work.

"So you said. I won't expect you to eat with the rest of the staff in the kitchen quarters if you cannot make the climb downstairs." He made it sound as though she were breakable or, worse, an invalid. And she took exception to that until his finger turned up her chin, and their gazes collided. "What is your preference for your morning meal?"

"Whatever your cook puts together for the rest of the household will be sufficient, Mr. Riley."

His jaw clenched. Had she displeased him with her answer? She wanted to ask but found herself speechless instead, when he took her arm in his, alleviating the pain from her bad ankle. It was impossible to hold back the sigh of relief that his support offered. Escorting her over to a matching pair of leather chairs, he settled her in the one that faced the gardens.

"A post came from the employment agency for you," he announced, as though her receiving a post had been expected. "I left it on the desk for you."

Though her body was strung like a new violin bow, she hoped he didn't notice the tension suddenly assailing her. What if her old employer had contacted the agency to give them a story that painted her as an unsuitable employee? What lies would Sir Ian have made up about her? If the agency wrote a note to her, what had they already told Mr. Riley?

She swallowed back her nervousness. "I didn't think they would have anything to say."

"They most certainly should have, for placing you were they did." There was a note of underlying anger in his comment. And she wondered again how much he knew of her employment with Sir Ian. If he contacted the agency for her yesterday, it was likely they told him which house she'd served in.

"You should know that I have a vested interested in the agency that placed you. And their services are always available to any woman in need of a safe job place."

She looked at him, unsure how she was meant to reply. He seemed so sure of himself, which was expected of men. But she knew that a woman with even the hint of a poor reputation could easily be tossed out into the street as if she were no better than a pile of kitchen refuse.

"I failed to mention that a very close friend of my mother's runs the agency," he said. "They assured me that your last employer would not find another placement through them."

Her head was spinning with the information he might have garnered in going to his mother's friend. Would he know what happened? He'd revealed something decent about himself in telling her that. He did not condone the actions of a man who took advantage of his power. And she hated to admit that it allowed her to trust him enough that the constant fear that cloaked her dissipate a little.

Too many questions were swirling around in her head, and she decided it was best to change the topic. "Your house is very beautiful. The library, especially."

When he looked her over from head to toe with a scrutinizing expression, her lungs were robbed of air. Did he find her lacking?

That she cared was worrisome. She was usually more levelheaded than to fall victim to a handsome face. But there was a masculinity and prowess to his nature that made her feel so utterly and foolishly feminine. Like he would catch her if she fell...which he'd already accomplished today.

"You can use any room you desire to do your work. Meals can be brought up to the library, if that is your preference," he said.

She looked at the stately room where she sat. It was something out of fairy tales or a room reserved for the women born into the upper echelon of society. She wasn't a fairy-tale princess, and while she was an earl's daughter, she certainly hadn't been born into great riches and privilege. She felt undeserving.

"I couldn't possibly..." She shook her head. "The rest of the staff might think less of me if I were given such an advantage." Staring at a loose thread on her sleeve, she was unable to voice just how important it was for her to fit in. It wasn't like she'd ever lived with a plethora of servants when growing up—only a cook, who also helped to clean the family cottage where they lived when her father's health started to fail some years ago.

After her father's death, the family finances had plunged to dangerous lows. It didn't help that her brother liked to gamble.

The worst thing for her wasn't the idea of losing her childhood home; it was realizing just how little her brother thought of her. His debts had amassed so high that in exchange for clearing them, he had promised her to a man she loathed. A man far crueler than Sir Ian had been.

She wanted that life far behind her, and in order to do that, she must wholly embrace her role as a working woman. And a tiny part of her wanted to believe that Mr. Riley was the man who would give her exactly what she wanted.

Mr. Riley walked over to the entrance and rang the servants' bell before taking a seat across from her.

Shyly, she glanced at him from beneath her lashes. Why did she find herself speechless when he remained broodingly silent? She was normally a better conversationalist than this.

"What tasks will you have me accomplish today, Mr. Riley?"

A maid interrupted them before he could answer. She was young, not more than sixteen, and slight. She had a face full of freckles and large brown eyes that gave her an air of innocence.

"Havin' yer breakfast here today, Mr. Nick?" The girl's accent was thick and difficult to understand.

Amelia recoiled at the common way the maid addressed the master of the house. But then she realized that Mr. Riley was nothing she would expect of a successful businessman. And he was nothing like her brother or the men he allowed to stay at her home in Berwick.

"We are. Joshua's usual will suffice."

The maid left without bowing.

"Are the staff always so informal?" Her brother would have had the poor girl tossed out of the house.

"Olive has lived here since she was ten. Then, she was nothing more than a soot-covered, terrified child. She refused to speak for the first three years in my service, not even to the other women. I'm glad she found her voice. She can address me any way she pleases," he said with a finality that brooked no further questioning.

"How wonderful that she can speak freely without being seen as disobedient." Amelia stared at her entwined hands in her lap, not sure if she'd said too much. Everything he revealed about himself spoke of an admirable and honest man. It was hard to distrust him.

"You never need fear speaking your mind in this house," he said gently. "It is something I encourage."

This all had to be a dream. She never expected to meet a man like Mr. Riley. Never expected to not have to live with some sort of guarded fear.

With frightening reality, Amelia realized just how much she wanted to know more about the man who hadn't thought twice about plucking her out of an abysmal situation. What he'd revealed about the maid settled her feelings of being offered this job so hastily. So much so that she resolved to stay on longer than a few days. Perhaps she'd give it a week, to see how she felt.

Mr. Riley sat poised and still in his chair, studying her with watchful regard as she digested his words. There was no doubt in her mind that he was a kindhearted man. And her respect for him grew by the second.

"Olive is a very lucky girl to have found employment in your house," she said. It went without saying that she believed herself to be just as lucky as Olive.

He leaned forward, his elbows on his knees. "Back to your original query, Miss Grant. How familiar are you with navigating high society and the *ton*?"

Was he testing her? Wanting to prove he hadn't made a mistake taking her in, she thought it best to give him no reason to question her ability. "Enough to sort through your invitations."

She didn't tell him that she knew Debrett's backward and forward.

"Then that is exactly what you shall do today. My correspondence has been sorely neglected for the past few months."

She breathed a small sigh of relief, knowing that he wasn't having second thoughts about hiring her. "Mr. Huxley showed me your appointment calendar and the stack of invitations yet to be answered. Are there any additional tasks you want me to complete?"

"The invitations will take you a few days. But I'll leave you with my appointment book, and as you learn more about my businesses, you will know how to book my days. We'll worry only about those items this week, Miss Grant, as I don't want you overworked when you have already sustained injury on my watch."

She took affront that he thought her unable to take on tasks because of a turned ankle. "I assure you that I'm more than capable of taking on additional responsibilities."

Lips pursed in an unmovable line, he looked at her for a long, silent moment. She had the impression he was judging her on her word but did not offer her request a yea or nay.

She was desperate to know more about him. Clearing her throat, she asked, "What exactly is it that you do, Mr. Riley?"

"When I was younger than you are now, I invested in a number of properties and ventures. Most have succeeded very well over the years. Not wanting to pigeonhole myself, so I've dabbled in just about everything. In the beginning, some ventures failed, but the majority have thrived and have allowed me to amass a collection of successful interests. Now I mainly focus my attentions on acquiring properties."

The more he spoke, the more of an enigma he seemed. In Berwick, she'd never heard of a Mr. Riley, but that might have more to do with his not being a peer than anything else. She was not oblivious to the happenings around town where some of the more prominent members of the *ton* were concerned, but Amelia knew next to nothing else about the city or its array of inhabitants.

That was why it had been so appealing to get lost in the crowd—in a city difficult for her brother to locate her, should he care enough to find her. And she suspected he would when his debts climbed, as they were sure to do.

"How will I know which invitations you wish to accept?"

"Huxley will provide you with the names of anyone I choose not to associate with and those who have aligned themselves with my ventures. As for the rest…I will trust your judgment."

"No questions asked?" She couldn't hold the shock back from her voice.

"No questions asked, Miss Grant."

"What if I make a mistake?"

"I can assure you it will not be the end of the world."

"Thank you for giving me this opportunity." She knew she'd be lost if not for his generosity.

"I have other motives for taking you in." She stiffened as he stood from his chair and walked toward her. "You have nothing to fear from me."

Then what other motives did he have for hiring her? It was evident he required a secretary. But Sir Ian was in need of a governess, and that hadn't turned out in her favor.

"I see where your thoughts are leading you," he said softly, as though worried he'd said too much.

She looked at him sharply. "And where is that?" She cringed at the harshness in her tone. She could not forget her manners when Mr. Riley had shown her nothing but kindness.

He sat on the edge of the ottoman that separated the two chairs and reached for her face. She winced at the first soft glide of his fingers across her bruised cheek.

"It pains me to see this reaction in you." With gentle fingers he grasped her chin and tipped her face up so he could meet her eyes. He looked at her as though he saw right through her. "You won't always flinch away from me."

The promise in those words sucked the air right out of her lungs.

Under other circumstances, the perceptiveness in his sharp slate-gray gaze might frighten her. Instead, the quiet patience she saw there made her feel safe. She knew with every fiber of her being that this man would protect her from knowing any more harsh realities. Protect her from the likes of any more Sir Ians. And that thought stilled the anxiety inside her.

"What do you want from me?" she whispered.

His gaze never broke from hers as he caressed the side of her face, rubbing his thumb over the mark left by Sir Ian. "No one will ever hurt you again."

Her lips parted with the promise and conviction in his voice. She thought about what she should say, but she was unable to formulate a coherent sentence when he was touching her.

"Do you feel it?" he asked, as he leaned in closer, his sharp eyes piercing right through to her heart. "Do you feel something undeniable happening between us?"

The pitter-patter in her chest had her heart beating overtime the nearer Mr. Riley drew. How could he feel how she did? Was such a thing even possible?

"I know your curiosity will win out," he said without needing her to answer.

It was so hard to define what she felt. But it couldn't be denied that she felt something she'd never felt around any other man.

His thumb brushed over her parted lips, the motion slow and seductive. Erotic. She struggled to take another breath, afraid to dispel what had started between them. She never wanted the intimacy of their stolen moment to end.

Mr. Riley's thumb brushed against her tongue as she darted it out to moisten her dry lips. Tasting the salt of his skin, she closed her eyes, trying to find her equilibrium in her world that was fast spinning out of control.

Senses heightened with the absence of eyesight, she was still shocked when the warmth of his breath brushed across her lips a moment before his lips sealed over hers. His lips were soft but unrelenting, searching yet patient. He pulled at her mouth in a coaxing manner and tasted her bottom lip before covering her mouth again and stealing the breath she exhaled in surprise.

She should discourage his advances. Push him away. But she was lost to his touch. And while she relished the feel of his mouth on hers, she needed to anchor herself. Stop this madness.

Instead of doing what she *should* do, her hands fisted in the soft material of his wool coat, and she pulled at his lips as he'd pulled at hers. That she even knew how to do such a thing astonished her.

She was running on pure instinct now.

With his hands buried in her hair, the hairpins pressed painfully against her scalp. She knew she should care about what she was allowing, but she didn't stop him, and she certainly couldn't stop herself. He lifted her from the chair and pulled her body along the solid length of his, never releasing her lips from the sweet torture he delivered. She moaned into his mouth and hated the need that filled that sound.

He confused her and made her yearn for things she had no right to want.

He pulled away from her suddenly, and it left her swaying where she stood. Her eyes snapped open, and she stared at him, bewildered. *Lost.*

She reached for the arm of the chair to steady herself, as Mr. Riley had moved away from her to stand at a decent distance—something she should have done from the beginning.

The door opened, and a maid entered the room, carrying a silver tray. Another staff member followed her, an identical breakfast tray in her hands. Amelia and Mr. Riley stood there in silence as their breakfast was set out. She didn't dare look at him again and dropped her gaze to the pale blue swirling design in the Aubusson rug.

She swallowed against the nerves that made it difficult for her to speak. She couldn't even look at the staff who had entered the room. They would know what she'd done—they might have even seen what she'd been engaged in. She'd lowered herself to no more than a whore.

Tears welled in her eyes, blurring her vision, as the two servants left the library. Mr. Riley's black polished shoes came into view a moment before he lifted her chin to look at her again. Why did she feel so lost?

"There is nothing to be ashamed of."

She wanted to believe him. But… "There is everything to be ashamed of." She shook her head, hating that she had to apologize, knowing that if given a chance to repeat the sequence of events that had led to that kiss, she'd commit all the same sins again and again.

What in the world was wrong with her?

"Why did you kiss me?" She wasn't sure she wanted to hear the answer, but a part of her needed to know. And talking was safer right now.

"I have wanted to do that since you first stumbled into my path. Do you feel something growing between us?"

She'd been ignoring that feeling, thinking and hoping it would pass with time. She'd assumed she'd developed hero worship after Mr. Riley had rescued her and then taken care of her when she'd been at an ultimate low.

She couldn't deny the truth now. She did feel something for him; something not easily defined as mere lust but a deep desire to learn more about him and why he made her feel so out of sorts with what she thought was right.

Not that she would ever admit to that.

Who was she to garner the attention of this man? Women probably threw themselves at his feet and begged him to ruin them on a regular basis. That thought left her feeling cold. She eyed the door, longing for escape.

"Don't leave, Amelia." He stepped closer to her, near enough that she could kiss him again if she so desired. She ignored that desire. "Work for me as we planned. Just stay."

There was a kind of desolation in his voice at the thought of her abandoning him. But that was impossible. And she was reading too much into his request. Logically, she knew she couldn't feel this sort of attachment to someone she had just met. Someone she didn't really know.

"I'm afraid of what I will do," she admitted, more for herself than for him.

"Then don't think about it. Go with what your instincts tell you. If there is one thing I have always done, it is to follow my first inclination. I might be in a very different position today, had I ignored those natural reflexes."

He caressed her cheek again. She nearly nestled into his palm before realizing what she was doing. With a heavy sigh, she pulled away from him before she made any more mistakes. This was not a good way to start her first official day as his secretary.

She couldn't help but ask. "And what do your instincts say about me?"

"I don't need my instincts to tell me where this is going. It is more base than that. I desire you. And there is nothing that can stop me from fulfilling and exploring what I want. You will be mine in the end, Amelia."

Her heart picked up speed at his admission. Her breathing grew more rapid as she assessed him. She desired him too. She, Amelia Marie Somerset, who wanted nothing more than to escape one vile man's sick craving to marry her and claim her, was willing to let the man in front of her ruin her because she felt so much different with him than she had with anyone else.

What would she lose of herself in the process of courting dangerous games with this man? Focusing on the hard angles of his face and the steady expression he wore, one thing was certain.

This man would ruin her.

And more startling was the realization that she would do nothing to stop him.

CHAPTER SIX

Their breakfast trays had been set on a walnut parlor table in the library. Mr. Riley removed both lids, revealing steaming mounds of scrambled eggs and mash with a generous side of sausages. He carried the dishes to a small decorative table that faced the gardens before turning back to Amelia, offering his arm.

The last thing she should be doing was touching him again after all that had transpired, but she knew she would look silly refusing his aid when she could barely walk well enough on her own. He escorted her to one of the chairs, sliding it closer to the table once she was seated.

"Olive will bring tea up shortly, unless you prefer coffee in the morning," he asked.

She pushed her fork around on her plate, feeling out of sorts for breakfast when she had to face Mr. Riley after their heated kiss. "I prefer tea," she said almost absently.

"As do I. Though coffee after dinner can be quite refreshing."

His attempt to engage her in simple conversation to put her at ease was working, but she couldn't ignore what had happened between them or the fact that they'd almost been discovered. "Do you think the maids saw us?"

"Is that what has you worried?" He pointedly looked at her food, which she had yet to take a bite of.

"They might think less of me. And I wouldn't want to give anyone the wrong impression as to why I was hired."

Mr. Riley nodded his understanding at her uneasiness. At her look of confusion, he added, "There is a creak in the old floorboard at the top of the stairs. I had already pulled away by the time the second creak sounded."

"That is not reassuring. They would have sensed something more." Her face had been furiously hot, and she hadn't been able to meet either servant's eyes as they set out the food.

"My staff is trustworthy, Miss Grant. They would never whisper a word of their suspicions if they believed or even suspected something was happening between us."

Mr. Riley filled his fork with mash and eggs together and ate it with a gusto she'd never seen a man eat with. He enjoyed food as much as he enjoyed women. That thought had her forkful of eggs stopped midway between her plate and mouth. How would she even know or be able to contemplate that?

What basis did she have to know he enjoyed women with *gusto*? Certainly, he was practiced in the art of seduction. It had taken her less than a day to fall victim to his kiss. These thoughts simply wouldn't do. She needed Mr. Riley out of her head, but how could she do that when he sat across from her, watching her? He was always watching her.

"It does no one any good to start the day hungry."

She was ready to give him a retort when she noticed the scraping and bruising across his knuckles, and her words froze in her throat. She dropped her fork and grasped his hand, pulling it closer and angling it toward the sun coming through the windows. "This must hurt. Let me ring for one of the maids to bring ice."

He chuckled and slid his hand from hers. "Nothing I'm not used to. I spent a larger part of my youth bloody and broken. Fighting paved my path to success."

She scrutinized him with renewed interest. "You were a pugilist?"

"That colors it too cleanly. More like the fighter you wanted to bet on in the ring."

The steady stride of someone coming down the hall stopped her from asking more questions. Was it normal for a man in London to fight for money?

"Good morning," Huxley said upon entering and taking a seat at the table.

Mr. Riley merely nodded and took another mouthful of his hash and eggs.

Amelia turned to the older man, thankful to have someone else in the room to break the tension between her and Mr. Riley. "Good day, Huxley. What will you show me today?"

Before he could answer, Mr. Riley said, "Miss Grant is itching to get her hands dirty. Doesn't want to get bored taking care of the appointments. Go over the newspapers and rags with her. Show her what to look for."

Amelia looked quizzically between the men.

Huxley must have noticed the questions forming on her tongue and said, "Watching the interests of the company. Verifying any gossip that makes its way through the servants about certain business partners and other interested parties."

"You do this every day?" What did they hope to find in the paper that they probably hadn't already heard through word of mouth?

"Just double-checking who the parties mentioned are and what activities they are tied to." After placing his napkin on his empty plate, Mr. Riley stood.

When she pushed her chair out to follow suit, he rested his hand atop hers, the act at once possessive and intimate. The look he leveled at her caused the air in her lungs to stall and her face to heat. That he could affect her with just a look should have her questioning her sanity in staying in his employ.

Surreptitiously, she glanced over to Huxley, hoping he didn't see her reaction to Mr. Riley. He was focused on the untouched sausage on her plate.

"We're not so formal here," Mr. Riley said to her. "Enjoy your breakfast before getting on with your day."

She gave him a small smile and settled back in her chair, hating that she missed his touch the moment he stepped away from her. Hating that she didn't want to lose his company so soon in the day when only moments ago she was glad for Huxley's arrival.

"Make sure you find a cane for Miss Grant, Huxley. She shouldn't be walking around the house without support."

Huxley grunted at the request, as his mouth was full with one of the sausages he'd been eyeing.

When Mr. Riley was gone, she said, "We can arrange for your own plate before we begin the appointment books."

"No need; been down to the kitchen already—didn't want it going to waste." He pushed out from the table, assessing her for a moment. "I will find a cane for you to hobble around on; then we can get started."

Huxley left to do just that, and it gave her time to think over the events of this morning. What had she been thinking? Pressing her fingers against her mouth, she swore she still felt the touch of Mr. Riley's lips upon hers.

She closed her eyes and tried to banish all thoughts of her employer from her head. It didn't work. Instead, she fantasized about having more time alone with him, more time in his arms before the maids came in with breakfast. Had they had more time alone, she wondered just how far Mr. Riley would have taken that kiss.

When Huxley returned to the library, he had a gentlemen's cane. The top was lacquered black with a band of silver around the base of the handle. As she stood, Huxley held it out to her. It was a bit tall, but it did make walking easier.

They worked companionably through the morning, sorting all the invitations she would respond to that afternoon.

"What will you do when I take over the secretary position?" she asked Huxley.

"Mr. Riley needs a trusted man down at the wharf. He owns a strip of land there. Needs someone to run the operation, as the books are looking funny."

"Funny, how?"

"Someone thinks they can steal from Mr. Riley's pocket without being caught."

She felt as if his words were a warning to her. "How disappointing, considering Mr. Riley's evident generosity toward those who work for him. Or so I have noticed since coming here."

"He's a hard man, Miss Grant, and has had a hard life. And the man you see—any man, really—behind closed doors isn't always the same man outside his home."

This comment seemed like a warning, but what was he warning her from? Did he suspect something more than an employee-employer relationship between Mr. Riley and her?

Truthfully, Huxley's words could be applied to even the likes of her brother, who was charming, confident, and a man of the world in a public setting. Behind closed doors, he was none of those things; he was a monster, bent on harsh cruelty and a dark hatred that had her living in fear for too long before her escape.

She swallowed those memories, feeling a tremble overtake her hands for the briefest moment before she tempered her emotions. Squeezing her hands into tight fists, she met Huxley's gaze head on.

He assessed her for a long moment, and she wondered if she'd given away something of herself in her silent contemplation and in her reaction to his words. Her stomach chose that moment to rumble, saving her from having to offer a response.

Checking his pocket watch, Huxley handed her the cane. "Might as well take lunch. Everyone wants to meet you."

Why that surprised her, she couldn't say. She hoped she wasn't a disappointment to the staff or that they saw her as usurping any of their positions by being here. A silly thought but valid, considering her terrible luck with employment to date.

"And where does the staff convene at this time of day?" she asked, limping out of the library with the aid of the cane and toward the stairs that led to the lower level.

"They'll be assembled in the dining hall." He paced evenly next to her, though she could tell he was ready to catch her, should her footing not be true.

"How many people are employed by Mr. Riley?"

"Aside from us, four housemaids, a footman, and a cook. As well as the housekeeper and her son, Devlin, a boy of nine years, and the groundsman who lives above the old carriage house."

As they neared the bottom step to the lower level, the noise grew louder around her, making it sound as though thirty people worked here, not ten. The kitchen hall seemed to be a very busy place. As she and Huxley stepped into the large rectangular room, everyone paused and looked up at her. Olive was darning a sock but gave her a big grin before going back to her work, tying off a stitch.

"This is Amelia Grant, the new secretary who will be tending to Mr. Riley's direct affairs outside of the house," Huxley said by way of introduction.

"Good afternoon," Amelia greeted them. "I'm pleased to meet you all. I have already met Olive and Hannah." Amelia smiled at the two women she'd seen in the library that morning. Hannah's deep brown eyes were warm and inviting, her posture comfortable where she sat at the table, working on fine embroidery at the edge of a pillowcase.

"Nice to be properly introduced, Miss Grant," Hannah said. Her voice was soft and accented, and Amelia guessed her native tongue was German. Hannah's hair was so blonde that it was almost white, and she wore it pulled back in a neat chignon.

A woman with twinkling blue eyes and a kind smile took Amelia's hands in her own. Her skin was smooth and untouched by age, despite her gray hair. "Mrs. Coleman. I am the housekeeper. Mr. Riley has needed someone in your position for a long time. We are all so glad to have you join us."

"Thank you," Amelia said, not sure how she should respond to the kindness from the staff.

"My son runs errands, so you'll meet him over dinner. Devlin is presently out delivering letters for Mr. Riley."

While the maids wore gray dresses, Mrs. Coleman's was a rich, dark blue. The other two maids, whom she hadn't met— twins, easily set apart, as one had a scar that slashed through her right eyebrow and arched around her cheek—stood from the table and in tandem said, "Jenny" and "Josie." They were red-haired, robust women who stood a few inches taller than Amelia, with hands worn and craggy from a life of hard work. Jenny, the one without the scar, had kinder brown eyes than her sister, as though life hadn't been as cruel to her. Both spoke with a soft Scottish lilt.

Amelia dipped her head. "A pleasure."

"Liam, miss," a tall lanky boy of no more than twenty years said, extending his hand. Amelia didn't hesitate to accept his hand, even though it was not at all proper for a lady to do. Height alone told her this was the footman. His blond hair was parted to one side and pomaded tidily in place. An apron covered his uniform, as he was in the midst of polishing the silver.

A rotund, balding man came forward and clasped his hands on either of her arms, as if giving her a good measure up. "You can call me Joshua." He looked her up and down, the motion made eerie as one eye—made of glass—stayed in place as he did so. "Just a wee thing you are. Give me a month to fix you up to a better state."

She wanted to argue that she was perfectly healthy but bit the inside of her cheek. It was important that she make a good impression. They did all have to live under the same roof, and Amelia had every intention of befriending each and every one of them.

She smiled. *New beginnings,* she kept thinking. The staff here were nothing like those at Sir Ian's. New beginnings, indeed, and by all appearances, the fresh start she'd intended when she'd arrived in London.

"It is a pleasure to meet you all. I was lucky to have landed in this position and couldn't be more grateful for your welcome and your kindness."

"How did you end up in Mr. Riley's service?" Jenny asked. Josie jabbed her elbow into her sister's ribs.

Of course they would be curious to know where she came from and what she'd done in the past. "My fall here was not so glamorous. As that is literally how I met Mr. Riley."

"Is that the way of it, then?" The housekeeper came around the table and took her arm, waving off Huxley. "Let me show you where everything is down here, though I'm sure it's not much different from the last household where you were engaged."

"No, not much different from the last." She kept her smile to herself, since Mrs. Coleman was referring to the layout and not the situation, which she found to be the exact opposite of the last place.

"So you fell into service here?" the housekeeper said.

"Did Mr. Riley not tell you he had hired me?"

"He did, but where you came from and how he acquired your services is your own business," Mrs. Coleman said. It sounded like a warning that she shouldn't ask the others how they'd ended up in Mr. Riley's employ. She had no problem respecting their privacy, considering she needed to keep a tight lid on her past.

"And what of Huxley?" Amelia asked. "Did he not inform you of how Mr. Riley and I crossed paths?"

"Huxley's a kind man and knows something of everything, but he's mum on anything to do with other people's secrets that are under Mr. Riley's protection."

The housekeeper's assessment didn't surprise Amelia. She had a feeling that finding out any information through Huxley was like prying open a lock without a key. Actually, it was probably more difficult than even that.

"I see," Amelia muttered.

"We're all lucky to have found work here. Everyone has had some misfortune along the way. You shouldn't expect anyone to reveal a past best left forgotten."

"I will heed your warning."

After showing Amelia where the linens, larder, pantry, and storage areas were located, she was shown the housekeeper's office and the place the men, including her son, bedded down at night, in the event that Mr. Riley ever needed to get a message out at an odd time of day.

When they entered the servants' hall once again, everyone had cleared away the items they'd been working on so Olive could set out bowls for the midday meal. A pot of stew and two loaves of bread were placed at one end of the old wood table, which was almost as large as the room and could probably seat twenty. The food's aroma wafted to Amelia's nose and smelled divine as she ladled thick chunks of lamb, carrots, and potatoes into her bowl.

As everyone took their seats to eat, conversation started on the gossip around town. While this was no different than the talk around the table at her last place of employment, there was one thing that Amelia noted almost immediately. Talk was focused on the people who had regular dealings with Mr. Riley or his businesses.

The servants were pooling their information together from what the housekeeper had heard from the shopkeepers during her morning errands at various shops; the maids revealed what they'd heard from the coal deliverer. All the while, Huxley wrote key points down in a small leather notebook he carried in his pocket. He didn't write down everything, just a handful of names. She wondered if she would have to do this as Mr. Riley's secretary—gather gossip and apprise him of it.

Between mouthfuls, Jenny said, "While Baker's son was doing his usual deliveries to the lords' and ladies' houses this morning, he stumbled across Sir Ian Hemming in the street. He was in a bad way, with his face right bloody and broken from a good beating. Baker wanted to fetch the bobbies, he did, but Hemming's valet convinced him all was fine. Took him—well, practically carried him—inside."

Amelia's spoon stilled between her bowl and her mouth. Her breath felt frozen in her lungs. Sir Ian had been hurt. She swallowed against the nervous lump forming in her throat. Tears pricked her eyes as she thought of that vile man. Wasn't it this morning that Mr. Riley told her that he had close ties to the employment agency? Her head spun as she thought of the painful-looking bruises she'd spied on Mr. Riley's knuckles only a few hours ago.

Could he have…Would he dare…

She brushed her fingers over her cheek where Sir Ian had hit her.

Amelia set her spoon down, unable to eat another bite. Her head was spinning with questions that couldn't be answered, questions she couldn't put voice to. But she needed to know the truth. Needed to know if Mr. Riley was somehow involved. Why would he do that for her?

"Did the baker find out what happened to Sir Ian?" Amelia asked, and all eyes turned toward her soft-spoken question.

Huxley's pencil stilled over the paper as his eyes met hers. She could see the questions burning there, but he didn't say a word. She wasn't sure if she'd said something wrong or if that was not a question they cared to answer. All Amelia knew was that Mr. Riley had saved her from a fate she didn't want to contemplate. But she reminded herself that Mr. Riley was not a peer of the realm. He could not be protected if he hurt someone above his station.

Not wanting to examine too deeply why she felt compelled to protect him, she focused on the fact that she owed him for his kindness.

"I have never heard of such a thing happening. Not without provocation. And even then…" She hoped that the curious inflection coating her voice would appease those around her as explanation of why she asked about that evil man's welfare.

Did everyone know how awful Sir Ian was? Or was she the only person with firsthand knowledge in that respect? Then she wondered if Mr. Riley's servants knew any of Sir Ian's servants and if they might have talked about the governess who had left without word.

As nice as the staff seemed around the table, she didn't want any of them knowing her business. It was bad enough that the evidence of the cruelty delivered to her in her last job marked her face. At least the bruise was fading fast with the salve Mr. Riley had given her to aid in the healing process.

"Didn't care to ask," Josie said, her eyes narrowing on Amelia.

Amelia wasn't sure if Josie disliked her or was just trying to figure out why she'd asked the question at all. "I am a country girl. Events like this are uncommon in the country," she admitted.

That seemed to satisfy everyone's interest at the table.

"Perhaps the valet thought it best to wait for Sir Ian to decide his next course of action—though that won't happen until he can talk again. Jaw was broken, from what I heard. And his eyes were so swollen, he could barely open them."

Amelia curled her hands under the table, squeezing them together. She must remember to bite her tongue. She was too new to be asking questions that pried into Mr. Riley's business, no matter that she was his secretary and would work closer with him than anyone else around the table, aside from Huxley.

Taking a deep breath and shaking off the sudden discomfort she felt at the mention of Sir Ian's name, Amelia focused on her lunch, even though her appetite was gone; it was like dust gumming up in her mouth, but she ate it nonetheless. Her thoughts were focused solely on Mr. Riley, recalling the way he tended to her cuts as gently as he'd checked her ankle when he'd first found her.

There was no denying what was staring her so blindly in the face. Mr. Riley had known what Sir Ian had done to her.

But what was she supposed to do with that realization? She couldn't confront him, no matter how badly she wanted to. A secret part of her was thrilled at the thought of Mr. Riley seeking some form of justice on her behalf, no matter how wrong those actions might be. No matter how much she should be against the very idea.

She would keep her assumptions to herself for now, though she wondered if the rest of the household suspected anything, Huxley in particular. She couldn't bear to look at any of them with the thoughts swirling through her head. She kept her eyes averted and focused solely on her food as she listened to the rest of the gossip they'd dug up in the last few days.

The maids gave Huxley other tidbits of information they'd heard through various delivery people, as did the cook. They were fonts of information that had her wondering if they'd been hired not only because they'd needed a job, as she did, but because of their ability to worm through all the gossip that came their way and pick out the parts that might be relevant to Mr. Riley's various ventures.

While she listened, she learned—that the son of a ship merchant was selling his wares higher to Mr. Riley than the other companies owned by men of a higher station, and the rumors speculating what Mr. Riley's next property acquisition would be. Huxley was right; Mr. Riley dabbled in a bit of everything.

Amelia remained silent throughout the meal, absorbing every bit of information about her mysterious employer.

The one thing she came away with, after sitting with Mr. Riley's household, was that he'd garnered the undivided trust of his staff, which made him a good man in her estimation. She had a newfound respect for him.

As she thought back to her morning with her employer, she could recall with perfect clarity how the press of his mouth upon hers felt. Her face heated, and she set her spoon down and wiped her mouth with the napkin, hoping it covered her red cheeks long enough that she could get her thoughts and emotions under control.

If Olive or Hannah had seen or even guessed what had gone on when they'd brought breakfast to the library, they gave no indication of it. Amelia wondered now if that was because they honestly hadn't suspected anything or if Mr. Riley could do no wrong in their eyes. Just because he could do no wrong didn't give her reason to believe the staff would treat her with the same regard, and she must remember that above all things.

After an hour, they all parted ways to continue on with their duties. Amelia left with Huxley, heading back up to the study to continue going through the papers. When they sat down to work, she looked longingly toward the library. Her companion must have noticed her waning attention.

"If you prefer the library," he said, "we can set up a desk in there."

"Only if that is Mr. Riley's preference." Odd, but Mr. Riley had asked her that very thing this morning.

"I assumed you liked the view," Huxley said. "Won't matter much to Mr. Riley."

"I think we should move my desk in there, then. The gardens are very peaceful."

"Distracting, more like."

She laughed. "Do you find them so?"

"Women's prerogative."

"I have known plenty of gentlemen with an inclination toward a green thumb," she said, amused.

He harrumphed his response before they focused on the stack of papers again.

CHAPTER SEVEN

The sky darkened outside, shrouding the library in shadows as night drew nearer. After moving her desk into the library, Huxley had left her to her own devices, telling her that dinner was served at seven thirty. It was well past that hour now.

She'd been determined to finish sorting through at least one stack of invitations and was confident in her choices for Mr. Riley's attendance. Of course, Huxley had counseled her at great length, giving her clear instructions on whom she should send regrets to, which had narrowed her stack considerably, though it hadn't stopped her from reading the contents of each and every letter so she could learn more about her employer.

By all accounts, he was deeply desired company. His invitations ranged from balls to soirees in renowned houses with marriageable daughters to lords and ladies with the grandest of estates. There was even an invitation to attend the opera from a widow who had more money than sense, or so Huxley had informed her.

Two letters were personal in nature and had evidently been mixed into the stack in error. When she realized what she was reading, she looked around her to make sure she was alone before continuing.

The first letter was addressed to Nick, without his last name. The handwriting slanted deeply to the right and the ink smeared across the page, telling her that the person wrote with his—or her—left hand. All it said was, "As requested. More to follow." It wasn't signed.

Enclosed with the letter was a list of addresses in Highgate and associated names. Beside the names, a monetary value was clearly indicated, perhaps the worth of the property or what the person owed. Some individuals were given a second number between one and three, which could be the number of owners on each property, she supposed.

The second letter was very neatly penned, and she assumed it was from a woman. The name on the bottom certainly wasn't helpful in determining the writer's sex; it was signed Ser. Again, it was addressed to Nick without his last name. The letter was dated three weeks ago, so she hoped it wasn't too important.

This letter detailed the start of new classes in a school and enrollment figures from the first week through to the end of the previous month. There was a note advising Nick that she'd hired Cece as an assistant in her classroom.

Did Nick own a school too? What an odd choice, considering the rest of the businesses in his conglomerate, which mostly seemed to be properties.

She stuffed both letters back into their respective envelopes and placed them in a separate stack to carry to the study when she retired for the evening.

Penning the last address of the evening on the invitations, she wiped off her pen on a cloth, put the lid back on the inkwell, and sat back in the chair to watch the lights grow dimmer outside. Gas lamps began to glow and replace the sun's light, but it wasn't enough to blind her view of the cloudy sky. For the first time in a long time, she felt content. And safe. It brought a small smile to her lips.

She startled when something heavy thudded on the desk in the study.

She stood from her desk, knowing she should go into the study and make her presence known, but stopped on hearing Huxley's angered tone. "He has taken a percentage of the profits coming in. Selling merchandise off the ship before it's logged in our books."

Amelia recalled the gossip discussed in the staff quarters over luncheon. She shouldn't be standing in the shadows, listening to their exchange, but the only escape was through the French doors to the balcony. She couldn't leave without drawing their attention now, so she decided to stay put in the library until they left.

She hated that she had reduced herself to eavesdropping. She made her way quietly over to the wall of books, took down a volume, and then curled up on the sofa to read, hoping she could tune out the voices and play ignorant, should they realize she was there.

"He's already a ruined man," Mr. Riley said with a finality that left no room for disagreement. Whether the manager of the shipping company had ruined his own name or Mr. Riley had done it for him, she couldn't say, but she thought perhaps it might be a combination of both. The edge of ruthlessness should have frightened her, but Mr. Riley filled his home with misfits and people in need, which made it difficult to find fault in his character.

Silence descended for a full two minutes, and she thought her ruse had been discovered, but then they discussed other business matters for almost twenty minutes before Huxley made his excuses and left. The creak of the chair in the second room meant Mr. Riley was also wrapping up his affairs for the night, so she could leave undetected. She held her breath and waited as time ticked by. Why she thought she should have such luck...

A small lamp turned low on the table next to her shed just enough light to allow her to read. So when Mr. Riley walked toward the tall windows, hands tucked in his pockets, she made no sound to give away her position. He wouldn't have seen her on entering, given the position of the chairs and sofa, but that didn't mean he wouldn't notice her once he left.

As she contemplated how to make herself known, Mr. Riley said, "How was your first day?"

He didn't turn to face her when he spoke. Would he sack her now that he knew she'd been listening?

"Quite well." She cleared her throat delicately as she stood from the sofa. "The staff were welcoming, and Huxley was a font of information as we went through a good third of the paperwork today."

Should she apologize for overhearing his conversation? For not making him aware that she was in the library. Perhaps she should pretend not to have heard his conversation at all, but that didn't feel right.

"I should have said something when you first came in," she said.

He turned around and faced her. She wished she could understand why he affected her the way he did, because not for the first time, she found herself speechless under his intense scrutiny. It was as though he could see right through her and knew her every thought. A silly notion, but one that gripped her every time she was alone with him.

"I should retire for the night." Her voice was a whisper that barely filled the silence around them.

He didn't respond, just studied her in his silent way for a long moment. Though she had every intention of doing just as she said, she couldn't find the strength to leave the room. There was so much to be said—about what had happened this morning and how they should move forward from that.

With a leisured grace and dominant air that should have had Amelia retreating, he approached her. She held her breath until he was but an arm's stretch from her. She had to put distance between them. What he wanted spoke so intimately in her mind that she knew she would lose herself too soon to this man if she didn't learn a little self-preservation fast.

She swallowed against the trepidation building in her throat when she couldn't find the words she needed to tell him to give her some space. "We cannot repeat what happened between us this morning. I won't be able to look at myself in the mirror if I lived under false pretense and deception. If we continue on amorally, it will not be long before we are discovered. That's not a chance I'm willing to gamble on."

Suddenly, they were a hand span apart. Mr. Riley caressed the back of his knuckles over her good cheek. "How can I make it any clearer that you'll be mine in the end, Amelia?"

Why? Why did he want to pursue her so persistently? And why did she want him to do exactly as he promised?

She closed her eyes, wishing she could just as easily close off her desire toward this man.

"I need this job," she whispered, almost afraid to break the spell that had washed over them.

"And it is yours. That has never been in question."

"Would not your actions be considered taking advantage of your position?" she boldly asked. She snapped her mouth shut, shocked she had even suggested it.

He surprised her with a calm response. "I might be master of this household, but I am not a master over any person, including you. You will come to me of your own free will and on equal footing, Amelia. I won't have you any other way."

His determination and conviction had her stomach in a flutter. And the feeling wasn't wholly undesirable. "You sound so sure." But with every word he uttered, she felt herself inching closer to him, trapped under his seductive spell.

"I always am when I know what I want." He stated it as if it was nothing more than fact.

When his gray eyes ensnared hers, she swallowed hard and held his gaze, believing every word he said. If she stayed, she would succumb to the need and desire burning brighter in her every time she was with him. She would succumb, because his resolve made her want to lean into him—kiss him—and damned be the consequences.

He reached behind her head and pulled the hairpins free, letting sections of her chignon fall around her shoulders. She supposed she should have stopped him but couldn't bring herself to do that. She wanted to know what he was about, what game he was playing to try to win her over of her own free will.

When he was done pulling out the last of her pins, he tucked them in the pocket of his waistcoat.

"And what would anyone think if they were to see me in such a state?" she asked.

"I can fix it later."

"Later?" she said in a soft, intrigued whisper. What was he doing to her?

"No one will disturb me in my study during the evening. The place is ours for the night."

"I know nothing of you."

"What is it you want to know?"

"Why do you want this?" *Why do you want me*, was what she'd meant to ask.

"You remind me of someone I once admired a great deal."

"But no longer?"

"She died a long time ago."

Her head tilted back, her lips parted expectantly. "You don't know me well enough to confess admiration."

Mr. Riley's hand held the back of her head, fingers woven tightly through her hair as though to hold her still, should she try to flee, but she had no such notion. It didn't occur to her that she should turn away as his mouth lowered to hers. It didn't occur to her that she should stop him as his lips drew closer and closer to descending upon hers.

His kiss was gentle and coaxing—it was meant to titillate and persuade her into wanting more. And did she ever want more. He was seducing her slowly and winning over her resolve to remain a professional working girl with every brush of his lips against hers. She was losing herself to this man, and when she thought about it now, that didn't seem like such a bad thing, at least not while he was kissing her.

Amelia didn't care that he hadn't answered her question. Any protest she wanted to utter as his lips parted over hers was also forgotten, and he sucked the top and then the bottom lip, pulling them between his before repeating the process. She was lost to his touch.

She should feel great shame for her actions; instead, she felt foolishly prideful at his devoted attention.

Taking all this to heart, she must never forget her roots or the past that had led her to this particular moment in time. With a force of will that she had thought was all but gone since the first brush of his lips, Amelia found a small vestige of pride for the woman she was raised to be and turned her head away, breaking their kiss and denying the one thing she wanted most right now.

A ragged breath rushed from her lips. Tightly squeezing her eyes shut, she recalled the last image of her brother, raising his hand against her in anger. That thought alone was enough to douse cold water over the moment, putting her in a palpable chill. She wrapped her arms around her middle as goose bumps rose along her arms.

Because she denied Mr. Riley her mouth, he pressed his lips to her cheek. His hand was still wound tightly through her hair, but she didn't try to shake him free.

"This cannot happen." To her surprise, her voice didn't waver, and she could not have been more thankful that she was holding herself together. Losing herself in this man—to any man—was a very bad idea, and she needed to erect walls between them, fast.

"This will be, Amelia." He kissed her cheek once more. This time, the press of his mouth was like a brand of ownership being burned against her skin. And she wanted him to brand more than her mouth.

Knowing he was reluctant to stop—she felt his hesitancy to release her—she said, "I need to retire for the evening if I'm to get an early start on the remaining invitations."

Hand sliding away, he let her escape the comfort of his embrace.

As she turned to leave, he called to her. "Amelia."

She couldn't turn to face him. If she did, she knew she would do more that she would regret come morning. It was time to take charge of her life, of her future, and if she was going to do that, she needed to avoid moments alone with Mr. Riley.

"Your hair pins," he said, reminding her.

She pinched her lips together, angry that she'd forgotten. Where was her mind? She turned back to the object of her deepest affection, but she couldn't look him in the eye. She might see something there that would draw her back into his arms, and she had to fight her attraction to him. *It will pass with time*, she told herself. Pass, if she ignored it.

She held out her hand, hoping he'd relinquish the pins so she could be on her way.

Instead of giving them to her, he turned her around and pulled her hair back, twisting it around until she had a bun low at her nape, and then he pinned it in place. His hands rested on her shoulders when he was done, squeezing them gently. She felt the heated fan of his breath against the small bit of skin exposed around her nape, and then his lips were on her. She swallowed heavily, closed her eyes once again, and soaked up the feel of him.

"Stay with me tonight," he said.

She shook her head. There would never be any escaping him, even if she tried to avoid him. "You mistake me. I'm not the kind of woman you think me to be."

"I never make mistakes," was his sure response.

Because there was nothing she could say to that, she leaned away from him to retrieve her cane. It took everything in her not to look back at him as she limped steadily out of the library. This time, he didn't call her back.

Where was his self-control? Nick pressed the flats of his hands against the desk. He wanted to follow her upstairs. He wanted to go to her even though she was gone. He wanted her to himself, damn it.

To be ruled by desire was to be ruled by emotion. And men ruled by emotion made mistakes he couldn't afford to make. His life was built on quick decisions. Some—very few—of his choices had undesirable outcomes, but for the most part, he did well and had found a great deal of success.

He couldn't gamble on Miss Grant for so many reasons, the first being that he didn't want to lose her. The one thing he couldn't figure out was exactly what he wanted from her. Or why her at all? *Lillie*, he reminded himself. Though now that he was getting to know Miss Grant, there were striking differences between the two women. But that didn't change the fact that every time he looked at his secretary, he saw a little bit of Lillie.

It was no secret that he had a knack for finding and taking in broken souls, and perhaps that was where the issue lay. He'd had his pick of women over the years, but they had all been vapid and empty inside. Then there was Victoria, whom he'd broken off with only a week ago, but he'd never wanted her like he wanted the woman walking away from him now.

None of those women had looked at him the way Miss Grant had, with her heart open and mind ready for any challenge. There was a tenacity to her that he didn't often find in a woman. By all appearances, she had an unwavering spirit that wanted nothing more than to be free, and that feeling was familiar to him. Women like her didn't hide in the shadows for long. They weren't afraid to experience life to the fullest. Did she want to experience the fullest with him? Because he could give her that. He wanted to give her that. He wanted to cloister them up in his bedroom...

There he went again; allowing himself to be ruled by this desire and the strange sense of feelings he had for Miss Grant. Avoiding her just wasn't possible. Keeping away from her, even knowing she wasn't ready for his advances, was impossible.

He wanted her in so primal a fashion that the fine line he walked as a society man was on the cusp of shredding whenever she was near. While no one would mistake him for a gentleman—nor did he pretend to be one—no one would ever question his acuity as a businessman. Except perhaps when he was with Miss Grant. Because he had no inclination to work when she was around. He wanted to arouse her curiosity of him.

Entering his study, he poured a dram of scotch into one of the crystal tumblers stocked on the sideboard. Taking his drink over to his desk, he sat heavily in the chair. He forced himself to sip the spirits, giving Miss Grant ample time to fall asleep. Once finished, he blew out the candles and turning down the lamps in the study and made his way upstairs.

Unable to keep away from her, even though he'd let her escape earlier, he tapped his knuckles feather-light on her door. If she was awake, would she open the door to him? He braced his arms around her doorframe, a sorry attempt at holding himself back. It was better she left him in the hall. Better that she refuse him, or she might consume his every thought, his every need. Not that she didn't do that already. God, what was wrong with him? She didn't need this from him.

After a few moments, he tore himself away from her door and headed down the corridor to his bedchamber, doubting sleep would find him easily.

CHAPTER EIGHT

Amelia woke with a start. As she scrambled to a sitting position, she reached down to cover her legs, prepared to defend herself.

Had she been dreaming of *that* night again?

She wasn't certain when the last time was that she had slept through the night uninterrupted. And it wasn't just the incident with Sir Ian that caused her sleeplessness. She wrapped her arms around herself, rubbing her hands up and down her upper arms as a chill brushed right through to her bones.

There was a clock on the dressing table, but she couldn't see it in the darkness that cloaked her room.

Amelia stared at the intricate plaster design on the ceiling, trying to make out one angel from the next, as she listened to her surroundings. Everything seemed to have gone silent in the house; all she could hear was the pounding of her heart in her chest, though the pace slowed with each breath she took. She was wide awake now.

Just as she resigned herself to getting up for the day, a second crash thudded from somewhere deep in the house.

Shooting fully out of her bed, Amelia flinched as a vicious yell came from the hallway, followed by another crash. Was there an intruder? She grabbed the night robe that Jenny had loaned her and cinched it tightly at her waist.

Hurrying from her room, she saw Huxley standing outside Mr. Riley's room. The candle stub in the holder burned low as he stared at her through narrowed eyes that were not the least bit tired-looking. "Back to your room, Miss Grant," Huxley snapped. "There is nothing you need worry about here."

She stood her ground for reasons she didn't want to consider, her chin jutting out and her back ramrod straight as she stared at him without flinching from his cold gaze. "I heard something fall or break, I'm not sure which." She didn't have the slightest idea how she *could* help. Nor was she certain that Huxley intended to enter Mr. Riley's bedchamber.

With his usual scowl firm on his face and the candlelight flickering harshly over his scars, Huxley looked intimidating, and Amelia might have found him so if she hadn't already known that he had nothing but kindness in him.

"You cannot scare me off so easily," she whispered. When she brushed past him and reached for the door latch, he settled his hand firmly over hers.

"I'm telling you once more: leave this with me."

She turned to look at him so that he could see the resolve burning in her eyes. She would not be persuaded from the path she intended to take. If Mr. Riley needed help, she would never walk away. Especially considering everything he'd done for her.

Huxley didn't say another word; he only backed up a step to allow her admittance, although with a look that almost dared her.

Before she could think about what she was doing and what she might see, she lifted the handle and pushed the door open. Twisted in his sheets, Mr. Riley lay in the middle of a monstrous four-poster bed, mumbling incomprehensible words as he tossed around in the grips of a nightmare. The only evidence of something being knocked over was a three-stemmed candelabra on the floor, but she wasn't here to look for the source now; she was here to assist Mr. Riley.

Huxley came into the room close behind her, his face somber, but not surprised by what he saw. Was this a regular occurrence? That was not a question she would dare ask. At least not right now.

There was a moment of regret as she approached Mr. Riley, and her face started to burn red as she realized that he did not wear clothes to bed. Though there was no feeling of desire as she approached his twisted, agonized form—only worry. All she wanted to do was help him as he'd helped her, to stop what pained him in his sleep in hopes that one day someone could help her through the nightmares that haunted her sleeping hours.

She took the candle stub Huxley had been holding and edged closer to the bed, using her softest voice to call Mr. Riley back from whatever tortured him in his sleep.

"Mr. Riley. You need to wake."

The pain that gripped his face broke her heart, and she hated to see him reduced to a man drowning in so much pain. Sweat beaded across his forehead and drew a damp line over his temples. The closer she got to the high bed, the more she realized that perhaps Huxley had been right when he'd told her to leave. But she couldn't leave now. Mr. Riley needed her.

Well, maybe not her, but he needed someone to help him, and she refused to walk away from anyone in need.

She set the candle on the nightstand next to the bed. His body was level with her chest, as the mattress rested on a high platform.

"Mr. Riley." She kept her voice low, soothing, hoping he would hear her if she kept repeating her request. "Let go of what pains you. Come back to us."

How could she break through his nightmare?

She reached toward his forearm, only to have Huxley yank her violently away. "You don't want to touch him. He isn't quite right when he is in this state."

"Best you head back to bed, Miss Grant. I can handle this."

There was something about Huxley's stark gaze that frightened her. Amelia wrapped her arms around her midsection and nodded. Leaving the candle behind, she made her way out of the room. She paused at the door to look back at Mr. Riley, still twisting around on his bed, mumbling incoherently.

Huxley caught her gaze again; he was waiting for her to leave so she wouldn't be witness to whatever came next. Reluctantly, she closed the door. She released a ragged, broken breath with the finality of her action.

Hand over her heart, she found her center after a few deep breaths and leaned on the wall as she headed back to her own room. Her ankle throbbed worse than it had before; she'd been foolish to run to Mr. Riley's aid without taking care of her injury.

She sat on her bed listening to the old creaks in the house, as one question turned over and over in her mind: what secrets haunted Mr. Riley so deeply?

And then she had to ask herself if Huxley would mention to Mr. Riley that she'd seen him at a great disadvantage. She must bring it up with Huxley first thing in the morning.

She was quite awake now, so decided she might as well get dressed for the day, even though it was close to half past four. Too early to break her fast, she resigned herself to getting some work done in the study. She had every intention of finishing Mr. Riley's invitations today and finalizing his calendar so that she might be available for more important tasks, preferably something more challenging; she disliked being idle.

Mr. Riley didn't come down to the study all morning. The first person she saw was Huxley, who advised her that breakfast was being served in the dining hall. Before she could ask him what had come of Mr. Riley the night before, Huxley held up his hand, stalling the words before they could leave her lips.

"Don't ask questions to which I can give no answers. Just forget last night."

She pinched her lips together. That was one thing she couldn't promise to do. How did Huxley expect her to forget what had happened? Couldn't she at least inquire as to Mr. Riley's state of mind once he woke? "If his nightmares are a regular occurrence, it might be in both our best interests to know how I should deal with the situation in future."

"You'll not need to deal with anything, Miss Grant. A man needs to keep some of his life private, and prying would be unwise."

Not satisfied with his answer, she boldly asked, "Are you suggesting that my further examination of the events last night will cost me my job here?"

Huxley wasn't expecting the question, she knew, because he turned from her suddenly and repeated in a far sterner voice, "Breakfast is being served in the dining hall."

Taking up her cane, she followed Huxley down to the kitchen, angry with herself for caring, and especially angry with Huxley for being such a stubborn mule about the whole situation. His warning, however, was unlikely to deter her from going to Mr. Riley again, should she hear him tossing around from another nightmare.

Whether Huxley had informed her employer about her witnessing the events of last night, she couldn't say. But she had to assume they discussed it, because she didn't see Mr. Riley for the remainder of the day.

CHAPTER NINE

It had been a feat but one she'd conquered without Huxley's help in all of two days. Amelia stuffed the last response in an envelope and set it on top of the stack of letters and RSVPs that needed to be posted in the morning. She sat back in her chair with a triumphant yawn and wondered what Huxley would have her do tomorrow.

Voices carried to her from the next room, just as a light flickered on in Mr. Riley's study. She recognized the soothing tone of her employer's voice, but there were two other gentlemen with him. Not wanting to repeat her rudeness from two nights ago, she rose to her feet just as Mr. Riley came into the library.

"Why are you still here?" His eyes lingered over the desk where her accouterments were neatly lined up.

"I wanted to finish the invitations and correspondence before the day was through."

She reached for her cane, but Mr. Riley reached it first, and his arm came under hers to guide her into the study. She hated to admit that she'd been counting down the hours until she would see him again.

Why did she always find herself breathless in his presence? It meant she was full of foolishness, and she silently scolded herself for that.

Delicately clearing her throat and focusing her thoughts away from the steady warmth of his body so very near to hers, she said, "I planned to head to the kitchen before I went to bed."

She winced at the suggestiveness of her words. Did he think she was inviting him to eat with her or join her in bed?

"Let me introduce you to some friends before you retire for the night," he responded.

As they walked into the study, two men stood from the leather chairs.

"Landon Price, Lord Burley," Mr. Riley said, indicating the shorter man, though he stood taller than Amelia. "This is my new secretary, Miss Grant. And she is currently handling all correspondence, so your wife will not need to read Huxley's chicken-scratch writing anymore."

"A pleasure to make your acquaintance, Miss Grant." Lord Burley's hand engulfed Amelia's as he bowed slightly and kissed the back of her knuckles. His hair was dark, though gray feathered through it at the temples, and his eyes were a rich brown.

"Likewise," Amelia responded.

"Landon and I share an interest in wool shipments," Mr. Riley said, explaining their relationship further. Amelia recalled accepting an invitation for Mr. Riley to a soiree at Lord Burley's house next week. "Landon is trying to convince me to visit his farm in Scotland, so I can see firsthand the start of the process."

"Aye, my wife thinks you need some time in the country. Help you get rid of the tension you always carry about you."

Amelia heard a slight Scottish lilt in Lord Burley's comment. Before she could ask him about his farm, the other man stepped forward, his hand out in invitation. When she put her hand in his, he turned it over and brushed a kiss across the back of it.

"Hart," he said. "I have known Nick for about as long as I can remember."

It was difficult to tell if he, too, was a peer. In fact, she wasn't altogether certain if he had just introduced himself with his first name or his last. The man's clothes spoke of similar wealth to Mr. Riley's—the fine material was pressed and without a wrinkle, even so late in the day. His waistcoat was a checkered silver and blue silk that complemented his light blue eyes and fair coloring. His smile was alluring, and it probably had seduced many an unsuspecting woman, but it didn't have the same effect as Mr. Riley's intense stares had on her.

She frowned with that thought.

"Will Miss Grant be replacing Huxley?" Lord Burley asked.

The last thing Amelia had planned this evening was to sit with Mr. Riley. Her stomach chose that inopportune moment to rumble in protest. She hoped no one heard it, though Mr. Riley glanced over to her, amusement dancing in his eyes.

He turned back to his guests. "She is taking over his old position, yes," Mr. Riley corrected Lord Burley. "I won't keep you, Miss Grant."

Amelia ducked her head cordially to everyone in the room. "It was a pleasure to make your acquaintances. Good evening, Mr. Riley."

She couldn't be sure, but she thought Mr. Riley was reluctant to release his hold on her elbow.

Mr. Riley's guests bid her a good night, allowing her to make her escape. She wasn't sure if she was happy to have had such a short interlude with Mr. Riley or disappointed that she hadn't spent more time with him alone. She furrowed her brows, not overly impressed that her thoughts were so consumed by her employer.

When she arrived in the kitchen, no one was about. The hour must be later than she suspected.

Although she was not sure whether she was allowed to avail herself of whatever was in the kitchen, her stomach's grumbling protest decided her path. Searching through the larder, she found a half a loaf of bread, a plate of covered cheese, and some butter. She settled herself to making a sandwich and sat on the stool off the side of the room to enjoy her dinner. She'd think twice before forgetting dinner again.

The steady pace of someone approaching stopped her midchew. She hadn't done anything wrong by coming down here—or at least she didn't think so.

The master of the house stepped into the kitchen area, one eyebrow quirked when he saw Amelia sitting in the chair.

He was down to his shirtsleeves and waistcoat. When he crossed his arms and leaned against the doorframe, she could clearly make out the sinew of his arms flexing beneath the crisp white linen.

"You do know that if you miss a meal, Joshua sets aside a plate," he said. "On cold days, he keeps stew warm on the coals."

She swallowed her half-chewed bite of food as she tore her gaze from his strong body and looked him in the eye. She shook her head. In the silence, she took the opportunity to slide off the stool and straighten out her dress where it had folded at her hips.

"You needn't get up on my account," Mr. Riley said.

"I beg to differ." She walked—well, limped—over to the chopping board in the middle of the room and set her sandwich on a cloth napkin. When he continued to watch her every move, she asked, "Is there something you need from me, Mr. Riley?"

He stepped into the room, his presence having a devastating effect on the rate of her heartbeat.

"Many things, Miss Grant. Many things." He stared at her in a way that had a new awareness skittering across her body and replacing the hunger pangs with something that made her ravenousness for something other than food.

She knew very well that he didn't require her in a secretarial sense, and she swallowed against the bubble of nerves that gave her goose bumps from the not entirely unpleasant sensation she always felt when they were alone together.

She picked up her cane and leaned into it, partly for support and partly in fear that her jelly-like legs would give out at any moment. "I must meet Huxley at eight tomorrow morning. Unless you would like me to get someone for you."

"As I was saying"—he walked over to the larder and bent down to one of the lower shelves to pull out a plate wrapped in cloth—"Joshua always prepares extra plates when someone misses dinner." He set the dish on the cutting block in front of her.

"Are you not hungry?" she asked.

"I ate at the club, Miss Grant. But thank you for your concern." He pulled the stool over to the table. "I insist you take a seat."

She did, not out of obedience, she told herself, but because the food smelled heavenly as she unwrapped it, revealing a pie decorated with a rabbit on the top to identify the contents. It was still warm to the touch, and she felt her mouth water; this was a far better meal than the one she'd prepared. There was even a fork tucked along the side of the dish, but she hesitated to pick it up; she put her hand back in her lap. It seemed strange to eat while Mr. Riley watched her. She swallowed against the hunger building in her and tore her gaze from the tasty-looking pastry.

"Don't wait on my account," he said.

It was silly to feel nervous around him. But questions had burned on her tongue since the last night they'd seen each other, and only Mr. Riley could shed light on those answers.

She picked up the fork and stabbed it through the pie crust, which was flaky and looked delicious. She took a bite, her mouth melting around the still-warm filling of rabbit, turnip, raisins, and other ingredients she couldn't distinguish. The pie was sweet and savory at the same time.

While she ate, Mr. Riley watched her with quiet regard. She pushed the plate toward him, wondering if he'd come down here to find an evening meal or if he'd followed her once his guests had left.

He took the fork from her hand and scooped up a bite for himself before handing the empty utensil back to her. She tried not to think of his mouth having been where she now placed hers, but she allowed the utensil to linger in her mouth longer than needed.

When she offered him the fork again, he shook his head.

"I insist you eat your fill."

She pulled the plate closer and picked through the last half of the pie, feeling more than full but enjoying it too much to let it go to waste.

She wasn't sure what prompted the question, but she said, "I wanted to ask what you did to your hand." Mr. Riley didn't so much as cringe. Perhaps she had assumed wrong on what had caused his cuts. Even now, he unashamedly displayed his bruised and abraded hand in plain sight. And she didn't pretend she hadn't seen the damage to his knuckles.

"That, Miss Grant, is a question I believe you do not truly want answered."

"Why would you think that?"

"Because the answer might unsettle you."

She looked away from him and back down to her pie. She forced herself to take a few more bites. Needing to hear the truth from Mr. Riley's mouth became imperative, and before she could think better of her question, she blurted out, "Did you have anything to do with Sir Ian's current circumstance?"

He unfurled his hand and laid it flat on the table as he continued to watch her. More than ever, she needed to know what his involvement had been, though she feared she already knew the answer. Had in fact always known the answer.

"It's a crime to exert force over those who are weaker than you are. And that so happens to be one thing I cannot and will not tolerate from anyone." He reached across the table and lightly touched the side of her face with the back of his hand. "If I had something to do with his current circumstance, what would you do?"

Amelia swallowed. Sir Ian had deserved what he got. And thinking that might make her a terrible person, but if someone hadn't dealt harshly with him, as she presumed Mr. Riley had, Sir Ian might do far worse to the next unsuspecting worker under his care. Though that didn't explain why was she so forgiving of Mr. Riley when she should be appalled. Because no one had ever stood up for her before now, not even her own flesh and blood.

"I'm not entirely sure what I would do." She scrutinized him for a moment; there was no denying that he would be much stronger than Sir Ian. "I suppose I would ask why."

Could you possibly ask a stupider question, Amelia?

"Can you not guess?" he asked.

She could only mentally shake her head at herself. Because he wanted her and had admitted as much. What disturbed her was not that he'd just admitted to Sir Ian's injuries, but the fact that she was thrilled he'd cared enough to right something that had gone so wrong for her.

She set her fork down, not sure how to extract herself from his company without seeming rude. This man twisted up her thoughts, and she needed to get away from him before she admired him any more than she currently did. He stood and took her plate.

"I can do that," she said, making her way to her feet too.

"Easier for me, I think." He disappeared into the next room but was back at her side within a minute. "Let me accompany you upstairs." It was a friendly offer.

She nodded. She couldn't very well say she wanted to go alone because he might ask why. And what answer would she give him? *Sorry, Mr. Riley, but I'm worried that I will ask you to kiss me again if we don't go our own ways.* That certainly wouldn't do, so she took his proffered arm and let him lead the way.

He was kind enough to pause at each stair landing to let her sore ankle rest. Who knew three flights of stairs could wind her so easily?

Unable to keep their silence, halfway up their ascent, she asked, "Did you sort out the business with your manager changing the ledgers?"

Mr. Riley's hand tightened at her elbow. Was he surprised by the question? "Not yet."

He didn't expand on that, so she would ask Huxley for an update in the morning. If she was to be his secretary, it would not be in name only. "Mr. Riley."

"Miss Grant."

"I think I should make a few things clear."

Before they cleared the top landing, Mr. Riley backed her up against the wall. An ornate picture frame, at least five feet tall and just as wide, dug into her shoulder and back. He loomed over her, forcing her to tilt her head back to look up at him. She noticed a hint of mischief in his eyes. It was odd that she didn't feel threatened by his show of dominance.

"What should be made clearer?" he asked.

"My position, for one. I will not be shielded from business dealings. I cannot do my job efficiently or very effectively if I'm not given all the information I require to do my job."

"Fair enough." Mr. Riley braced one hand against the wall near her arm and leaned in closer.

"When I ask you a question, I would prefer that you did not skirt around it."

"So you want to know what happened to the manager. Nothing, actually. We are waiting to catch him in action."

"Why, when you already know he has stolen from you?"

"Because I will make an example of him. Stealing is a whipping offense, Miss Grant. I will have the full letter of the law behind me when I deal with him. He is not the first to try to take advantage of me, and he certainly will not be the last, but action taken against him will stay the hand of most men who are on the fence between making the right or wrong decision."

"Thank you for your honesty."

"What other questions have I skirted?"

"You are forgiven for anything you have not yet answered, but I want you to be straightforward with me in future. It is only fair, given that we are to work so closely."

"How close?"

She swallowed, but didn't duck away from him. She liked his nearness, his dominance.

"If you do not take this opportunity to run from me, Miss Grant, I might do something you will regret later."

"The last thing I want to do is run from you." She snapped her mouth shut. Had she really just admitted that to him? Why couldn't she have said because her ankle hurt too much to attempt the feat? Her breath audibly hitched in her lungs.

"I could think of better ways to make you breathless." There was so much promise in his words, and it was hard to ignore what he meant. But she had to, or she'd lose her train of thought.

He caressed the back of his hand over her cheek. "After the abuse you have suffered…"

She reached for his hand, bringing it between their bodies, ensuring that she couldn't step tighter into the circle of his arms as she craved. Her fingers wrapped around his much-larger ones. "It is different between us." Different from any of her brother's friends who had made unwelcome advances toward her. "The last thing I feel when I'm with you is fear."

"I will not hurt you, but I cannot pretend to be a good man either."

So he could easily break her heart if she allowed this desire to bloom into something more. As long as he was forthcoming about that.

He stepped closer. Close enough to crush their hands between them. Her body trembled at the nearness. She knew she was about to make a monumental change to their relationship, one that might jeopardize their professional relationship—not now, but down the road. And she couldn't steer herself away from the imminent danger. She didn't have the wherewithal or the willpower.

His arm snaked around her lower back to pull her forward, and he crushed her pelvis tightly against his, with her skirts pressed up against him and between her legs. She was sure the only reason she was still standing on her jelly-like legs was because his hand was placed possessively over her lower back, holding her up.

"I want your complete surrender."

She bit her lower lip and swallowed against the lump of nerves sizzling like a slow burn through her whole body. What did complete surrender look like?

Her voice was barely above a whisper. "What if I cannot give you that?" She couldn't think straight when Mr. Riley surrounded her as he did now. She couldn't think straight whenever he was even in the same room as she was.

"You will," he said with conviction.

Her breath froze in her lungs with his declaration that she would be his. If she were honest with herself, part of her wanted him to make that decision for her; maybe she'd regret her actions less that way.

What would it mean to be his?

Before she could find her voice, he kneeled and lifted her into his arms. The action caused the breath to whoosh from her lungs. She knew the right thing to do would be to protest, beg him to put her down. But she couldn't bring herself to do that.

"Where are you taking me?" she finally managed, though her voice was husky with a need she did not fully understand.

"Don't worry, Miss Grant."

He looked at her with those stormy gray eyes and just like that, she was lost. She couldn't even voice that she wasn't worried. Not when she felt so safe in his arms. Not when she wanted to be where she was in this very moment and stay there for an eternity before reality crept back in.

"I would never do anything you're not ready for," he added.

Those words should have frightened her, brought her back to her senses, or at the very least made her think about what she was allowing to happen. But they did no such thing. She wanted to know what happened when she didn't run from what she felt for this man.

Shame should burn in her for the feelings bombarding her right now, but the truth was, curiosity won over.

Amelia wanted to give Mr. Riley more than she'd ever given anyone, not because she owed it to him, but because she wanted to explore things with him that she'd never explored with another. She wanted to give him a part of herself she'd never openly shared.

Why now? Why him?

He set her down on her feet just outside her bedroom door. Her hands and arms were tucked between them, and she had no desire to put space between them.

He gave her a chaste kiss on her forehead and stepped away from her. She was feeling weak-kneed and had to lean against her door, or she feared she'd slither right down to the floor.

"Good night, Miss Grant." He turned away from her, tucking his hands in his pockets as he walked toward his room.

She opened her mouth to call him back, but what would she say? What exactly did she want from him? It was better that he'd left her. She needed to think about what had happened, what she'd almost allowed. She needed to give herself a good shake and wake up from this fairy-tale-like dream she thought she was living.

Chapter Ten

When Amelia opened her bedchamber door, it was hard to miss the large ivory box placed neatly at the foot of her bed. She paused on the threshold and turned her gaze to the rest of the room. Nothing else was different, aside from the unmistakable presence of a gift.

The idea of receiving a gift since she and Mr. Riley had come to an understanding of what their future held felt wrong, and it degraded what was between them. Though had they really come to an understanding?

He'd told her that he would have her surrender, and she hadn't disagreed.

Closing the door behind her, she made her way to the bed. She could ignore the box and worry about it later. She had only come up to her bedchamber to freshen herself up for dinner. The lavender bow around the box was elaborate and perfectly tied. It was smooth and satiny as she pulled it loose. Tentatively, she lifted the lid, and her hand flew to cover her mouth in surprise.

A blush-rose dress was folded neatly inside. A note rested on top of the material. Flipping the heavy parchment open, she read the rough scroll:

Miss Grant,

   It would please me if you would join me for an evening out. Jenny will come around to help you ready.
—*Nick*

Amelia sat heavily at the corner of the bed, fingering the edge of the note. Why had he put her in a position where she'd have to explain what had happened between her and Mr. Riley? She was certain Jenny would want to know why he'd purchased a dress for Amelia at all. What would the staff think of her? Hot shame washed over her face. She *should* decline the gift and have it returned to Mr. Riley at once.

Reaching into the box, she pulled out the dress. There was a heavy layer of plum pulled into a becoming fall at the base of the back and layered in with the blush. The front was decorated in layers of lace and mauve satin. She laid the dress out on the bed and found a pair of matching pink gloves in the bottom of the box, with a wooden fan trimmed in the same lace as was on the dress. She spread out the fan to reveal a painting of an elegant woman wearing ivory, sitting in a swan-shaped sleigh, with a man pushing her through a snowy backdrop. It was a work of art. And apparently Mr. Riley left no detail untouched.

At the brush of knuckles on her door, she snapped the fan shut and put it back in the box. Jenny popped her head in. "Mr. Riley sent me up to have you readied."

Unable to face the maid's scrutiny or judgment, she focused on the evidence of Mr. Riley's gifts spread out over her bed. "I cannot imagine why he should want to take me anywhere."

"I take it he didn't tell you all your duties." Jenny came into the room and stood beside Amelia. Amelia fingered one of the lace bits on the back of the dress that was shaped into a rosette. "You will be there to even out the numbers of a client dinner. I'm glad I have not the tact or elegance you have with language. Cannot much imagine me squeezing into a dress like this and then minding my manners all evening."

That brought a smile to Amelia's face. Jenny had a good, kind heart and knew exactly how to ease the doubt that niggled at the corners of Amelia's mind.

"Not sure how we will style your hair, as you're to be ready in an hour, but we should at least get you dressed and proper-looking for your role tonight."

Amelia wanted to ask what role that was, but didn't have the courage to say it outright. She started to remove her clothes as Jenny walked over to the wardrobe and pulled open the doors. She rummaged through a drawer tucked into the bottom of the cabinet, fishing through the materials and making a mess of the neat stacks Amelia had made when cleaning out the room.

"Found what we need," Jenny said, revealing a small bustle made with bunches and frills of fabric that would help drape the dress properly at the back.

With Amelia standing in her chemise and corset, Jenny went about securing the bustle around Amelia's waist. She was dressed and perched carefully in front of her mirror in no time at all.

"Were you a lady's maid?" Amelia asked.

"My mum was. Spent my youth in a grand house."

Amelia didn't ask why Jenny had left the grand house, fearing that it would mean having to reveal something of her own past. "Well, I think you would make a wonderful lady's maid."

"Let's see how you feel after your hair is done. I'm not as accomplished in that department."

"Why not just pin it up and see if we can find a strand of beads to weave through it?" Amelia suggested.

"Wouldn't have thought of that. Let me call for Mrs. Coleman." Before Amelia could protest, Jenny walked over to the bed where the servants' bell was tucked behind the canopy's fall of fabric.

Jenny returned to Amelia's side and went about pinning pieces of hair into an elaborate bun on top of her head. The young woman had a way of making it look more intricate a style than it really was. Amelia stared at her reflection in the mirror, a little in awe to see herself dressed up. She had never worn a dress of such beauty. In fact, it was more lavish than anything she'd ever seen.

It wasn't long before Mrs. Coleman came into the room, and she seemed not at all surprised that Amelia was being readied for a grand affair. Jenny explained what they needed, hoping there was something in the house they could use for Amelia's hair. Mrs. Coleman squeezed Amelia's shoulder, her eyes misting a little as she looked her over. Then she was gone. Amelia wanted to ask why she'd caused such a reaction from the housekeeper, but bit her tongue.

She must pretend that her being dressed for the evening was a normal affair and that Huxley would have filled this task of accompanying Mr. Riley before her arrival, but there was a niggling doubt at the back of her mind saying otherwise. So what exactly did the rest of the household think of her? Did they assume she was Mr. Riley's mistress?

Clearing her throat, Amelia asked, "Why do you suppose a secretary is needed to attend this meeting?"

"Mr. Riley needs another set of eyes and ears," Jenny explained. "Think of it as a test. He's gonna need to know how you interpret people, your impressions of them. This will be the best setting to get to know the people he has aligned himself with."

"Why would Huxley not attend?"

Just as Jenny was twisting the last strand of Amelia's hair into the bun, Mrs. Coleman came back into the room holding out a strand of onyx beads.

It looked like a necklace, but it was only the length of a choker. Jenny took it and wrapped it through Amelia's hair like a flower wreath on May Day.

"There," said Jenny stepping back, admiring her handiwork.

Amelia walked to the middle of the room so she could see the full look in her small mirror. A gasp of shock escaped when she saw the image staring back; she barely recognized herself.

"Why should I attend at all? I'm still trying to understand everything Mr. Riley does." She smoothed her hand over the front of her dress. "I feel awkward and fear Mr. Riley's business partners will find me lacking. Surely he has a friend who can attend in my place."

Mrs. Coleman stepped toward her and brushed a stray piece of hair from Amelia's temple. "He used to attend these events with Miss Victoria. But they have broken off."

Amelia's breath caught as a stab of hurt nicked her heart and knocked down her confidence a smidgen. Of course he'd be romantically involved with other women. Women far more beautiful and refined than she, and likely far better trained in the art of innuendo. Far more aware of what he wanted. She felt lacking in an entirely different way now.

"This is not me." This time she said it more for herself, looking at her image in the mirror that seemed so alien. Maybe in another time, another place, she could have had this, but now…

"Were they engaged?" She pressed her lips together. How could she ask them such a question?

Both women chuckled, and Jenny shook her head. Amelia understood then what Victoria's and Mr. Riley's relationship had been, and she hated having that knowledge at all. And though she shouldn't care, she wondered if Mr. Riley had broken off with Miss Victoria prior to Amelia's joining his house. And why should that be relevant? She swallowed back the disappointment she felt.

She hated the idea of asking another stupid question, so she didn't ask more on what the night ahead might bring. Without another worrying thought, she cleared her throat and announced, "Shall we go downstairs and end the suspense?"

Without waiting for a response, she did just that, pausing at the door when she saw the cane. Should she bring it? She rotated her foot, feeling the now familiar ache of her ankle and grabbed the cane on her way out the door.

She might feel silly, hobbling around with a support usually reserved for old crippled men, but it was better to use the cane than fall on her face and look like a fool in front of the people dining with Mr. Riley.

Though she made her way to the study fully expecting to wait for Mr. Riley to join her, he was already sitting behind his desk, head down as he read the newspaper.

Mr. Riley looked up as she approached his desk. His eyes didn't leave her face as he stared at her. "You look delicious enough to consume."

She felt her cheeks burn and had to dip her head to hide the blush that seemed to have also stolen her voice.

He came around his desk and took one of her gloved hands, raised it to his mouth, and kissed her knuckles. She dared to look at him then and could see the gray of his eyes eaten up by the black of his pupils. She swallowed, not sure what she should say, or how she should react to his forward nature. She slid her hand from his grasp and tucked it behind her back as she faced him.

"Where will we dine this evening?" she asked.

"South Langtry."

While Amelia might not be familiar with London, there were some places everyone knew. "I have heard wonderful things about the establishment."

"I should hope so. Hart owns it."

"Oh…" What did she say to that? After responding to invitations and forgotten correspondence the last few days, she knew that he mingled with the upper echelon of society. Why shouldn't one of his business partners be the hotelier who happened to own the nicest, most luxuriant hotel in all of England?

"Why did you not warn me about tonight?" she asked.

"I didn't want this to be an ordeal or for you to fret over it. It's a dinner with the closest of my friends, and we do this once a month. You'll have to grow accustomed to such affairs while working with me."

"Because you broke off with your mistress?" Amelia slapped her hands over her mouth. How dare she utter such a thing—and right to her employer's face.

"My mistress?" Though he said it like a question, she could see in his eyes that he knew precisely what she was talking about.

Amelia cleared her throat and turned away from him, wanting to escape his company but unsure how to do just that when she'd only just arrived in his study. "I'm sorry. I meant nothing by it."

"Oh, quite the contrary." Though his tone was even, she couldn't tell if he was angry that she'd mentioned it or that she knew he'd had a mistress.

"I should perhaps clear up one misconception," he said.

She spun around on her good foot so she was facing him again. "And what is that?"

"Victoria is no man's mistress. And she'd resent anyone for even thinking it."

Mr. Riley stepped close enough that she could have touched him if she stretched her hand out just a little. While she was tempted to reach for him, not only to keep her legs from giving out under her but to merely touch him, she remained motionless. Of course that didn't stop him from skimming the back of his hand over her temple as he pushed an errant curl from her forehead. "So naïve in the art of sex, Miss Grant. I will educate you yet."

"I have seen things that might make you take a second look at me," she said, challenging him.

Mr. Riley grasped her hand and swung them both about so she was pressed against his mahogany desk. He leaned suggestively over her. "I am interested to know more about what you think you know, Miss Grant."

"Perhaps another time. We do have a dinner party to attend." She had never dared to be so outspoken with anyone. What had provoked her now? Oh, she knew what nettled her; she was looking right at him.

His face was but inches from hers, his eyes glued to her parted lips. "We have time to explore the finer qualities of your lips."

She wasn't sure how to respond to that, not that she was given the opportunity to say anything. Mr. Riley hitched her up enough that she was perched precariously on the edge of his desk as he pressed between her legs. She felt a cool draft on her calves as he exposed her lower legs to the elements of the room so he could better settle himself in the V of her spread thighs.

His mouth was a scant inch from hers when he spoke in a soft, seductive tone. "Do you think you can teach me something? I dare you to try."

She'd stepped into territory she didn't quite understand. She didn't know how she was supposed to respond to him or how she was supposed to act, now that she'd crossed into unfamiliar ground.

"I can see your thoughts turning over right now," he said. "Just act, Miss Grant. I promise you will not regret it."

How could he know that? Any self-respecting woman would frown on the thoughts she was having right now. Apparently, *any self-respecting woman* didn't extend to her.

"Regret is a peculiar word," she said. "We are taught to regret—"

Mr. Riley's lips melded with hers, though "melded" seemed too tame a word. They meshed and smashed and drew her in. Her resolve to resist this man was torn down a little every time she was in his company. She wanted him with a fierceness and desire she couldn't explain in words. Sex, she understood, but this gut-deep desire that consumed her so wholly befuddled and confounded her.

His lips were unforgiving as they parted hers so his tongue could swirl around her mouth, giving her an unfamiliar feeling to which she was so far from adverse to that a soft moan passed her lips, only to be swallowed up by his hungry growl.

She felt so hot, so desirous and needy, that she panted against him, her breathing coming in great rushes through the parting of their lips. Her hands curled into the lapels of his jacket and she tasted him back. She let her tongue search as his did. Let her body feel the weight of him crushed against her.

"You tempt me beyond all reason," he said against her forehead before kissing it. "Let us leave here before you find yourself strapped to my bed."

Her eyes widened at the suggestion, which he seemed to find humorous, for he chuckled as he eased off her and pulled her from the desk. He tipped up her chin to look at her full on. "Not so experienced as you think. I plan to teach you a lot, Amelia."

What this man did to her and made her feel was so foreign, yet it felt so right.

"Am I to replace Victoria?" she asked. "Be your mistress in name, even if she wasn't?"

"There is no denying that you will be mine, but you are your own woman. I will not label you, other than to introduce you as my secretary. Our trust in each other needs to be absolute if we are to work well together."

She turned her gaze to the dark library. "What makes you so certain you can have the best of both worlds?"

"Because I always get what I want."

As they entered the dining hall at the South Langtry Hotel, Nick couldn't help the possessiveness he felt over Amelia. Discreetly, he placed his hand at the base of her back and led her through the maze of tables as the maître d'hôtel showed them to their seats. Discreet, though, could be used subjectively, as anyone and everyone could see that he had a new lady at his side this evening. And tonight the world would know that Amelia was his alone.

As they approached the table, Nick realized they were the last to arrive; they had been delayed in his study, but it had been the traffic stalling the carriage ride that had made them late. Not that arriving last was a cause for concern; tonight was casual and spent, for the most part, among friends.

There was a familiar face in the crowd Nick hadn't expected to see. Her ostrich feather was perched high among a fall of blonde curls, and her dress was a damask that gave her the effect of being swathed in gold. Nick merely raised one eyebrow as he stared in Victoria's direction. She gave him a mischievous smile as she tipped her champagne against her lips.

Victoria sat between Hart and Meredith. Meredith he'd known for a short time, as she'd married his friend Landon last fall.

Landon had once been a business rival until they had sat down and strategically come up with a plan for bidding on properties to each of their preferences instead of outbidding and inflating the value of said properties every time they had cross dealings.

Sitting beside Landon was Lord Murray. Not a friend by any estimation but someone who owned the latest plot of land that Nick wanted to buy, just north of London. The land wrapped around some of his and Landon's other properties. Murray was a known gambler with luck that should caution his daring but instead made his estate a prime target for those more capable in managing it.

Heddie Burton, the woman next to Murray, was a well-known actress and dancer for a number of shows around town. She was as sought after for her beauty as she was for her brains. Nick thought her no more than a perfectly trained courtesan. She took on paramours like she did productions, changing them frequently when bored with them or when they ran out of money to spend on her; he couldn't tell which. She'd been with Murray for three months now, and this was her second dinner at the hotel with them.

"Sorry to have kept you waiting," Nick said.

"Not at all, old chap," said Hart as he and the other men at the table stood to acknowledge Amelia.

"For those who haven't been introduced to my new secretary," Nick said, "let me present Miss Amelia Grant."

Amelia bowed delicately, like a lady might do when introduced to a room of possible suitors. Nick hated the thought of that as much as he hated to share their evening with everyone present at the table.

They all gave their introductions as he pulled out the chair next to the actress for Amelia, who was currently extending her hand to those she didn't yet know. She asked Hart and Lord Burley how they had been since they had last met. A perfect conversationalist.

While rounds were made, Victoria remained in her seat, ever the voyeur in any situation. Nick didn't fail to notice the furrow creasing her brow.

"Victoria," Nick said by way of greeting.

"Nick," she replied, though her response came at a moment of silence and had everyone looking between them.

"Miss Grant," Nick said, "This is Victoria Newgate."

"A pleasure," Amelia said with a dip of her head.

"Shall we start with the first course?" Hart motioned for the bowls of soup to be set out on the table by the restaurant's staff. It was a cream of asparagus, not Nick's favorite but Amelia seemed to enjoy it.

While Nick sat next to Hart, he spent most of the first course listening to Amelia and Heddie discuss the newest plays to see in town, and he occasionally added a bit when he could say he'd seen something. Overall, his new secretary seemed to keep Murray's guest entertained and unfocused on the conversation Lord Burley was having, of which Nick was only getting pieces.

When the second course came, white wine was poured for everyone. He could tell Amelia wasn't used to eating and drinking in this style, as she finished only half her fish and drank but a quarter glass of her wine.

By the third course, Nick realized he'd paid little attention to Victoria and Meredith and had said barely more than a few sentences to Hart, as his attention had been focused on Amelia.

When Victoria made a point of staring at him, he said, "I didn't expect to see you tonight."

"Hart wouldn't let me miss dinner."

"You're right," Hart said. "I couldn't allow it. You wanted to decline at the last minute when I had no one else to invite."

Hart had recently broken off with an opera singer he'd been seeing for almost a year. The separation had been a public mess.

"You must tell me, Miss Grant," Victoria said, "how is it you took over for Huxley? I thought that man irreplaceable, Nick being as hard to please as he is."

"Huxley is still very involved," Amelia responded. "It will be a miracle if I can get him to hand over the reins to me."

"And how has Nick treated you?"

Before Amelia could reply, Nick settled his hand over hers and squeezed it as he pushed out from the table. "If you will excuse me for a moment." Lord Burley snickered in his direction as Nick walked around the table and leaned close enough to speak in Victoria's ear. "Take a walk with me, will you?"

"I rather like the company," she said, laughing a little too gaily.

"In case my tone wasn't clear, that was me telling you to follow me out."

Victoria placed her folded napkin beside her bowl as Nick pulled her chair out from under the table. "If you'll excuse us a moment," she said.

Though he wanted nothing more than to have her follow behind him for her rudeness, he took her arm to keep up appearances as he led her toward a private terrace. The air was cool, and the night surrounding them was filled with fog.

"Why are you here, Victoria? I thought we agreed to end things amicably."

"I can't help that we have the same friends. And I didn't think *amicable* meant never seeing you again."

It hadn't, but she'd thrown him off by being here tonight. Nick crossed his arms over his chest and leaned against the wall.

"Fine," she said. "I wanted to see this new secretary of yours that Hart was going on about. She's a bit meek for you."

"Jealousy does not suit you, Victoria. You know better than most that Miss Grant is filling a role that had grown vacant with Huxley's expanding role in my businesses."

Victoria leaned closer to him, her finger tracing a path down the middle of his waistcoat. "I do not like how things ended so suddenly between us."

"We both know it wasn't sudden." He curled his hand around hers so she wasn't tempted to further explore him and gently maneuvered her away from him; not that he was tempted by her forwardness; he wasn't, but she needed to understand that their relationship was over. The only woman he wanted was Amelia.

"I miss your company all the same," she said, turning away from him to lean against the iron railing and gaze out over the city. "You're wasted on someone like Miss Grant."

"I have never known you to unfairly judge a woman you do not know. She was in a difficult position before I found her."

Victoria spun around, one eyebrow quirked. "She is not so hard on her luck as you would have me believe."

"While her past might be less complicated than yours, it was just as difficult for her to escape."

He knew Amelia was hiding something from her past—the name she'd given him was false. In fact, she'd done such a fine job of hiding her true identity that he hadn't yet figured out just who she was or where she'd come from. He knew she was from Berwick, and it would be easy enough to inquire about Amelia that way, but he couldn't, in the event that she was running from someone she'd left behind.

Victoria stepped closer, stretching one dainty finger toward his chin. "And what if I am jealous?" she asked, with a pout playing on her red painted lips.

"We did not end our affair so that we could play cat-and-mouse in future."

"Then stop trying to cut me out of your life."

That hadn't been his intention, but Victoria could think what she liked. Amelia was his only concern. "Miss Grant is complicated," he admitted.

"Oh, I can see that. You haven't taken your eyes off her all evening." He looked at her sharply, and she spread her hands as though she were blameless. "I'm not the only one to take notice."

"I don't want you taking anything out of context, Victoria. If I start hearing rumors…"

"Tsk. Darling. You have obviously forgotten the woman I am. Discretion is my middle name."

"Perfect. Then I trust you to have a wardrobe prepared for my new secretary. I'm afraid she has nothing suitable for the meetings she will be required to attend in the coming weeks."

Victoria raised her eyebrow. "From which of my shop girls did you order the blush gown?"

"Darcy."

"Then I shall ensure that discretion is met and your new *secretary* is appropriately attired."

Nick nodded his thanks. "Keep your assumptions to yourself."

"It's not me you should worry about, Nicky. You men think you're so devious and sly, when you are all an open book. Everyone at that table saw your intentions, clear as day."

"Then it's a good thing we're among friends. I mean it, Victoria. I do not want you asking about Amelia either."

"Amelia, is it? Already on a first-name basis? You do move fast, or were you already hot on her tail before you broke off our arrangement?" She traced one of her painted nails over his lower lip. "Don't worry, Nicky. I will keep your secrets. I always have."

She had, but if what Victoria said was true—that he'd been obvious in his attention toward Amelia—he'd have to be more circumspect. If there was one thing Nick had managed to accomplish, in addition to his wealth, it was an equal measure of enemies. Amelia was too gentle a soul to ward off some of the uglier parts of his life.

"Everyone certainly must be wondering where we are," Victoria pointed out.

"Then we should not keep them waiting."

He vowed to ignore Amelia for the rest of their dinner. If he could convince his friends that Amelia was only his secretary, then that was what the rest of the world would believe. Only he needed to know that she was so much more.

CHAPTER ELEVEN

Amelia wasn't sure where Mr. Riley and Miss Newgate had gone off to, but her stomach flipped at the idea of their needing a moment of privacy. She'd taken one spoonful of her lemon sorbet before giving up—her appetite was gone, ruined really.

Heddie, her dining companion, proved to be an interesting and entertaining woman. Perhaps that was natural for someone in her profession. Though Heddie was guarded about personal details of her life, she did share a number of humorous stories from her time in theatre.

"There was a time during *Midsummer's Night Dream* when the stage was large enough to accommodate a horse. Well, that horse found himself particularly full from all the apples and carrots we fed him off stage. Relieved himself right in the middle of the show and kicked his foot out. The actor on stage with me got a horse mud pie right in the face."

Lord Murray couldn't seem to contain his mirth, for he laughed and snorted at the end of her tale. Taking a long swallow of his champagne the wrong way, he sputtered and coughed enough to draw the eyes of everyone around them in the restaurant. Heddie gave her companion a few good thumps on the back until he stopped hacking.

While everyone was laughing at the story, Amelia grew sicker to her stomach as the minutes ticked by and Mr. Riley had yet to return to the table.

"Had I met you before my wife, Heddie, I'd be a man in trouble," Lord Murray insisted.

"I wouldn't let you steal me away from the city and all that I love to be sealed up in that dratted old castle you call a home in Highgate."

At the mention of Highgate, Amelia snapped to attention. "A castle?" she said inquisitively.

"She exaggerates, Miss Grant. It's just a drafty old house."

Did Mr. Riley intend to purchase Lord Murray's drafty old house? Before she could ask more about Highgate, Mr. Riley and Miss Newgate entered from the opposite end of the room.

She was a beautiful woman, shorter than Amelia but voluptuous, and her corseted-waist was cinched to perfection. Her hair looked like spun gold, and her dress looked like it had been dipped in the precious metal. It was obvious that Victoria Newgate was a woman with a great deal of wealth.

Men turned when she walked past them. Mr. Riley seemed entranced by her conversation and laughed about whatever it was they discussed.

Why should it matter to Amelia how Mr. Riley acted around the other woman? She was forgetting her position. Something she shouldn't dare do. She looked away from them so they wouldn't see her staring, and she focused on the other guests at the table.

Mr. Riley took his seat, his elbow brushing against Amelia's as he placed his napkin in his lap. "Sorry to keep you waiting," he said as he took a spoonful of his sorbet.

She didn't respond, just gave a slight smile as she looked at the woman sitting across from her. When their eyes met, Victoria gave her a wink and laughed about something Lady Burley had whispered. Amelia dropped her gaze to her bowl. She was so far out of her element right now that she just wanted the night to end.

Coffee was served around the table after the last setting was taken away. When Amelia brought the small white cup to her nose, she was immediately repelled by the strong smell and set the cup down untouched.

"It's bitter and perhaps an acquired taste," Mr. Riley said, sliding the glass tray of sugar cubes closer to her cup. "This will sweeten it."

"I'm not sure anything will make that smell pleasant enough to drink," Amelia said.

Mr. Riley dropped a sugar cube in her cup and stirred it around with a spoon. "Try it," he insisted.

She looked at him, forgetting once again that there were other people at the table. "Can I trust you, Mr. Riley?" She wasn't asking about the coffee; she was looking at Miss Newgate across the table.

"Implicitly."

Placing her lips against the cup, she took a small sip of the liquid and was immediately repelled by the stringent assault on her tongue. She set it down. "I'm afraid I likely will not acquire a liking for coffee anytime soon." She pushed the cup away so she wouldn't have to smell it.

Hart chuckled and said, "Before long, you will crave it after dinner. I used to hate the stuff."

"Then why did you continue to drink it?" Heddie asked, sipping her own coffee.

"Sometimes coffee was the only decent drink available when I traveled," Hart said.

"Where did you travel?" Amelia asked, genuinely curious. The idea of traveling had always fascinated her, but she wasn't sure how one went about planning a trip.

"Egypt and Morocco, mainly," Hart said with a shrug, as though everyone traveled to exotic locations.

"He's being modest, darling," Victoria said to Amelia. "Those were only his favorite places. Hart is a bit of a travel bug. Every few years he practically itches to see something new and disappears for months at a time. When he remembers he has friends back home, we receive a letter from some far-off locale."

Victoria had perfect teeth and a perfect smile. Amelia couldn't help but compare herself to this woman who so easily drew Mr. Riley's attention. Was it possible they were still lovers, even though the Jenny had said otherwise? She hated that she wanted to know the answer so badly.

"Well," Lady Burley said, directing her words to Amelia, "if it's any consolation, I have never been outside of Britain."

Amelia liked Lady Burley very much. Where Victoria had managed to say everything in a lofty air that seemed like an insult, the other woman merely brushed it off, as if there was nothing overly spectacular about the exotic locations Hart had visited.

"I used to visit an aunt in Scotland, but I have not been farther north than that," Amelia chimed in with a smile. She could say that she'd at least been somewhere else.

"Whereabouts? My mum was Scots," Heddie said.

"Edinburgh." Amelia was surprised to have Mr. Riley's complete attention. He looked at her as if his knowing something she rarely talked about made a difference to him. "But my aunt died when I was twelve, and we didn't have any family left that way, so I haven't visited after that. What about you, Mr. Riley? Have you traveled the world far and wide?"

"Never had a desire to travel. My life and my businesses are all on English soil."

"Because you haven't thought of the possibilities elsewhere," Hart said with laughter in his voice, as though this was a topic they discussed regularly.

"We are in very different businesses, my friend," Mr. Riley said with a finality that ended the conversation.

To Amelia's surprise, Mr. Riley stood to wish everyone a good night. It seemed they had another engagement, as did some of the others.

"It was a pleasure to see you again, Miss Grant," Lord Burley said.

"You and your wife were wonderful company for my first dinner out," Amelia responded.

When she said good night to Victoria, the woman kissed both her cheeks and then held Amelia at arm's length to look at her. Was she assessing her? Looking for flaws? Amelia felt her cheeks grow warm under the other woman's regard. "You will keep him in good order?" Victoria asked.

Amelia opened her mouth to respond, but how was she to reply to that? Her job was, in a sense, to keep Mr. Riley in order.

"Vic," Mr. Riley interjected, "always inserting yourself in my affairs. Miss Grant, you must ignore my friend. She knows how disorganized I can be and cannot tolerate any sort of chaos."

"Yes, well…" Victoria started to say, but Mr. Riley kissed her cheek, and he and Amelia left in the next instant, having concluded their good-byes.

"I feel I should apologize for her forwardness," Mr. Riley said as he and Amelia made their way out into the street.

"She seems very brazen. I dare say, I have not met any other woman like her."

"That almost sounds like a compliment, Miss Grant."

Mr. Riley hailed a cab and opened the low door for her. She stepped inside and took a seat on the bench, and Mr. Riley gave direction to the driver before following her inside.

"Are we not finished with the evening?" she asked. She thought he might drop her off at the house while he attended to his other engagements.

"Far from, my dear. We're dressed, so we might as well enjoy a night around the city."

"Will your friends be joining us?"

He shook his head, that intense gaze of his focused fully on her again. She swallowed back any further questions. She wouldn't refuse him the night; this might be her only opportunity to wander around London and explore the places frequented by men and women of means.

Before long, the driver pulled up to a two-story brick building with no sign to identify it.

As Mr. Riley assisted Amelia out of the carriage, he flicked the driver a coin and said, "Double that and your usual fare for the night if you wait until we are through here."

"I will wait right here, good sir," the driver said.

Mr. Riley took Amelia's elbow and led her to a small café. It was stuffed to the brim with patrons, half of them shouting and singing along with the piano player in the background, the rest gaily milling about.

She wasn't sure what type of music played but the patrons enjoyed it enough to raise their ale and sing along in boisterous volume. Some patrons danced on a small section of the floor that had been cleared for that purpose. Both she and Mr. Riley were jostled as they made their way to the center of the loud room. When she was pushed into Mr. Riley's side, he put his arm around her to shield her from the rowdy crowd and continued to pull them forward.

"You should use your cane to clear your path if the louts will not move for a lady," Mr. Riley said clearly, without having to shout over the noise.

"I couldn't," she mumbled, doubting he even heard her.

A polished mahogany bar stood dead center in the room. It curved along the top edge and bowed out in the middle to accommodate shelving behind. Various bottles of liquor and wine filled the shelves, as did an array of different glasses. Beveled mirrors were mounted on the back wall behind the bar, making the room look grander than it was. Leather-cushioned stools lined along the bar like soldiers standing guard, every one of them occupied by men and women mingling together. There were large water fountains at both ends of the bar, filled to the top with ice.

Mr. Riley placed an order and then took Amelia's hand and led her to a booth with a round table in the middle; it might have seated four comfortably, but there were six people seated there. One of the men at the table saw Mr. Riley and motioned for the others to vacate the booth. No words passed between the men, but the two heavily painted women gave Amelia a knowing look before the men led them away.

Amelia was fairly certain they were prostitutes, but she didn't say a word. Instead of sliding into a seat across from her, Mr. Riley sat next to her, his shoulder so close to touching hers that she could feel the heat radiating off him. That she wanted to sink into his warmth in front of a room full of patrons was a thought she'd dissect much later.

"What is this place?" she asked, though the question sounded better in her head. She knew it was a tavern, but she'd never been to one, other than the Hound & Hare in Berwick, and that was a good deal less lively than this place.

"People come here for the atmosphere. You can escape the day and enjoy yourself with a drink. They also sell the best glass of absinthe this side of London."

Before she could ask more, a barkeeper approached their table. He held a tray laden with a glass, a small pitcher of yellowish-green liquid, and a tumbler filled halfway with what looked like whisky. A smaller fountain of water with ice, like the one on the edge of the bar, was carried in behind the barkeeper and set on the round table in front of them.

Mr. Riley nodded his thanks to the man, and they were left alone again.

"Why did you bring me here?" Amelia asked.

"You seemed to be enjoying yourself at Langtry's, and I thought you would like it here. Besides, I was not ready to end our night with dinner."

She didn't know how to respond to that because she hadn't wanted their night to end either. Instead of responding to his candor, she watched him set up the odd-colored drink.

He filled one glass with the peridot-colored liquid, setting an odd-looking perforated spoon over the rim and placing a sugar cube in the middle. She knew it was absinthe, but she'd never before had it or seen it prepared. It was a fascinating process. When that was done, he set it under the spout of the fountain. The nozzle was loosened enough to let out only a few drops of water to wet the sugar cube.

Closing off the flow of water, he looked at her as though waiting for her next question.

"Why did you invite me to dinner tonight? I wasn't needed in the capacity of secretary."

"Correct, you were not needed in that capacity," he agreed, but did not elaborate. "I admit that I wanted to see you lose a little of the reserve you cloak yourself in whenever we're together."

Not all the time, she thought. There had been too many slip-ups with this man, too many instances where she'd forgotten who she was, who she was trying to be—what she'd been trying to escape.

How she wished her father were still alive. Her whole life would be different. The things that had happened…the things her brother had done since their father's passing…

She closed her eyes for only a moment, and Mr. Riley twisted the nozzle again to release the water until it was more than a drip. When she opened her eyes again, she saw him focused on the drink he was preparing. She stared at him for a moment, fascinated by the firm set of his jaw, the crow's feet at the corner of his eyes, and his overall bearing. He was a man who stood out.

When the liquid in the glass started to cloud, Mr. Riley turned off the water again. Sliding the glass toward her, he tipped what was left of the sugar in the glass and stirred it into the drink.

She wondered if he saw the hunger in her eyes that said just how much she desired this man.

"The cloud is called the *louche*," he explained, though she couldn't seem to tear her gaze from his eyes. "It is from the oils in the alcohol blending with the water. The color also tells you when it's the right consistency for taste."

Removing the spoon, he pushed the glass back toward her.

"Try it. See if you like it."

For some reason, she didn't think he was talking about the drink.

She picked the glass up tentatively, not sure what she would think, but the smell that reached her nose was surprisingly more pleasant than she had anticipated—like black licorice and anise-seed cake served on special occasions.

"If you recall, you thought I would enjoy the coffee too," she teased.

"Then I ask you to trust me once more. I endeavor not to steer you wrong again."

She tipped the glass against her lips ever so slightly. The liquid that slipped past her lips was more chilled than she expected and stronger than she anticipated, but it glided easily over her tongue, a little sweet and a little tart all at once.

Lowering the glass, she noticed that Mr. Riley was focused on her lips. When he leaned closer, she worried that he planned to kiss her in front of all the people in the café.

She cleared her throat. "Why did you break off with Victoria?"

His eyes snapped up to hers. "We cannot make each other happy."

She didn't mention that they looked quite happy talking and walking together earlier tonight. That would make her seem like an old jealous shrew. Instead of saying anything more, she took another sip of her drink. This time she was expecting the strong flavor and took a bigger swallow than she probably should have. She laughed a little at her stupidity, and some of the absinthe dribbled between her lips and the glass. She set the glass down and looked for a cloth to wipe it away.

"Do not worry," Mr. Riley said.

She looked at him for a moment, panic causing her heart to race and pump blood furiously through her veins. He couldn't mean to act rashly in a room filled with people she didn't know but who obviously knew him. Before she could swipe the liquid away herself, his hand reached up, his thumb catching the drop of liquid from her chin, and then settling against the middle of her lip, sweeping back and forth.

Her lips parted, and an anxious breath rushed out.

Though it felt like an eternity and that they would be caught for their open indiscretion, his touching her was but a stolen second of time. His warmth was done before she knew it, as though time had only suspended the moment for them, and no one else had been privy to the intimacy that had passed between them.

When he pulled his thumb away, he sucked it into his mouth, making the encounter more intimate.

Looking back at her glass, she realized she had drunk more than half the liquid. Come to think of it, she was feeling a little lightheaded, though she attributed that to Mr. Riley's close proximity, which was too close and too far away all at the same time.

Mr. Riley paid her no mind for a moment, giving her time to think about his actions, about her willingness to accept them without thought of what it would mean for her future. He'd told her that he'd have her in the end, but she hadn't taken into consideration the true weight of those words.

Before she knew it, Mr. Riley was preparing a second glass of absinthe. Her mind whirled in so many directions that she was too afraid to say anything—too worried she'd say the wrong thing. But she was gathering up the courage to find out what he wanted from her.

"Do you mean to make me your mistress tonight?" She frowned at herself. That hadn't been what she'd meant to ask, and she was thankful he was at a loss on how to respond. Unable to look at him, she spun her glass by the base on the table.

His fingers lightly pinched the edge of her chin and turned her head so she was forced to face him with her accusations, though why call them that? She wanted exactly that, didn't she?

"I have told you that you will come to me of your own free will. You will not be my mistress. I want more than a bed partner from you."

"What else is there, where men are concerned?" Wasn't that what her brother's friends, and then the man her brother had promised her to had thought? That she was only good for one thing. That lying on her back for a man was the exact path she was trying to avoid.

"I ran away from home because my brother was unkind and cruel at every turn." She left out the part about her being sold to another man to pay off her brother's debts, as that didn't have any bearing on this conversation.

"I will never force you to do anything. But Amelia…" Her name caught her attention, and his eyes stared into hers once again. "You want this. Stop looking for reasons to deny your desires." His finger traced along the inside of her wrist.

She swallowed her denial. It would have been a lie, and of all people she didn't want to lie to, Mr. Riley topped that list.

"It is so easy for a man to say he will take something when he wants it. When a woman takes what she wants, it often is at the cost of her reputation, her worth."

"You're confusing me with the men your brother failed to keep away from you."

"I could never mistake you, Mr. Riley." His previous comment gave her pause, as she realized what he'd said. "How did you know his friends were a problem?"

"You just confirmed my suspicions."

Drat. That had to be the effects of the absinthe. "Have I ever given you reason to believe I was running from him?"

"I suspected you were running from something other than your last employer when we met. You were too calm and collected about having been subjected to Sir Ian's abuse," he said matter-of-factly. "I would have expected histrionics, at the very least. You remained defiant in the name of self-preservation. Only a woman used to that kind of treatment would act as you did."

She gave him a quizzical look. "Do you know a lot of women who have been in the same type of predicament?"

"Too many." The tone of his voice was dark, almost as if it was filled with pain. She wanted him to elaborate but didn't know how to ask that of him.

To lighten the mood, she said, "This might seem silly, but I never feared you. Not from the first moment we met. You're a good man. Or at least you have been nothing but kind to everyone who works for you."

He made a sound in the back of his throat that said he disagreed with her assessment.

"Did you only help me because you saw something you wanted? Saw something you could have if you did one small favor for a woman down on her luck?"

His face was right in front hers, his mouth scant inches from touching her mouth. She should pull back but couldn't find the strength to continually refuse him.

"You describe exactly how I view my work, my acquisitions in properties and businesses alike," he said. "I take what I want without regard to anyone else. Sometimes my intentions are not pure, nor to the benefit of others. What you do not have is an accurate picture of what I see in you."

"Then explain it to me," she said, frustrated that she hadn't guarded her tongue. She pulled away from him and drank down half the contents of her glass. She would probably regret how much she'd imbibed come morning and how much her tongue had slipped when it should have stayed. But Mr. Riley did not seem angry with her, more curious about what she thought—or at least, that was the impression she got, being slightly tipsy from the alcohol.

"I always find a way to get what I want, Miss Grant. Right now, that just so happens to be you. Do not mistake me for the gentlemen you grew up around. I'm nothing of the sort. I claim no good manners, but I will not hurt you as they did."

"How do you know they were gentlemen?"

"Pigs, the lot of them from your comment about your brother. But I know you come from a privileged background. I see it in your poise, in your every movement, in the way you talk. I have always known."

"Oh," she said. She hadn't thought she was so easy to read. At least her tongue wasn't so loose as to reveal her identity. Though she could admit it was only a matter of time before she would have to reveal that part of herself.

Mr. Riley's large hands wrapped around hers where they were folded in her lap. He brought one up to his mouth and kissed her knuckles and then each of her fingers. Before he let that hand go he kissed the inside of her wrist, the action possessive.

"Trust me to take care of you, Amelia. I will not hurt you."

"That does not negate the fact that you want exactly what my brother's friends wanted. I will not sell myself to the highest bidder. I came to London to escape that fate." My, she was bold while drinking absinthe, but for the first time in so long, she didn't want to take the words back. They were the truth, and it felt good to speak her mind. "Why should I stumble and fall after making it this far?" she added.

"Because I will catch you," he said without pause.

His words melted some of her resolve. She had wanted to barrage him with questions until she understood everything that made him tick. Until she understood why he needed to possess her so badly when there were surely dozens of other women willing and ready to fall at his feet to do his every bidding.

It amazed her that she even thought that, but she'd watched everyone around her tonight. Almost half the women at the restaurant seemed smitten with Mr. Riley, as though they wanted to catch his eye so that he would choose them. But she, plain old Amelia, had been the one on his arm.

Mr. Riley stood from the bench and gave her his hand. "We should enjoy the music. Dance with me."

"My ankle—"

"I'll keep you steady. Leave your cane here. This will be our table for as long as you wish to stay."

After all her denials and speeches tonight, she still took his hand. She could admit that she liked feeling lost in his arms. Just because she liked it didn't mean she was entitled to have it. But when they stood there on the small dance floor, it was as if there was no one in that room but her, Mr. Riley, and the piano player.

The song changed to something less lively and more ballad-like. Mr. Riley didn't hesitate to spin her around, making her use her good foot, before his hand pressed against her back and brought her body up tight along his.

"Put your foot with the bad ankle over my shoe."

"I couldn't." She started to pull away, but Mr. Riley only tightened the grip he had on her. "It will look indecent," she said.

"And here I thought the absinthe had loosened your inhibitions enough that you would trust me for at least one night."

"I do trust you," she said, meaning it.

"Then do as I ask."

Despite all her points about men being made equal, she realized Mr. Riley stood alone in her opinion. Instead of squabbling further, she set her foot atop his, and he immediately started moving them around the floor as though they'd done this a thousand times. She laughed gaily, feeling like she was flying in his arms. They spun around, moving between and around other dancers with ease.

She had wanted to be lost in his arms, and that was exactly what she got. His hand was pressed tightly to her back above the small bustle and fall of her dress; his other held her hand like you would for a waltz. Their pelvises were crushed together, though all she could feel of him was his strong thighs as he moved through the steps of some unknown dance. Her chest was crushed against his as well, and while the rules for dancing were to keep space between partners, she liked how close he held her. Relished it, actually.

When the song ended and a livelier piece was played, Mr. Riley didn't stop; he merely adjusted his grip, held her tighter, and spun her around faster. Both her feet were atop his at this point, for she couldn't keep up with the quick steps of the piece the piano player pounded out.

She laughed halfway through the set, not remembering the last time she'd been able to just let go and enjoy herself as she did now. It was exhilarating. Freeing. It was a perfect night, and one she would never forget.

Gasping for air and from their laughter, Mr. Riley spun her around on her good foot and set them in the direction of their table. She couldn't say why she was out of breath, as he'd done most of the work and all she'd had to do was hold on.

"Wherever did you learn to dance like that?" she asked, still breathless as she slid back into her seat. One of her curls had fallen, and she had to pin it back in place. She was afraid to see herself in a mirror right now, but she imagined her cheeks were flushed and her hair a mess of curls popping out everywhere. She had to fan herself to cool her blood.

"My mother taught me to dance, if you can believe it," Mr. Riley answered. "And the girls who worked with her."

"What did your mother do?"

Someone had set another glass with ice on the table in their absence. Mr. Riley fished a few out with tongs and dropped them in her drink as he slid it toward her.

Amelia spun the glass around, letting the ice chill her drink. "Why did you not order one?"

"Because I prefer whisky." He leaned in close to her, not that anyone could hear their conversation with all the noise, celebrations, and good times going on around them. "Besides I would rather taste it from your lips."

She stared at the swirling contents of her glass. "I do not know how I'm supposed to respond when you say such things."

"Then act instead. Do what I know you want to do."

She looked at him sharply. "You ask impossible things of me."

"They are only impossible if you allow them to be."

Mr. Riley leaned back in his seat, one hand raised and swirling his whisky round and round in the tumbler as he watched her puzzle out his words. She wasn't sure if she was supposed to be stunned and surprised, or if she was supposed to take on his challenge.

She merely lifted her glass to her lips and drank the last half of her absinthe straight down. A third glass was produced and prepared for her. It all happened so fast that before she knew it, she had drunk it all down, and Mr. Riley was pulling her to her feet. She felt quite spry, as though she were floating. She closed her eyes and concentrated on the music. "The piano player is quite good."

Though she expected no answer, Mr. Riley said, "He is. Came over from New Orleans, in America, and brings a special flare of that Creole music with him."

They were on the dance floor again, her bad foot atop his, the other moving along with him. "How do you know the piano player?"

"He was a stowaway in one of my shipments. The captain wanted to toss him out to sea and feed him to the sharks. When I saw the look in his eyes, I knew all he wanted was to find a place to build a new life."

Yet another admirable thing he'd done to endear him to her further. Did this man have any faults? Not only was he the most handsome man she'd ever met, but he had riches she could barely comprehend as she dug further into his business. Most important, he had a heart of gold for those struck down by bad luck and poor circumstances. It made her feel so…unaccomplished.

"Do you have ties to this establishment too?" Amelia asked.

"Are you asking if I own it?"

She nodded.

"I do not. But the owners are friends, of sorts."

"Of sorts? I thought friends only came in one sense of the word," she teased.

"They come in many varieties, Miss Grant," he said with a flourishing swirl around the floor, weaving in and out of other dancers.

"I do not think I have ever enjoyed dancing as much as I do with you."

"I will take that as a compliment to my skill."

"I like this side of you, Mr. Riley," she said, gazing up at his stern expression.

"And what side would that be?" He didn't crack the smallest hint of a smile, but surely he knew what she was talking about.

"Your playful side. You're always business-like or very serious… You're different tonight."

"Is that so? Well, perhaps I should take you dancing more often."

She pulled him to a stop after one too many spins. She had to grasp the front of his waistcoat and hold herself still while her head straightened out. She laughed as she tried to focus on the crowds around her.

Goodness, she must be more careful about imbibing in spirits in future. Finally, some of the faces became clearer; she even followed a top hat bobbing around the perimeter of the crowd, the gait awkward in its up and down motion…and familiar.

Amelia suddenly straightened, her heart in her throat, as she waited for that hat to turn her way. She only caught a glimpse of her brother's face before she ducked behind Mr. Riley's large form.

"I fear the spirits have gone straight to my head," she said in a rush.

Mr. Riley knew immediately something was wrong, for he looked around the café to see what had caught her eye. Thank heavens, he wouldn't know what or whom to look for.

He led her back to the table to retrieve her cane and his hat. "The carriage awaits our departure," Mr. Riley said.

He tucked her arm under his and led her outside. Amelia looked at every one of the faces they passed and searched for that familiar hat again, but she didn't see it anywhere. Had she imagined seeing her brother? Perhaps it was someone who looked like him. But the walk…

She felt dizzy, unbalanced, and stumbled a little in her path. Mr. Riley lifted her up in his arms and strode with purpose toward the carriage. Amelia tucked her face into his shoulder, thankful she hadn't had to ask for his assistance and glad to be able to hide her face.

When they were in the carriage, Mr. Riley took her hands between his and watched her in that silent way of his. "Are you going to tell me what frightened you enough that we had to leave so abruptly?"

"No reason. The absinthe—"

"I can tolerate a lot of faults and vices in people, but lying is not one of them. Not from you."

Pressing her hands against either of his knees, she leaned in close to him. The carriage hit a rut in the road, and she flew right into him, face first, which worked, she supposed, in her favor. Mr. Riley's hands clasped her arms to keep her steady.

She didn't quite mean to make it so clumsy, but after swallowing back any further denials, there was nothing left to do but kiss him. And she seemed to be mucking that up too.

Mr. Riley turned her so she sat across his lap, her arms wrapped around his shoulders. His hat was knocked to the side and fell to the seat with a muffled thud.

With her lips parted, she looked at him from her elevated position, not quite sure how to initiate what they had been working toward all night. His eyes were hard, the color so cold that it could easily send a chill down someone's arms. But to her, they were inviting. Even forgiving. She could definitely get lost in his eyes.

"Now you are avoiding my questions," he said evenly, as though the kiss had little effect on him, but she knew it had, for he was caressing his fingers up and down her side, over her ribs, where one seam of the corset pressed against the dress.

"It would be a shame for our night to end. It has been… magical. And I'm afraid that magic will be nothing but a figment of my imagination, come morning."

"This isn't something I'll let you forget," he said with so much promise that she believed him.

But they would resume their normal roles when morning broke. She would play the part of his secretary; he, the powerful industrialist.

She slid her arms away from his shoulders, feeling quite silly sitting in his lap. She was unsure how exactly to extricate herself, but it didn't seem to matter, because Mr. Riley's hand grasped her side to hold her right where she was.

"What are you doing?" she asked.

"That you even have to ask tells me you kissed me on a whim, to try to distract me. You will not be able to keep secrets from me forever, Amelia."

Gazing into his eyes, she knew he was giving her a reprieve this once. Her heart skipped in worry at the thought of his knowing what her brother had done to make her leave her old life. What the man who thought to marry her had promised.

Surely the absinthe was playing tricks on her mind right now. It was impossible for her brother to find her. How would he know she'd come to London instead of somewhere more familiar, like Edinburgh?

When the carriage stopped, Mr. Riley reached around her to open the door and assisted her to her feet before they exited the carriage. After handing her the cane, he placed his hand on her lower back as he had at the restaurant. That show of possessiveness thrilled her so deeply that she mentally chastised herself for her reaction.

When they were inside, Mr. Riley backed her up against the door and placed his arms on either side of her shoulders. He leaned in close to her face, close enough that she could smell the coffee on his breath. It was much more pleasant a scent on him. She wanted to taste his lips to see if he tasted as good as he smelled, now that she wasn't focused on distracting him.

"What do we do now, Mr. Riley?"

He set her cane in the umbrella stand next to the door. She swallowed the nervousness that suddenly choked her.

"Our night is far from finished," he said. Then he swept her up into his arms and headed for the stairs.

CHAPTER TWELVE

Hitching Amelia higher in his arms, Nick turned his back to her door and reached behind him to find the doorknob. Twisting it, they rushed backward into her room. Her grip had tightened around his shoulders, and she felt a giddiness wash through her at the sudden thrill and excitement of their stolen moment.

This is wrong, her mind screamed. She needed to stop this. She needed to think about her choices. But the words asking him to set her down and leave simply wouldn't form on her tongue. What she wanted was to forget about everything else, including the pesky voice of reason trying to ruin her perfect night. And while she might still feel slightly lightheaded from the absinthe, it was not ruling her actions.

Mr. Riley set her down on her feet. Her body slid along his on its descent.

Holding on to his jacket, she tipped her head up and stared into his eyes. "Why do I feel this way around you?"

He rubbed his hands over hers, holding her close. "And how is that?"

"Confused. In need of something I do not understand and for which I cannot find words." She closed her eyes, not believing she was admitting this much to him. "Desperate for your touch, for your lips pressed against mine…for your hands around me as they were in the carriage."

Perhaps that was the absinthe talking. She doubted she'd have said any of that, had she refrained from indulging in the green liquid.

When she cracked her eyes open, it was hard to miss the hunger that dilated his pupils. Releasing her hands, he caressed her jaw and chin. She backed away from him, not sure if she'd made the right decision in inviting him into her bedroom, not sure about confessing her feelings at all.

She stumbled on her bad foot and reached out to catch herself on the cushioned bench at the end of her bed. Mr. Riley was there in an instant, lifting and carrying her over to the side of the bed. He set her down with a gentleness she couldn't have guessed he harbored when he looked positively ravenous and ready to devour her.

She closed her eyes again, took in a steady breath, and released it. She repeated this process as Mr. Riley kneeled in front of her and pushed her skirts up so that they were gathered above her knees. Any proper young lady would have asked him to stop, but she didn't have it in her to do so. She didn't want to be proper when she was with Mr. Riley.

Instead, she stared at his bowed head and considered leaning close enough to run her fingers through the thick waves of black that fell forward around his collar. His focus was on untying her boot. He removed the boot on her good foot first and then carefully worked on the second, loosening all the laces so it fell off her foot and into his hand without having to be tugged free.

She jumped when his fingers caressed the side of her ankle. He looked up, alarmed. "Does this hurt?"

She shook her head, at a loss for words. Nibbling her lower lip, she hesitated before saying, "I know I should ask you to leave, but I do not want you to go."

He stood, suddenly looming over her, forcing her to tilt her head back to look up at him. With his fingers under her chin, he looked at her with a longing she imagined was mirrored in her own eyes. A longing that a man of his bearing and standing should never have for someone like her, she reminded herself.

She was his secretary; he was her employer—two very important facts that she could never forget. Yet that was precisely what she had done to let this man undress her.

"What am I meant to do?" she asked.

"That is up to you. But no more than you are willing."

She shook her head. Confused by what she should do, what she wanted to do, and what she guessed they were about to do.

Accepting him was never a question. She wanted this just as much as she wanted a decent life and a job to support herself and to be a self-sufficient woman, which seemed contradictory. But she could acknowledge that Mr. Riley would be a vital part of her immediate future.

With his hand gently cupping the back of her head, his lips drew nearer. His breath was a warm whisper over her lips. He stopped a scant inch away from her parted mouth. She craved his kiss.

"Tell me when it's too much," he said.

She searched his eyes and nodded once, as he seemed to be waiting for her response. Before she could inhale her next breath, Mr. Riley's tongue was sliding into her mouth and curling around her tongue. Her actions at first were tentative, never having kissed anyone before Mr. Riley. Her tongue followed his, never exploring on its own.

With his hand tangled in her hair, he guided her back against the bed, bringing his much larger frame over her slight one, though he didn't press his weight upon her. Not knowing what to do with her hands, she fisted them in the material of his waistcoat on either side of his wide chest.

She grew bolder with their kiss, touching parts of his mouth with her tongue, loving the smooth slide against his teeth. Soon, their kiss left her panting, not for breath but for a deeper sweep of his tongue, for want of her breasts smashed against his chest as when they had danced, for his full weight covering and crushing her into the bed. She arched up against him, needing all that and so much more.

Their lips parted only to join and taste and feel again and again.

Wanting more but not sure how to put words to those desires, she unclasped her hands and tentatively spread one of her palms over his shoulder, sliding it higher until it rested on his upper back. She could feel his strength in the coiling of his muscles as he braced himself above her. His body was all tension and vibrated so hard that she wanted the last tether of his control to snap.

It was that moment she realized he was being careful— holding himself back. She wanted all of him.

Feeling braver by the moment, she snaked her other hand around his neck, her fingers tickling the line between the edge of his shirt collar and the soft strands of his hair. Like a wolf in wait, he stilled.

She opened her eyes so she could read the expression in his eyes. He was staring right back at her. She knew precisely what the gleam in his eyes meant, and she wasn't afraid of the desire radiating off him, like coals burning out of control.

"Have I done something wrong?" Her voice was barely above a whisper.

"There is no going back from this."

She understood that perfectly well. She wanted whatever *this* was.

He continued to stare at her, his arms braced on either side of her shoulders. Did he want her assurance that she wanted this?

"Amelia." Her name on his tongue was a seductive growl in her ears, and the sound had her mouth parting on a small sigh. "You're mine and no one else's."

"I only want you."

He kissed her hard, his mouth rougher, needier this time. The feel of his teeth grazing her lips and her tongue tore a moan from deep in her throat. This time, when he pulled away, she almost followed his mouth with hers, not willing to relinquish the kiss she'd been craving since they arrived home. This was precisely what she wanted.

"I will never let you leave," he said with a finality that might have frightened most women, but he didn't scare her.

"Why do I feel this way about you?" she asked. "I don't plan to leave when I have only just found my place here."

Her answer seemed to satisfy him, and his body came down on top of hers, though he kept most of his weight off her. The hard press of his manhood was a very clear indication of what he wanted, and had she not been trapped by her dress, she would have rubbed against it, wanting to feel his virility over every inch of her burning flesh.

Feeling bolder by the minute and desperate to shut off any warring thoughts about her actions, she lightly scratched her nails across the back of his head and scalp. If she was going to be reckless, she might as well embrace this new side of herself to the fullest.

"I do not know how to ask for what I want. I want you to show me."

Her words drew another groan of appreciation from deep in his chest, and that sound vibrated from her breasts all the way to her mouth, where his tongue did a wicked dance around her tongue, eliciting sounds from her she couldn't hold back. Didn't want to hold back.

Finally, he pressed his full weight onto her, his hands caressing her upper arms, working their way higher until she was forced to loosen her hold in his hair. With her arms stretched above her head, he clasped her wrists together with one of his hands, leaving her helpless and unable to move. She liked being trapped by him. Liked that he had all the control.

She tugged at her hands, testing his hold. In response, he tightened his grip, giving her a clear indication that he was in charge right now.

"Do not move," he said with a light bite to her lip that he soothed immediately with the caress of his lips.

Amelia found herself obeying because she wanted nothing more than to please him. Her mouth meshed tightly against Mr. Riley's as they lost themselves in another kiss.

The seductive abrasion of his short clipped beard against her face made her want to feel that delicious friction the rest of the way down her body. Her rigidness dissolved as his free hand explored a path over the side of her breast, until it finally stopped around her ribcage.

Body arching off the bed, she wanted to be closer to him. His hand tightened around her side, holding her so they were crushed, breast to chest, pelvis to groin.

She let out a surprised yelp when her body jerked forward as he worked the buttons free at the back of her bodice, tearing a few in the process. He found the ties on her overskirt and the buckles that held the bustle with an ease that told of his experience in removing women's clothing. When he was finished, he pulled her skirts down and over her hips and released her wrists so he could shed the outer layers of the dress he'd given her.

Sitting her up, he pulled the bodice off next. He stared down at her for a moment, his hand tracing over the bones in the corset as he spanned the width of her waist. It was a simple corset, nothing grand enough for the dress she wore, but it was all she had. Little green sparrows were embroidered around the edges, top and bottom; she hadn't thought much about it until now.

She swallowed, not sure if she could touch him while he explored every part of her. There was just enough give in the corset that he yanked the front of it lower and tore the chemise away to expose her breasts to that penetrating gaze of his. It didn't occur to her that she should protest. Though his motions were rough, his hands were tender where they cupped her breast above the bindings.

He released her breast and crushed his mouth against hers. His tongue stole past her lips with an authority she would never question. The kiss robbed her of breath and squashed any objecting thoughts. There was nothing except the feel of their bodies crushed together, his tongue dancing and sliding wickedly over and around hers, tasting so deeply that he stole her breath away.

Her heart hammered so hard in her chest that she thought Mr. Riley might feel it. His mouth moved lower, tasting and nibbling a path over her chin, the slender column of her neck, and her collarbone. He shoved the chemise off her shoulders and then lay kisses there too.

"Mr. Riley."

He was suddenly kneeling above her like a predator in wait, wearing an expression that was half ravenous, half something she couldn't define, for she'd never seen that particular look in a man's eyes.

"Nick," he corrected her as he lowered his mouth to the top swell of her breasts. The hard edge of his teeth scraped lightly over her skin, causing her nipples to peak impossibly hard. She wanted him to suck those berry-colored tips into his mouth.

This time when her hands threaded through his hair, he didn't stop her; he let her explore the thick strands before she lowered her hands to his strong shoulders. The sinew flexed fluidly beneath her hold, mesmerizing her, encouraging and daring her to explore more.

A small part of her knew she needed to ask him to stop. But she'd come this far, hadn't she? She didn't want to turn back when it felt so right. She didn't want to stop when she'd never needed a man to do wicked things to her like she wanted Nick to do to her right now.

And she knew this wasn't the absinthe talking. This was all her. Her desires, her wants.

All the air whooshed out of her lungs the moment he drew her nipple sharply into his mouth. It had her arching off the bed to get closer to him. The sensation was unlike anything she'd ever felt, and it unfurled a new awareness in other parts of her body. The butterflies in her stomach seemed to rush lower, and she felt herself dampen between her legs. Slickness coated her inner thighs as she rubbed them together, desperate for a different kind of touch. Her heart was still racing a mile a minute, and she felt her breasts grow heavier in want of his hands and mouth all over them.

A high keening sound passed her lips when his teeth scraped over the tip of her nipple before he released it to move on to the next.

The cool evening air washed over her bared breasts when he knelt above her. She had a strong urge to cover herself, and he must have read that intent in her expression. "Don't hide yourself from me." His command was firm, and one she didn't hesitate to obey.

She watched him watching her, his gaze trailing along the path his mouth had just taken. How could a look be so erotic? Her breathing came faster, and goose bumps washed over her body. Her nipples were hard peaks of pink, just begging for his mouth to land on them again. She'd never seen herself like this, never imagined showing herself like this to a man. Never imagined wanting the things she wanted right now.

She licked her lips nervously, wanting so badly to ask him to do what he'd just been doing but unsure how she should voice that desire. She felt her cheeks flush at the very idea of speaking so bluntly. Before she could muster up the courage to speak, he turned her over so she was on her stomach, with the hard tips of her nipples rubbing across the wool blanket, giving her a new type of sensation that wasn't at all unpleasant.

Nick shoved her chemise out of the way, his rough hand trailing up the back of her legs and to the opening of her drawers at the inside of her thighs. Would he touch her *there*… her eyes slipped closed, and she bit her lip hard in anticipation and in trepidation. She shouldn't want such a thing, but the more he touched her, the more she wanted what was forbidden.

"How badly do you want me to touch you here?" His fingers grazed over her curls, teasing her. Not giving her enough. "Tell me."

"I want your touch." The blanket on the bed muffled her voice, but she couldn't find the courage to ask for something she didn't understand.

His hand slipped beneath the drawers the opposite way, cupping and squeezing her buttocks. The motion caused her breath to catch in her throat and come out in soft pants when she could no longer hold them back.

When his hand slid between the crack of her buttocks, she scooted away from his touch, in complete shock that he would touch her there. When she tried to turn over, he placed his hand over the middle of her lower back, keeping her still.

"Shhh…" he said, as though that alone would calm her. "I won't hurt you, Amelia, but I will know every intimate detail of you."

When she looked at him over her shoulder, she saw that he wore a resolute expression, like a stamp of ownership. That very look should have had her running, but she only turned and pressed her forehead into the mattress with a groan.

He didn't touch her there again. Instead, he loosened her corset. "Remove it," he demanded when he was done with the strings at her back.

She pressed either side of the corset's busk together to release the clasps at the front. When they snapped, indicating it was apart, he pulled it away. She could feel the lines where the bones had squeezed her skin, and she felt embarrassed that he should see her like that. Even though she was still wearing her chemise and drawers, she'd never been so underdressed in front of anyone.

There was a tie at the back and front of her drawers. Nick undid the back, letting the material fall away to reveal her whole backside. His hand slid between her and the bed until it was cupped over her stomach, and he pulled her onto her knees. With her back to his stomach and her rear tucked against the firmness at his center, he pulled the last tie holding her drawers at the front. The material fell from her waist to pool at her knees.

Nick's hand slid high enough to cup her breast, kneading and squeezing the tender flesh. Her head fell back to his shoulder, and her body relaxed into his as he massaged her in a way that should have made her feel ashamed but instead made her grind her body tighter into the hardness that pressed between the cheeks of her buttocks. The pins holding her hair dug into her scalp, so she pulled them free and tossed them to the bed as her hair unfurled and fell around them.

Her breath erratic and her skin on fire and in need of being touched, she shivered when Nick brushed her hair away from her shoulder and nipped the sensitive skin there.

"I plan to claim you tonight, Amelia."

She nodded her head quickly, unable to give voice to that exact desire.

"Say you want that," he ordered.

"Yes," she half moaned, half whispered, in a voice she barely recognized.

She had never wanted anything as much as she wanted Nick.

Nick's hand slid down between her breasts and over her belly button, pressing harder as his finger skimmed the crisp hair of her mound. Her breath caught in her throat as she waited for his next move. But he didn't move his hand any lower, just hovered there, out of reach, giving her time to accept not only his touch but what was about to happen.

There would be no going back from this. With the realization that she preferred to leap blindly forward, she ground her rear against Nick's groin, her legs spreading wider so she could feel him closer and tighter in the folds of her sex that ached so deeply for his touch. The wetness slicked over his trousers, giving her the ability to slide against the rigid hardness that lay out of reach of what she wanted.

Nick's lips feathered kisses and licked a hot path along her neck. He distracted her as his free hand slipped inside the front of her chemise and lifted one breast free of the material. He squeezed her hard nipple between his fingers, pulling at the taut tip, extending it further.

Amelia arched her back, thrusting her breast into his hand in unspoken need.

"Please," she begged in a hoarse voice.

"Please what?" Nick's breath was hot against her neck, eliciting a shiver from her. She wanted him to blow a hot stream of air everywhere on her, including the area between her thighs that continued to grow slicker with every stroke of his hand at her breast.

"Show me more," she said.

As his hands released her, she was immediately aware of how underdressed she was in comparison to him. Her thighs were flush to his; her very naked bottom was pressed against his clothed form. He gathered the hemline of her chemise in his hands and lifted it higher and higher until it was over her head. He tossed it aside.

Even though she had her back to his chest, she crossed her arms over her breasts. He didn't stop her, his hands were busy elsewhere, one curved over her side and hip, the other tracing every bone from her neck down along her spine. Though she didn't remove her hands from covering herself, she did relax into his touch. His lips followed the same path as his hand along her back, drawing a moan from deep in her chest the lower he went.

When she looked at him over her shoulder, he was watching her. His gray eyes, this close, seemed darker, stormier.

"Remove your drawers the rest of the way," he said softly but firmly.

Oddly enough, she felt embarrassed by her uncertainty, enough that she didn't want to move off his lap and reveal more of herself.

"Take your drawers off, Amelia." Though his voice was low and calm, there was unspoken demand in his words that promised reprisal if she didn't do exactly as he wanted.

Uncovering her breasts, she lifted herself from his lap. Her hands were unsteady as she leaned forward on her hands and knees to pull off the material.

Nick's hands caressed the cheeks of her buttocks. He murmured a sound of appreciation when she was fully naked. When she tried to kneel in front of him again, the palm of his hand pressed against her lower back to keep her where she was—on all fours.

"I like looking at you like this." His hand trailed over her hip and down her thigh.

Unsure how she should respond, she said nothing.

The rustle of material behind her should have made her more nervous than she already was; instead, she closed her eyes and imagined what Nick looked like beneath his finely made suit.

His hand landed on her hip, the touch possessive as he pulled her against his body, crushing her back to his warm, naked chest. One of his arms stretched along hers, holding him steadily above her. His skin was darker than hers; the contrast of seeing their arms naked and pressed together on the bed had her breath coming faster.

His other hand cupped her mound again; this time, his fingers delved deeper between the folds of her sex. He would feel her wetness, and that made her blush. He practically growled when he pulled his wet fingers away from her to push her legs wider apart. She would have jumped from the sudden move, had he not being covering her like an animal in rut.

His breath hot against her ear, he said, "Do you know what it means to be mine, Amelia?"

She had a few ideas, but her voice wouldn't work. She shook her head, all the while concentrating on his hand. His fingers were rubbing between the folds of her sex again, his fingers as wet as she was now.

"This is mine. I own it. I am the only one who will see it, touch it, or taste it." The roughness of his beard rubbed along her neck, the friction erotic with the dirty words coming from his mouth. "I am the only one who will ever fuck it."

The coarse way he spoke made her press back into his groin with a ragged breath. She never imaged she'd be in this position with a man, never imagined giving herself so desperately. It was new; it was exhilarating; it was so far out of the realm of what she expected that she anticipated and craved his next move.

He spread the folds of her sex more, slipping his fingers over the more sensitive parts, causing her to jolt a little at the unfamiliar touch.

"Shhh," he said, and the noise was calming. "I am going to make you climax all over my hand."

She had no idea what he meant, but his hand moved lightly over that private part of her flesh—first back and forth and then in circles that grew tighter and tighter the faster he moved. She felt wetness slick between her thighs and gather at her core the longer he rotated his hand over that part of her. Her breath grew more irregular as her heart raced in her chest and butterflies built low in her belly.

His fingers moved through the wetness, spreading it with each rotation. He thrust his cloth-clad penis against her backside. And to her embarrassment, she moved against his hand wanting more, wanting him to press harder than he was, wanting to never stop what she was feeling.

Her breath came out in pants, short and needy to her own ears. Nick whispered hoarsely in her ear that she needed to climax, that she was his.

There was no way to describe what she felt, and despite any reservations she had, her body had a mind all its own. She unfurled around him. She surrendered to the desire that clouded her better judgment.

Utterly and completely, she gave herself to this man.

She let go.

"Climax," he demanded. "Climax for me so I can claim this pretty pussy of yours."

It could have been his words or his motions, but she let go of the last of her reservations as she thrust back against him with the same urgency as he ground his hardness into her. Their bodies were slick with sweat, the hair on his chest abrading the sensitive skin of her back as their bodies moved together, as she reached for a finale that would end this mad delirium that had encapsulated them in pure ecstasy.

Noises she didn't know she could make built in her throat and passed her lips with each slam of their bodies, trying to fit tighter together. Then something spectacular and different and so unexpected happened. It was as though her body had been building toward this. The sensation of complete abandon slammed through her so hard that she let out an alien sound—it was so different from any of the sounds she'd made that it should have embarrassed and tempered her, but it did exactly the opposite.

She felt as though she were flying, her heart in her throat, her breath stalled in her lungs, as a rush of fluid wet Nick's hand so thoroughly that when he pulled it away, he said, "Beautiful." He smeared her juices over her nipple and areola as he tweaked and pulled hard at the tip, extending the sensation that robbed her of all ability to think.

"Nick?" she whispered. She wanted him to continue and to stop. It all confused her so much that she let him lead her further down the path of sweet destruction.

His hand was unforgiving where it kneaded her breast, but it didn't hurt; it felt good. Her body still moved, mimicking what they'd done before she'd felt the explosion of perfect sensation and release in her body.

Nick was loosening his trousers, his hands grazing against her as he shoved the material out of the way. His penis was a heavy weight on one cheek of her buttocks, and it caressed and bounced off her as he removed the last of his clothes.

That part of him was soft where it touched her, yet firm as she pushed back into him in unspoken need. When she tried to turn around on her knees, he came over her body as he had earlier, though this time there was no mistaking the feel of his cock between her thighs, where she knelt in wait.

The folds of her sex brushed that solid length of him as she swayed back and forth in his hold, never quite touching him as hard as she wanted. She felt his hand curl around his cock between her thighs, and he tilted it in a way that let the tip brush through the folds of her sex. Only it felt different and far more intimate.

When he pulled his hand away from his cock, she felt bereft and needier than she had before. He brushed her hair over one of her shoulders and kissed her flushed skin.

"Press your shoulders to the bed." His voice was hoarse in her ear.

She did immediately as he asked, hoping he'd reward her with that steely part of his flesh she was so unfamiliar with but wanted to learn everything about. He was behind her, his legs pushing out her knees so she was spread impossibly wider and open to his view. Her hands grasped the counterpane beneath her as she closed her eyes.

To her everlasting surprise, he continued to tease her with the head of his penis, circling it around her opening, slicking the entrance and building that sensation of need in her again. She wanted to reach back and touch him and learn him, the way he had with her body, but at the same time she didn't want what she felt now to stop. So she stayed where she was, pressed to the mattress, and absorbed every new teasing touch of his body against hers. He pressed himself against her entrance, making her pull forward and away from him when she felt the first sting of pain as he pressed the tip of his manhood inside her.

Nick managed to keep himself poised at her entrance. His hands held each of her buttocks, spreading the cheeks apart as he held her tightly enough that she wouldn't be able to pull away from him a second time.

"If I could take away the pain, I would," he said.

Fundamentally, she'd known it might hurt to be taken by a man, and she'd not worried about it until those words passed his lips. When she tried to move away from him, he steadied her hips.

"Do you still want this, Amelia? You can ask me to stop."

"I want this," she said, her voice muffled by the blanket. She repeated her words over and over again, knowing he needed her permission.

She realized too late that she should have said no. He thrust so hard and so true through the barrier of her virginity that she tried to pull away from the assault of his body finally claiming hers. Nick's hands never once let up at her hips, keeping him buried deep inside her and holding them still where they were joined, even when she rose from the bed to kneel in the position she'd been in before, though that made it hurt more, so she went on her hands and knees in front of him.

He didn't move inside her as tears slipped down her cheeks, droplets falling on the bed in front of her.

When she proved she had no desire to either move closer or away from him, Nick released her hips, his fingers sliding over her sides eliciting a shiver from her before he cupped both her breasts. As he leaned over her, his cock slid slightly from her tight sheath, which made her wince.

"The pain is temporary. It will get better."

There was a promise in his words she wanted to believe, so she relaxed, marginally. Nick moved his hand from her breast and over her stomach, rubbing in small circles from her navel down to the crisp hair between her thighs. Finally, he cupped her sex again. Spreading the folds to find the spot that had given her so much pleasure before, he circled the bud there. He kept rolling his finger around that sensitive part of her until her breaths came shorter and faster.

Kissing the shell of her ear, he said. "Now you will feel nothing but pleasure. Do you trust me?"

She nodded. She did trust him more than she ought, considering the length of time they'd known each other, but he'd done nothing to give her reason to doubt him.

"I need to hear it from your lips, Amelia."

He pulled her earlobe into her mouth and nibbled the end of it. She arched back in surprise, turning her pelvis up to him, pulling him deeper into her body. The burn from his originally seating himself within her was ebbing and her desire rekindling.

"I trust you," she whispered, just as he sucked her lower lip into his mouth.

Nick kissed the column of her neck, nibbling between each soft caress, never once letting up on the rotation of his fingers. Gradually, the sensation of complete abandonment came back, and she started to move against his hand, allowing the thick erection between her thighs to move inside her, and which, to her surprise, was not at all an unpleasant feeling. Her back arched and her body grew pliant yet desperate to feel the release she'd felt with only his hands.

The thrust of his penis was a new and different feeling, now that she was edging toward another release. He was slow as he pulled out and pushed back into her, careful with her, even though she felt the whipcord strength in him ready to be unleashed and given free rein of her body.

They were both wet with sweat as they moved and slid together. He pinched her nipple, twisting it to the point of pain before letting up and soothing the pleasurable hurt by massaging her whole breast with his big hands.

For each press of his penis forward, her pelvis arched back, trying to take him in deeper. As their pace increased,

Amelia was forced to hold on to the blankets beneath her so she wouldn't slide farther away from him. She wanted to grind that private part of herself hard against him, to feel him so fully inside her that he would be stamped into her skin and body as firmly as he was stamped into her mind.

"I will be the only one to ever play with this little clit of yours." The promise in his words made her moan. "You belong to me, Amelia."

She wanted to belong to Nick Riley. She wanted to please him in any way she could.

Nick stole her full attention again when he took her clit between his fingers and squeezed it. She let out a hoarse cry of pleasure, torn between grinding that part of her body against his hand and pushing back to take him in deeper. Her body felt on fire, ready for another climax. She curled her hands tighter around the bedding for purchase, desperate for any sort of leverage as she pushed and pulled away from him in equal measure.

The pace of his body moving in hers increased, making it hard for her to concentrate on any one aspect of their joining, of giving herself fully to him without thought to the repercussions. She didn't care about that right now; she cared only about giving him the same pleasure she felt. His hands grew rougher the faster he pumped in and out of her, never letting up, unforgiving in letting her reach her peak.

When she climaxed this time, her whole body stilled in his hold, the slam of his body against her backside only adding to the pleasure she felt as she exploded around his hand. A rush of fluid gushed out of her and seeped down her leg as he fucked her at a pace she no longer had the energy to reciprocate.

She fell to the bed, replete, out of breath, thrusting gently against his hand, trying to wring every ounce of pleasure from his touch and not sure if she wanted it to end. Nick let her go, grabbed her hips with both hands, and took her from behind like a beast, rutting her with a vigor she could not match.

He let out a roar as he too found his end. She could feel the hot injection of his seed filling her in a never-ending stream that pumped along her channel, until he slammed hard into her, buried to the hilt, and let her sheath milk the rest of him dry. He pressed into her periodically, as though making sure he was empty of his seed.

Her hips felt bruised where he'd gripped her. His hands trailed over her spine, the sweat on her body cooling fast in the room around them. His touch made her shiver, and her nipples peaked hard.

She wasn't sure what to do—if she should move or pull away—so she let Nick explore her in the aftermath of their lovemaking. Although the twitch of his cock subsided, his hardness did not. She held him inside her, as though her body didn't want to be apart from him. But she also felt stretched and achy.

"I'm going to pull out," Nick said. "Slowly, so you don't feel too much pain."

She nodded into the mattress, looking away in shame.

His hands cupped either of her buttocks as he pulled his still-hard length from her in slow increments. Every inch was a mixture of pleasure and pain. When he was fully out, she felt his seed trickle down the inside of her thigh in a hot stream.

She squeezed her legs together, curling them under her as she half sat up; to be seen this way made her feel at a disadvantage. While he'd seen her through the whole of their lovemaking, she hadn't once seen him. She was too shy to turn around and face him, too mortified to look him in the eye after what they'd just done.

Should she leave the bed and dress? She wasn't sure she had the strength to even move, let alone walk.

CHAPTER THIRTEEN

Nick drew Amelia's attention back to him with a kiss to her shoulder. The feather-light press of his lips had her eyes closing and her body swaying closer to his.

She crossed her hands over her breasts. They were sore and tender from his attention. When she turned to look at him, his face was a few inches away.

"What has you so skittish?" he asked.

"You," she whispered.

He placed his hands around her waist. She thought it was to keep her from fleeing, but she had no intention of running from what they'd just done.

"Are you hurt?" he asked.

She shook her head, but he was inspecting her body to make sure she was all right, and that melted her heart a little.

"No," she said. Mostly, she was starting to feel sore in places she had never felt anything prior to their joining.

"Then why do you keep averting your eyes?" he asked. The tone in his voice made her think she was hurting him by pulling back, so she met his gaze and held it.

"What am I meant to do?"

His hand cupped the side of her face, and he gave her a tender kiss on the mouth before answering her. "Exactly what you are doing."

"Is it always like that?"

He pulled her into his lap and held her. Parts of him poked at her, and it took everything in her not to look down and take in the sight of him. "It only hurts the first time. I won't hurt you again."

"I mean the other thing." God, her cheeks were flaming. "The parts that felt good."

He gave her a mischievous smile. "We need to get you in a warm bath before the pain really settles in."

Lifting her from his lap, he stood from the bed, his penis still hard. Her eyes were glued to that part of him. The sight of him naked was primal and breathtaking. His body was muscled everywhere, his stomach a series bumps and dents that moved like a rippling machine as he pulled his trousers over his strong legs. It was a shame he had to cover himself at all; she wanted to study him for hours.

Trousers donned, he snatched up her robe from the chair near her window and handed it to her. "You can wear this to my room." She realized she had to release her breasts and show herself to him if she took the wrap, so she stayed where she was until Nick leaned over the bed and kissed her full on the mouth. "Neither of us will be wearing clothes for the rest of the night, so your modesty is for a lost cause."

She took the robe and tied it around her waist as he pulled his shirt over his head and covered the dark hair speckled across his chest. She wanted to run her fingers over every part of his body.

Not bothering with the ties, the front gaped open and gave him a clear view of her breasts. He held out his hand, which she didn't hesitate to take.

Once her feet were on the floor, he scooped her up in his arms and carried her across the room. "What if someone sees us?" she asked, genuinely worried they might be caught.

"It is late enough that everyone will be in bed."

"Does Huxley ever sleep?"

Nick chuckled at that. "He's not here and will not be back for a few days."

She bit her bottom lip. Was she looking for an excuse to end their evening?

Nick opened the door, and after a cursory look down the hallway, he walked with purpose toward his bedchamber doors, which felt so much farther than it actually was.

"What we did…what does this mean for us going forward?"

"I was serious when I said you were mine. I will not let you go, Amelia."

"Why me?"

He looked her in the eye as he put her down on the edge of his high bed. His room was dark, except for the small fire burning in the fireplace in the sitting area at his back, so it was difficult to make out his expression.

"Why not you?" he returned.

He left her with those words as he went into the plunge bath, which was just off his bedroom. A light flickered on in that room, and she could hear the water being turned on.

Why would he choose her over a woman like Victoria, who was refined, beautiful, and already a part of his world? She hugged her arms around herself, pulling the robe tight around her body like a blanket. No, more like a shield.

Could she brave baring herself to him again? She was still coming down from the high of being in his arms. And while she knew she needed to distance herself from him, a larger part of her wanted the exact opposite. But how much could she insert herself in his life before she crossed a line between personal and professional? Hadn't she already crossed that line? She nearly snorted at that but was distracted from giving it further thought when Nick came back into the room, shirtless.

She hadn't been free to explore him when they'd been in her room. She hadn't seen any of him and wouldn't give up the opportunity, now that he was standing in front of her, and she had more light to see him.

The hair speckling his chest was as black as his beard; it covered his pectorals and trailed down his torso before stopping at his stomach. The trail picked up again beneath his belly button in a V-shape that disappeared in the band of his trousers.

The muscled lines on his stomach spoke of vigorous exercise. She had lived in the country all her life. Men took their shirts off on a hot summer day when they were working in the fields, but they had nothing on Nick Riley. He was sculpted like a Greek statue, every line of muscle defined, right down to his narrow hips. His arms were roped with sinew too, and her mouth dropped open with an appreciative sigh.

Her gaze trailed back to his eyes, and she saw a measure of pride in those stormy depths of his. "If you look at the rest of me that way, I won't be able to keep my hands off you much longer, Amelia."

Her breathing grew erratic again. She closed her eyes as he approached her. When the shush of his feet crossing the floor stopped, and she felt the heat radiating from his body and reaching out toward her, she put her hand out. Her fingers pressed into his chest as he leaned closer.

"I want to kiss every inch of your porcelain skin." His hands reached for the tie around her waist. Jerking the sash loose, the garment glided off her shoulders and caught in the bend of her arms. Hastily, she slipped free of the material, desperate to touch him again. Desperate to feel their bodies smashed together without any clothes.

She was no longer afraid of her nudity and hoped this newfound bravery didn't abandon her any time soon.

Trailing her hand over his chest, she traced along the line that cut cleanly down the center of him before fanning out her fingers through the spatter of hair on his chest.

"What happens tomorrow?" she asked, hating that she needed to know. "Do I become your mistress? Or do we pretend none of this happened?"

"I promise you, this happened. And I will not let you forget it. You are a free woman, to decide as you please, Amelia. I will never cage you like a songbird. But make no mistake; you are still mine."

"And what of the rest of the household?" She couldn't help but worry what they would think of her. She'd only just been hired, and now she was intimate with her employer. They could never know what transpired between her and Nick.

"They have nothing to do with us."

"They cannot know," she whispered.

"I agree that secrecy is probably for the better. For the time being anyway." He kissed her shoulder before standing again. "Come," he said giving her his hand yet giving her the choice to go with him. "Your bath awaits."

She didn't hesitate to go with him and stood unashamed and feeling braver by the moment, though she didn't expect that bravery to last past tonight.

The bathing room was quite grand and tiled in beige marble on the floors and halfway up the walls. The tub was bigger than any she'd ever seen, and its decorative brass-clawed feet rested in the middle of the large room. There was a dressing table and sink on one wall and a toilet on the other, all encased in blond wood. She'd never seen a full bath in any house, and the luxury of it had her speechless. Water still filled the bath, and Nick reached down to turn the taps off when it was three-quarters full.

Taking her hand once again, he helped her into the water, which was hot but not so hot that it would burn her, just enough to soothe her.

Nick stayed outside the water, his trousers still in place and sitting low on his hips. Though she could see the bulge of his penis straining against the material, he didn't seem to find any discomfort.

He reached down to gather a large sea sponge in his hand and soaked it with water. When he sat on the rim of the tub and squeezed the water over her thighs, she was mortified to see streaks of blood. She reached for the sponge and started to sink into the water in an attempt to hide herself, but the water was crystal clear.

"You have nothing for which you should be ashamed, Amelia. I should have been gentler." Now that she was sitting in the water, he squeezed streams of water over her breasts, making her nipples peak. There were a few abrasions and scuff marks from his beard blotted across her pale skin. Nick thumbed the scratches he'd left on her body. "I like seeing my marks on you."

She liked it too but couldn't admit as much. What was wrong with her to want a stamp of ownership marking her skin? It was so she wouldn't forget tonight when morning finally arrived. So she would know this had actually happened and hadn't been a dream.

"The water is more soothing than I thought it would be," she said, drawing his eyes back to hers. His gaze was pure hunger. She swallowed, not sure what to say, not sure what to do. She took the sponge from him and let it fall into the water.

"I have changed my mind," he said, standing suddenly to undo his trousers so he could pull them down his legs. The sight that greeted her caused her breath to catch in her throat, and her heart paused for a full second in her chest.

When he tossed his trousers aside and stood proudly before her, she took the opportunity to study his form. She'd never seen a man naked before tonight. Never seen that part of a man's body in any state or form, though she imagined men didn't walk around with a bulging piece of flesh day in and day out; she would have noticed it. In fact, it was as thick as her wrist, and she wasn't at all surprised that it had hurt so much when he'd entered her. The tip of it was a deep plum, and the heavy column was closer to his tanned skin tone. The hair at the base was clipped short and was the same color as the trail of hair snaking down the center of his abdomen.

Noticing where her attention was focused, Nick's hand curled around the base of his penis. "This is what you do to me, Amelia. Do you know how many times I have thought of tossing you on my desk, throwing your skirts over your head, and fucking you senseless whenever we are alone?" His words were crass and raw, and they made her sheath throb to have him inside her again. That was a new sensation for her, for she'd never felt it before tonight.

"And now?" she dared to ask.

The faintest of smiles tilted his lips. To her surprise, he stepped into the water with her, his feet between her legs. She scooted back in the water to give him more room until she was stopped by the curved backrest. Nick's hands curled around the edge of the bathing tub, and he leaned in close to her face, as though he planned to kiss her.

"Right now, all I can think of doing is having you wrap your legs around my hips so I can bury my cock deep inside you."

With his words, her knees spread wider, stopped only by the width of the tub. If that wasn't an invitation, she didn't know what was. Nick moved closer, the head of his penis brushing the curls of her sex. His arms surrounded her as he leaned over her.

"What if I also want that?" It was a challenge and a dare. Even though she felt a tinge of soreness in her nether region, she wanted this too badly to say no.

Hands holding tightly to the edge of the tub, she dared herself to be bold, to take what she wanted just once. Just *this* once. Curling one leg around his hip, she dug her heel into his backside to pull him into the V of her thighs. Still, he held back enough that he didn't enter her, his penis teasing her and just out of reach from its ultimate goal.

"I want to feel you inside me again. I want you to make me feel what I felt before." Amelia nibbled on her lower lip. "Before...when you were inside me, I never wanted it to end."

Her admission must have driven Nick over the edge, for he roughly grabbed her buttocks so he could tilt her pelvis toward him, and he slid inside her. He didn't slam deep and hard as he had the first time. This time he was slow, letting her get used to the welcome intrusion and adjusting to the size of him. He groaned when he was fully seated. Amelia wrapped both her legs around his hips, her hands on the edge of the tub the only thing keeping her afloat in the water.

Nick's mouth was harsh and brutal as it smashed against hers in a drugging, all-consuming kiss. His teeth scraped against her lips, and he sucked at her tongue so violently that their teeth clanked with every thrust of his tongue into her mouth.

Being with Nick this way felt...right.

She knew if she asked to stop at any point, Nick would have respected that decision. But she wanted to be reckless, carefree. She wanted to be the type of woman who had the world at her fingertips. As did the other women who had been at dinner tonight. But she was only playing part of that role now, indulging in intimacy she'd never before experienced. Lavishing in every new sensation Nick let her feel.

Her focus turned solely to Nick as his mouth landed on hers again, gentler this time. His knees found purchase between her legs, while his hands curled over the rim of the tub and offered support for her head as he slid in and out of her at a much slower pace. Being in the water, her breasts floated on the surface in their position, the wetness all around them lapping at her nipples like hundreds of tongues. Nick periodically dipped his head to suck one of her hard nipples into his mouth, eliciting moan after moan from her. Every time he did that, she felt her sheath tighten around his cock in exquisite pleasure.

She couldn't say how long their bodies moved together, but the water cooled enough that goose bumps rose along her arms and legs. Nick gently bit her shoulder and must have noticed that her skin was chilled.

He lifted them both from the tub, sloshing water around them and on the floor as he stepped onto the marble tiles. He remained buried deep inside her. Arms wrapped tight around his shoulders and ankles locked behind his back, she looked into his eyes and found herself breathless by the possessive determination in his gaze. It was a look that matched his earlier declaration; it said she belonged to him.

When she looked at the image they made in the mirror behind them, she could see a puzzle of scars crisscrossing Nick's back. She lowered one of her hands to touch the raised welts. She didn't know what to say when she looked back into his eyes, questions surely clear all over her face.

"Another time," he said.

"It hurts me to see that," she admitted out loud. And it had a thousand questions burning in her mind as to how such a thing had happened.

"Then I will try to clear it from your memory."

When he looked at her, the stamp of possession was clear—he owned her body and intended to show her that throughout the night. And she could admit he owned a little piece of her soul, but perhaps that was because she'd chosen him above everyone else. Others had tried to take what she wasn't willing to give, and she'd resisted and fought back, but when she looked at Nick, she wanted to give him everything she had to offer.

She hated that her lies stood between them. It was in that moment she knew she had to tell him the truth about who she was, and what exactly she was running from. But not tonight. She couldn't bear to bring any ugliness between them when everything was so perfect right now.

She kissed him full on the mouth as he carried her into the next room, her arms anchored around his neck again, though she couldn't get the image of those scars out of her mind.

There was no harshness as their mouths came together; it was a gentle tasting, as if she was familiarizing herself with him, and he was doing the same. It let her see a softer side of him, though she thought he was only being careful because she was still tender from their first lovemaking.

To her surprise, he didn't take her over to his bed but to the hearth flanked with an oversized chair on one side and a burgundy chaise on the other. There was a fire burning low and emitting enough heat that the droplets of water left on her skin soon began to evaporate.

Nick leaned over the chaise, pressing her back into the velvety soft material. Kneeling between her legs, he guided her knees toward her chest and seated himself deeper inside her. Her eyes fell shut, and her head tilted back, giving him access to her throat, which he rubbed his beard along. Though the position stretched her body oddly and gave her no control, it felt good to be trapped beneath this man, to give him complete power over her body—to do as he pleased with her, while she was at his mercy.

She wanted to touch every part of him, explore the scars on his back, and try to understand what that might have been like for him, but he anchored her wrists together above her head with his unmovable grip.

Then his body worked hard inside her, pushing deep, only to pull out and slam back into her. What was left from the water on their skin grew sticky and damp between them as Nick stretched her body to its limits of pleasure and pain. She was helpless to move beneath him and could only accept what he doled out. She didn't ask him to slow down his punishing pace; she begged him to give her release. Begged him to never stop. She couldn't say how long they moved in unison, but their bodies were covered in sweat again when he finally emptied himself inside her. After retrieving a wet towel from the bathing chamber, he wiped away the evidence of their lovemaking and carried her over to his bed.

They didn't join again, but he did worship every part of her body with kisses. She wasn't sure how late they were awake, never talking, only touching, but she eventually fell asleep in his arms.

CHAPTER FOURTEEN

Nick was nowhere to be found when Amelia opened her eyes and stared at the small stream of light spilling in through the split in her curtains. She stretched her hand out across her bed, and inhaled deeply, smelling the sandalwood of his soap and the amber in his cologne everywhere. She felt dampness between her thighs when she recalled everything they'd done. She wasn't sure when he'd brought her back to her room, but she was glad he'd thought that far ahead so they wouldn't be discovered together.

She rolled over onto her back, feeling aches in places she had never felt before and a lingering soreness everywhere. Her breasts felt tender, and even her nipples were overly sensitized as she stretched her arms above her head, and the material of her night rail scraped across the tips.

She felt like she'd ridden a horse for an entire day. As she sat up, she cringed at the residual pain in lower parts of her body. Taking her time, she swung her feet out of her bed and stood. Though her body was tired and slow, she felt better standing than sitting, probably because most of the soreness radiated out from her sex. She blushed as she recalled her evening with Mr. Riley. And then she blushed more, realizing she'd have to face him in the light of day.

She remembered every intimate detail of their time together, everything they'd done. She made her bed neatly so the maids wouldn't bother with her room. The quilt atop was a dark blue and hid any blood from their first joining last night, for which she was thankful. Her dress was in a heap on the floor, so she picked up the skirts and bodice and hung them in the wardrobe.

Changing into a chemise, she put on the corset she'd worn last night before donning a plain dress.

Rotating her ankle under the dressing table, she was surprised it felt so much better—perhaps that was because other parts of her seemed to hurt more, though she still took her cane with her, using it intermittently as she went down the stairs and headed toward the study.

What would today bring? What would Mr. Riley say to her, and how would he treat her now that she'd allowed herself to be tempted onto their current path of seduction?

She didn't spare another thought as she opened the double doors into the study. Today, she had every intention of tidying up Mr. Riley's paperwork before sorting through the mail and attending to her own duties. Then she would act as if nothing was different and join the rest of the staff for breakfast.

Of course, her good intentions could change if she ran into Mr. Riley. To her disappointment, he wasn't in the study, not that he seemed to go there first thing in the morning. So she went about her duties, reading his missives.

She paused when she handled a letter that looked like it was of a personal nature. Lifting the vellum to her nose, she could smell the faint trace of lavender on the paper.

Turning it over, she saw an unfamiliar name: Seraphina. Who was she? A lover? A friend? A relative? The last was unlikely, considering the lavender scent that infused the paper. But someone by the name of "Ser" had written to him before. Could that be the same woman?

Amelia sat heavily in the leather chair and she stared at it, wondering...She wouldn't dare invade his privacy, but...

"Good morning," Nick said from the door.

She stood from his desk and backed up a few steps. It wasn't quite embarrassment she felt at being caught sitting at his desk; it was more like guilt.

"I hope you slept well," he said.

"I did. Thank you." She ducked her head, not ready to meet his assessing gaze. "I did not expect you down yet. I was going through your papers to make sure everything is in order."

He came fully into the room, his presence dominating everything. After shutting the double doors behind him, he turned the lock. She swallowed, nerves making it difficult for her to breathe, let alone ask him what he was doing.

"By all means, do what you need to do," he said without inflection in his voice—she had difficulty reading his mood.

"There is a private letter for you. I did not want to open it."

"I have nothing to hide from you, Amelia." Her eyes shot to his. "Open it," he said.

She hesitated, feeling ashamed for thinking the worst. "I...I couldn't." She retrieved it and passed it to him.

"It's from Sera."

"Who is she?"

His smile was slow. "I think you're jealous."

She opened her mouth to deny it but closed it again. She was being silly. "I know so little about you, Nick. Everything I do or ask feels like prying." She still held the letter out to him. He took it and tucked it in his jacket pocket.

That predatory look was in his eyes as he approached her. She took another step back and was stopped by the wall.

"Sera, you should know, is my sister."

"Sister?" Oh, God, could she have sounded any more pathetic?

"Half sister, if you want to be precise. But still my sister."

There was so much that they needed to discuss, so much they had to figure out before they moved forward. All this time, and she had no idea he had siblings.

"I see your mind moving, Amelia, and can almost hear the thousand questions spinning around in that pretty head of yours. Perhaps you're wondering how we carry on during the day when our nights are filled with sin after sin." He stood but a hand span from her now, his hand tracing the top swell of her breast, where the barest amount of skin was exposed along the edge of the dress.

"I need to be honest with you—" she started to say.

His finger pressed against her parted lips, effectively shushing her. "I will be home late tonight, and I will not ask you to wait up for me, considering the hour you finally fell asleep this morning." He pressed closer to her. Her breathing grew erratic. "I want you to know that *we* did not end with last night."

"Help me understand what exactly you expect of me," she asked, at a loss for words when he stood close enough that she could smell the amber of his cologne. She wanted to burrow into that scent and rub herself against him like a cat in heat.

Reining in her desires, she recalled where they were. And while Nick had locked the study door behind him, they were taking too daring a chance.

"Am I supposed to carry on as if nothing has changed between us?" she asked.

"I leave that decision with you." His hand lowered, his thumb and forefinger taking her chin and turning her head to the side so he could press his lips against her neck. Her pulse fluttered with the simple touch, and he kissed her again.

Amelia's eyes drifted closed as she basked in the feel of his mouth on her, and all the feelings from the previous night slammed through her so suddenly that a moan slipped past her lips. She had to grab the front of his jacket to keep from swaying, to keep her knees from buckling under her.

When he lifted his head and looked at her again, there was a gleam of pure satisfaction in his eyes. She felt lost and found at the same time when she was in his arms and subject to his wicked ministrations. It was then that she wished they hadn't had to leave his bed at all. That their night could have carried on for an eternity. That the reality of morning didn't have to exist and make things awkward between them.

She lowered her hands, knowing they couldn't continue, knowing she needed to set boundaries between them if she wanted to do her job well. She cleared her throat delicately. "With Huxley away, what would you like me to spend my time doing?"

Huxley was still giving her direction, and he hadn't left her with a list of tasks to complete. And since he hadn't informed her that he was leaving, she assumed he had left rather suddenly.

Nick gave her just enough space to escape his domineering presence. She sidled out from between him and the wall and took a steadying breath as she walked toward his desk. Nick followed, though he must have sensed her hesitancy of the situation, as he didn't touch her again.

Reaching around her, he picked up a pen and turned a notebook toward him. He wrote down an address, tore the page from the book, and handed it to her.

She looked at the location and the name of a store, her brow furrowing. "What is this?"

"That is the address of Victoria's shop. If you feel so inclined, she is expecting you at some point for a fitting."

"I cannot accept this, Mr. Riley." Amelia pushed the paper toward him, but his hand curled around hers, pressing the address into her palm.

She would not be treated like his mistress. She would not let him treat her differently from anyone else in the house.

"As my secretary, *Amelia*," he said pointedly, as a reminder that she should call him by his first name, "you have a clothing allowance. It is required for the meetings and dinner parties you will attend with me."

"Oh." She felt foolish for not knowing that. And it made sense, considering how well Huxley was always dressed, though she didn't get the impression that he ever dined out with Nick and his associates.

"We have a dinner engagement tomorrow night, and I need you to wear something that will turn heads."

Her eyebrows scrunched together.

He must have read her confusion, for he said, "You will provide a distraction. Lord Murray and I have business to discuss, but his man of business tends to interfere as he has a personal interest in Murray's lands. I have no doubt you will be able to keep him engaged in a separate conversation."

She wasn't so sure about that, but she would do her best if that was what he wanted. "And what will I discuss with this person?"

"This will be a casual affair. You need only to be your charming self."

She had no real knowledge of what Nick's primary business purposes were, as he dabbled in so many things. "What do you want from Lord Murray?"

"His lands."

"Highgate," she said, remembering mention of it last night. "Heddie said he had a drafty old castle there. Is that far outside of London?"

"Not too far." His hands were at her hips, pulling her closer to his body. She let him. "What are you trying to delicately ask?"

"I want to understand why this is important."

"He has two hundred acres and holds the majority of the leases in the town. I have a personal interest in the area and plan to reinstate the house."

"Where will Lord Murray go if you buy his house and his lands?"

"He has two other properties, neither of which have my interest."

She arched one eyebrow at that and tucked the address into the bosom of her dress. She would visit Miss Newgate's shop, even though she had every reason to dislike the woman who had once held Nick's affections.

"I would like to see you tonight," she said.

"You may wish for a night of reprieve."

She shook her head; that was the last thing she wanted. "We have so much to figure out between us. There are things about me…about my past."

"You don't have to tell me anything you don't want to tell, Amelia. Your past will not change what's between us."

She wished she didn't have to worry about her past, but he should know the truth. Perhaps now wasn't the best time to bring it to the fore.

Before she could say more, Nick's thumb pressed against her lower lip and pulled it down enough that he could slip the tip into her mouth. Amelia closed her eyes and, feeling daring and bold, flicked her tongue against him. His mouth replaced his hand while her eyes were still closed. There was less urgency to his kiss today, and it was done in a way that made her crave more. Perhaps she would always crave more after last night.

He pulled away just as she curled her fingers into the sleeves of his jacket. "While you're a pleasant distraction, I will never make my meeting with Landon if we continue." His voice was hoarse, filled with desire.

She nodded her agreement, at a loss for words. She hated that she couldn't control herself around him.

Before turning to leave, he reached into his waistcoat pocket and pulled out a small pouch. Handing it to her, he said, "For your tea. The taste is a little bitter, but if you use some sugar, you will not notice it." Before she could ask what it was, he added, "It will help keep my seed from taking root."

Her cheeks warmed, and she had to turn her gaze elsewhere. She hadn't even thought of that.

"It is nothing for which you should be ashamed," Nick said and gave her a peck on the mouth before turning away again. "You will need to drink it daily."

She blushed. How could she not? This was all still new to her.

Taking out the paper she'd tucked in her dress, she looked at the address and decided to go directly to Miss Newgate's shop. Amelia would not be intimidated by her.

Nick had a tendency to trust those in his house above all. He felt a certain responsibility in safeguarding their welfare. Not one of them came from a past easily forgotten, though he tried to give them as safe a place as possible to overcome the obstacles of those pasts. When Devlin, his housekeeper's son, found him at Landon's club, the boy had a black eye and a swollen, bloody lip. Nick felt rage building in him.

Nick ushered the boy into a private room. Kneeling so they were at the same level, he placed his hands on Devlin's arms and inspected the damage done to his face. The boy's nose was intact, as were his teeth, from what Nick could see. It looked worse than it really was. Not that Devlin's mother would have agreed with that assessment.

"You need to tell me exactly what happened, Devlin," Nick said.

Tears filled the youth's eyes. While the boy was only nine, size alone made him look much younger. He was an easy target for violence, should someone want to hurt him. "Didn't catch his name, Mr. Riley."

Seeing blood in Devlin's mouth sent Nick over the edge. Whoever had done this would pay dearly. Nick held out his handkerchief for Devlin. When the boy took it, Nick saw a crumpled letter in the boy's hand. "What's this, Dev?" he asked, reaching for it.

Devlin gave him the letter, but Nick noticed that it was not addressed.

Tearing open the envelope, he quickly read the contents. He wasn't angry anymore; he was enraged.

There was no salutation, but the contents made it clear to whom it was addressed. Nick crumpled the letter in his fist. "Who gave you this letter?"

"Didn't know him. He was a gent."

"What did he say?"

"To get it straight to Amelia Somerset."

This was not how Nick expected to discover Amelia's real name. Damn it, he wished Huxley was around to do a little investigating while he dealt with the ass who thought he could raise his hand against a child. And then to threaten Amelia...He needed to find her. Make sure she was safe.

"Why did he approach you and not Amelia?"

"Saw us together, is all I can think. We walked some ways. I pointed her in the direction of Miss Victoria's shop," the boy explained.

"Then where did you go?" He didn't want to push too hard for information, but they needed to sort this out fast.

"Did my errands for me ma and got cornered when I left the market. Ma's gonna be angry about her carrots. I don't know where I dropped 'em."

Nick clasped Devlin's shoulder. "Don't worry about the carrots. Let's get you home safely so your mother can fret over you."

"Just a split lip. Had one before, and Ma didn't much mind—just told me to stay out of trouble."

If the situation wasn't as dire as it was, Nick might have laughed. But Devlin, he was sure, had been lucky not to suffer more serious harm.

Leading the boy out of the private room, he gave his excuses to Landon, promising to catch up with him another time. Devlin didn't say a word on their carriage ride home; he just watched the scenery pass by outside, which gave Nick time to think about the letter's contents.

When they arrived home, Mrs. Coleman was not at all happy to see her boy sporting bruises like he had been in a fight. "What have you gotten yourself into, Dev?"

Devlin's cheeks flushed, and he ducked his head, evidently embarrassed that his mother was admonishing him at all. "I was too slow and didn't realize there was the two of 'em, Ma."

"If you want to blame anyone, Marney, you should blame me," Nick said, giving her arm a friendly squeeze. "It's not your son's fault. The man who did this will be sorry he thought he could cross me."

"What did he think he would get from Devlin?" she asked, worry thick in her question.

"He was a fool and should have come to me, not your son. He will pay for what he has done," he promised.

She squeezed Nick's hand in thanks and turned her focus back to her son, dabbing away at the dried blood on his mouth. Mrs. Coleman gathered Devlin in her arms and looked at Nick over her son's dark mop of hair, tears awash in her eyes.

His housekeeper put Devlin at arm's length and focused on the cuts on his face. "You shouldn't have to worry about escaping any bad situation, love."

Nick was ready to slaughter the person who had done this. The slow burn of rage he normally kept at an even temperature was boiling over. All he needed was a direction to focus that fury. And the answers he needed could be found with his new secretary.

Nick ruffled Devlin's hair and headed up to the study, taking the stairs two at a time in his haste. There was always the possibility that Amelia was back from Vic's shop. When he opened the library door, he wasn't surprised to see her desk chair empty. Opening up her date book, he tore a page from the back and left a note for her, should their paths not cross.

Before he left, he went over to his books and pulled down his copy of Debrett's. Her name wasn't familiar, which said precisely nothing, other than he'd never had business dealings with her family. But he'd figure out just who she was on his way to Vic's store. If she was in any sort of danger...so help the person who laid one bloody finger on her. He'd break each of the man's fingers himself, and then bloody his face worse than he'd done to Dev.

CHAPTER FIFTEEN

Amelia curled her fingers tighter around the heavy drapes that enclosed the changing room where she'd been set up with a number of dresses to try. A shop girl stood behind her, yanking tight on the strings of a new corset. This corset was quite snug compared to the one she normally wore—that one had been well worn and had probably loosened over the past year. This one felt…impossible.

The girl tugged again, causing the air to whoosh from Amelia's lungs. Though she wanted to ask the girl to leave it loose, she refused to show any weakness when Victoria Newgate sat delicately in a chair, sipping tea as she watched Amelia with feigned interest. There was a look of disappointment in the woman's cat-like green eyes, only Amelia couldn't figure out what had put the other woman off her. Victoria could not possibly know what Nick and Amelia had done, so maybe she was reading that disappointment incorrectly.

"It simply will not do, Louisa," Victoria said as she stood, shooing the shop girl away as she approached Amelia. "Retrieve the twenty-one inch," Victoria told the girl, leaving Amelia alone with the woman who, by all appearances, immensely disliked her. It had taken every bit of courage Amelia had to come to the shop today.

Amelia let go of the curtain and reached behind her to release the ties on the corset. She took in a full, relieved breath when it sat loose around her torso. To her surprise, Victoria turned her around and pulled open the front of the corset, taking it off Amelia. Victoria laid the delicate material flat on a table to straighten the strings.

"It's all the rage to cinch down below a twenty," Victoria said. "If we cannot do that, I'm afraid the selection for your wardrobe shrinks drastically. Perhaps we can let out a few dresses if they are truly needed, but as it is, I will have to place an order."

It didn't surprise Amelia in the least that this woman would insult her. Though her words stung, Amelia didn't show how uncomfortable she was in Victoria's presence. "Why are you helping me at all when it's apparent that is the last thing you want to do?" Amelia asked.

"Because Nick asked me to," Victoria said, as if that was answer enough.

"And do you always do as he asks? Even when it is clear that you would rather be anywhere else but here with me?" Amelia snapped her mouth shut. It wasn't like her to be so candid or unkind. She knew why this woman didn't like her, and while Victoria might not know that Amelia and Nick's relationship had developed into something Amelia couldn't even put into words, this woman had only one reason to dislike her: Amelia could spend time with Nick as often as she liked and would attend functions that Victoria had once attended. But was that really reason for Victoria to dislike her? It seemed petty.

"I'm a businesswoman, Miss Grant. I do what I need to do to keep my shop brimming over with *business*. If that means catering to a few people I have no inclination to like, then that is what I will do."

"Well, I am glad for that clarification. I would not want to think there was a chance you and I could become fast friends," Amelia said, not caring to guard her tongue now. She had never met anyone so...so obstinate and rude and spiteful.

"I know your type," Victoria said. "You have wormed your way into the house of one of the richest men in England, and I know you plan to seduce your way into his pocketbook. I'm looking out for Nick's best interests, as a friend would do."

Amelia's mouth flapped, at a loss for words. That was the last thing she'd ever expected or wanted from Nick, though Victoria would have no reason to believe anything Amelia said that contradicted that. Thankfully, the shop girl returned carrying a small stack of corsets before Amelia had to come up with a retort.

The silence in the changing room was almost more than Amelia could bear, but she refused to say another word to Victoria.

The bigger size helped, though it still was a great deal more snug than her old corset. Victoria went back to sipping her tea, watching, and commenting periodically about how to bring in or let out the dresses that Amelia tried on. Not one was perfect, as apparently Amelia was not an ideal model for the clothes stocked in Victoria's shop. Amelia bit her tongue through it all, just wanting the ordeal to end.

At her wit's end from Victoria's insulting gibes, Amelia was glad when the last dress was removed and set aside by the shop girl.

"Victoria!" A man's voice shouted just beyond the curtain—a voice Amelia knew but had never heard raised before now.

"What in hell does he think he's doing?" Victoria said with a shake of her head. She strode from the room with purpose, whipping around the curtains that blocked Amelia before disappearing into the next room. Squeals and comments rose at the presence of a man in Victoria's shop.

"Where is she?" he said, loud enough that Amelia and— she was sure—the rest of the patrons in the store heard.

Before Victoria could turn Nick around, he ushered Victoria back into the changing room. His eyes searched the small room and found Amelia almost immediately. Was that relief Amelia saw in the steely depths?

"You know we don't allow men back here, Nick. You need to leave." Victoria's voice was firm and determined.

Nick's focus was momentarily pulled away from Amelia as he addressed his friend. "Leave us."

The shop girl had been edging toward the curtains before Nick had even commanded they leave, and she was gone from sight before Victoria crossed her arms over her chest to glare at Nick. It crossed Amelia's mind that gossip would start if Victoria left them alone too. The other shoppers present would speculate what was happening behind the closed curtains and leave Amelia's reputation in shambles.

She stopped that thought...she was not Lady Amelia Somerset, the Earl of Berwick's daughter. She was Amelia

Grant, secretary to industrialist Nick Riley. She didn't matter to anyone, and that brought a small smile to her lips that she wished she could have hidden better or at least saved for when Victoria wasn't around, because Victoria had noticed. No one would care about Amelia's reputation, though by the look on Victoria's face, she didn't like what might be said about her store.

"I have to insist you leave, Nick. You know my reputation is only as good as the service I provide to young ladies. You are making a scene I can ill afford."

Nick didn't seem to be listening to his friend. He approached Amelia but thought twice about reaching for her and stopped a good three feet away. Amelia stood stock still, shocked to see him here and unsure what to do when she was barely dressed.

Victoria threw up her arms and expelled her breath in pure frustration before picking up Amelia's serviceable gray dress and shoving Nick away before helping her get dressed. Nick didn't say a word; he just stared at her, as though he had a lot to say but not in front of Victoria.

When Amelia's dress was in place, Victoria said, "You both need to leave. I will not have you causing a scene in my store." She ushered them out beyond the curtain. It appeared the shop girl had cleared most of the patrons from the back area where the dressing rooms were, and Amelia was thankful she wouldn't have to face the women in the shop.

Nick placed his hand at the base of Amelia's back, following Victoria.

"Since you cannot be seen leaving here, Nick, you will have to use the service entrance," Victoria said unapologetically as she opened a door that revealed a narrow staircase lit with a few electric lamps. "It's three flights, but once you reach the bottom, there is another door that leads to the shipment yard."

"If this wasn't important, I would have waited," Nick said to Victoria but didn't take his eyes off Amelia.

Victoria snorted in pure disgust. "For some reason, I find that hard to believe." Victoria crossed her arms and looked pointedly at them both. "I will have two dresses delivered tomorrow. The rest will have to wait until next week. Now leave my store."

"Thank you," Nick said, motioning for Amelia to go ahead of him.

"Do not thank me. I will add a hazard charge to your bill," Victoria said, shutting the door behind them and leaving them alone in the dimly lit stairwell.

"I'm sorry I was here so long," Amelia explained. "I intended for this to be a quick trip—"

Nick's arms wrapped around her, and he slammed his mouth against hers. His teeth were harsh, his mouth unforgiving as he stole her breath away and left her panting for air. When he released her, she was left slightly dizzy and confused. Surely he hadn't come all this way and made such a scene just so he could kiss her.

His hands cupped either side of her face, and he looked into her eyes as though looking for something. What her tired brain should have asked was, why was he here at all? He'd told her he wouldn't be home until rather late, yet here it was in the middle of the afternoon, and he'd seemed frantic to find her.

"Has something happened?" she asked, because she didn't know what else to say.

"Yes." At the look of worry on her face, he added, "I feared something had happened to you."

"Me?" she parroted and hated that she sounded like an idiot, but she hadn't the faintest idea of what he was talking about.

He took her hand, and turned toward the stairs. "We need to leave."

She didn't say another word; she just blindly followed him down the rickety wooden stairs. When they reached the door at the bottom, he didn't pause, but he did let go of her hand the moment they found themselves in the courtyard Victoria had mentioned. No one paid them much mind as they let themselves out through a back gate and into the street. Nick didn't say a word as he called over a carriage and gave instructions on where to bring them.

"Why are we not headed back to the house?" she asked, once they were in the carriage.

"We have matters to discuss."

"Have I done something wrong?"

Nick opened his jacket and reached inside a pocket. He pulled out an ivory linen envelope and handed it to her. She looked up at him briefly before flattening the wrinkles and unfolding the parchment inside.

Without even reading it, she knew who had written it. Tears filled her eyes. She couldn't help it. Her time of freedom had been far too short. She looked at the ceiling, trying to hold her tears at bay, hating that her first inclination was to cry instead of fighting back against her brother. When she had better control over her emotions, she looked down at the words, reading them carefully.

"Do you know who wrote it?" Nick asked.

And she wanted to cry even more when she heard the gentle kindness in his tone. She could hear his desire to help her, and she couldn't appreciate that more than she did in this moment.

She nodded at his question, unable to speak, afraid her voice wouldn't hold together as she tried to fight the fear that was choking her from the inside out.

Nick reached for her hand, giving it a comforting squeeze.

"Why must you be so perfect and so kind to me?" She looked away from him, shaking her head as the words spilled from her mouth. "If you want me to leave, I can. I don't want to cause you any trouble. Or anyone in the house. I just wanted to disappear, but it seems my attempt at even that was unsuccessful."

"You're not leaving, Amelia. I have already told you—you're mine, and I will not let you go. Not even for this."

She looked at him then, her tears barely holding. She needed to be strong. She needed to stand up for herself.

"Who wrote the letter, Amelia?"

She supposed she would have to tell him everything now, relive the horror she had wanted to bury with her escape. Relive parts of her past if she was going to explain just what type of man her brother was.

"The letter is from my brother."

"The same man who promised you to another?"

"More like he sold me, as if I were a cart horse." She snorted. "Though I think he might put more value on a horse than his own sister."

Amelia watched Nick's expression change from anger to barely concealed rage with that revelation. The tick at the side of his jaw seemed more pronounced now than ever before.

"You should know who I am," she said.

"I know already."

She looked at him, perplexed. "Did my brother give you the letter directly?"

"No."

She narrowed her eyes. Something wasn't right here. "What are you not telling me?"

"Devlin walked with you this morning."

Her hand flew to her mouth and she sucked in a gulp of air. "Is he all right? Tell me my brother did not hurt him." Tears fell from her eyes this time, and she didn't bother to hide them or wipe them away. She knew just how vile her brother was, and he didn't discriminate against whom he hurt. The weaker they were, the easier it was to hurt them—this was something her brother lived by. "If Devlin is hurt…" She couldn't even bear to finish that thought. Bile climbed up her throat, and she gulped in air to keep her nerves settled.

"He got away. Came straight to me with that letter you're holding."

She wiped away her tears and looked down at the paper. "I was so careful." Her voice broke at that admission. "I don't understand how he found me."

"Shhh." Nick slid onto the seat next to her and wrapped his big arms around her shoulders. She cried a little into his shoulder, taking great heaps of air into her lungs to try to suffocate her fear.

"I can keep you safe." His words were a promise she wanted so badly to believe.

But she knew her brother better than anyone. Knew what he was capable of doing. Most of all, she knew he wouldn't stop until he had her where he wanted her. "I will not risk putting anyone else in danger. I cannot. It would be best for everyone that I leave."

"You are not leaving, Amelia." His declaration calmed her somewhat, though the distress she'd always felt in her brother's presence still threatened to strangle her. The urge to run again was so strong that she glanced out the window, seriously thinking about leaving this instant. She could go to Edinburgh; perhaps that was where should have gone. No, then she wouldn't have met Nick. He was the best thing to happen in her life.

While being in Nick's arms kept the panic at bay, she knew it would overwhelm her when he wasn't around to keep her feeling safe. How could she stress how terrible a person her brother was? How could she stress how dangerous his friends were? Would they be looking for her too? She couldn't bear to think about that. One problem at a time was all she could handle without shutting down and letting the fear bury her.

"I can see the wheels turning in your head, trying to formulate excuses." Nick thumbed away the tears that wetted her cheeks. "Your brother is no different from some of the men I have dealt with. I can protect you better than you can protect yourself if you try to run. But run, Amelia, and I will follow you."

She heard the warning in his voice and wouldn't dare disobey it. "There's nothing inside him. No love, no happiness, just this deep hatred that allows him to do horrible things. He is cold and calculating, and he has always done as he pleases, Nick. If he found me walking with Devlin, he may already know where I live. He may try to hurt someone else at the house."

"Let me handle your brother. He will wish he had stayed in Berwick."

Nick's hand caressed her arm up and down; the constant motion helped her breath calmly. When she had her emotions under control, they went inside and locked themselves in the library. Nick sat on the sofa next to her.

"When Devlin came to you," Amelia said, "my leaving was not a consideration, was it?"

"Your brother doesn't scare me." He leveled that intense gaze of his on her, and she believed him. "I have known people far worse than you could imagine."

She couldn't be so sure of that. "And what about Devlin? Tell me what happened to him."

"Nothing more than a scuffle that resulted in a black eye."

Amelia felt her lip tremble. Poor Devlin, he didn't deserve the violence that had befallen him. And she hated that she'd been the cause of that. She needed to make Nick understand what kind of man her brother was. "Jeremy always finds ways to accomplish what he wants, no matter how vile the method in achieving it," she admitted. "I can't recall a time when my brother was not cruel. Not even when we were young, and our parents were still alive. I would feel responsible if you or anyone else was hurt." She wasn't sure why, but she couldn't admit she'd stolen money from her brother, couldn't admit that she was in the wrong when she finally got the courage to leave.

"I won't allow him to get to anyone else," Nick promised once again.

Could he really? He must have seen the disbelief clouding her expression.

"I know a thing or two about the type of person your brother is. As does everyone else who works in this house."

Amelia spread her hands out and stared down at them. What had she done wrong? How had her brother found her at all? The name Grant meant nothing; she'd taken it from the side of someone's luggage on the train to London. Perhaps she should have changed her first name too, but she somehow thought that might not have saved her from discovery either. If she hadn't stolen his money, would he have followed her? It wasn't a great sum, but it would have kept him busy for a couple of weeks in his gambling hells.

Her mind hadn't been playing tricks on her the night before; Jeremy had been in the crowd. That was how he'd found her. By chance. She wondered if he'd followed her and Nick home. The thought that he knew where she lived made her feel helpless…and angry.

"If you cut me free, you will never have to worry about my brother." She had to offer to leave again. Even though she didn't have anywhere else to go. "I couldn't bear the thought of someone else inadvertently being hurt because of me."

She wasn't so sure he would let her keep her job if things escalated with her brother. And knowing her brother, that's exactly what would happen. He would find a way to get to her, and he wouldn't stop when someone got in his way—he'd plow right through that person if he had to.

Nick leaned forward, and tipped her chin so she had to look him in the eye. "I have wanted you from the moment you fell into my life. That does not change because your brother thinks he has some claim over you."

"You barely know me, Nick." Why did she keep reminding him of this? Because she cared about him. No matter the length of time they'd known each other, she couldn't help but care for him, and she wanted to protect him too.

"That hardly matters. Meeting by chance was just the start of us. You are mine to defend, Amelia Somerset."

"You say that now." She shook her head in amazement of his complete resolve to protect her. "Wait. How do you know my name? It's not on the letter."

"It was mentioned to Devlin."

She felt guilty that she hadn't been the one to tell him. "I was going to tell you. I tried to this morning."

"Hush." His thumb swiped over her lips, rubbing back and forth. "I am not angry that you did not tell me sooner. You had a right to keep your secrets for as long as you did. But now you need to be completely honest with me."

He was right. As much as it pained her to have to tell him any of this, she needed to tell him her story. Tell him how she'd ended up in London at all.

"My father was an earl." Nick only nodded, waiting for her to continue. And she found herself telling him everything, leaving nothing out of the horrors of her life. "My father was a good man and loved me as much as he loved life. The doctor said his heart gave out. He could not keep up with his lavish life. A life he could ill afford, though I didn't know that until he died. I was fourteen. Jeremy was sixteen and not old enough to take my father's seat, so he was appointed a guardian until he came of age.

"Lord Ashley groomed my brother into the monster he is. That's not to say Jeremy was not always like that; he was cruel as a child. He hated me. Did terrible things to me even when my father was alive, though it progressively got worse as I got older. He hosted parties at our house in the summer, mostly to gamble. I usually stayed out of sight."

A shiver of revulsion ran through her as she remembered the first time she'd been truly violated by her brother. Sensing her unease, Nick pulled her into his arms, her head resting against his shoulder as she told him about her ugly past.

"If ever I had met him," Nick said, his hand brushing over her hair, "I would have stolen you out from under his power."

"When I was seventeen, Jeremy declared me old enough to be considered a woman." Tears burned at the back of her eyes. "He lost a bet; it was a heavy wager and more than he could afford to lose. To put the amount back in his pocket, he let the winner grope me."

She pressed her hands against her bosom, not able to put words to what had happened. That had been the mildest of assaults she'd suffered at the hands of her brother's many friends.

The only reason she hadn't been sold to some man as a mistress sooner was that she was more valuable as a virgin. That didn't stop her brother from granting men other privileges. Mostly, they just touched her. She didn't tell Nick about those incidents.

"Jeremy lost our home to Lord Ashley on a hand of cards. The price was much steeper this time, and I was given to Lord

Ashley under the condition that he could do as he wished, as long as he married me. I hated Lord Ashley. He frightened me as a young girl, and I could not bear to be in the same room with him as I got older. I did not wait around long enough to find out what Lord Ashley would do to me."

Nick lifted her from his shoulder and placed his hands on both sides of her face. "You did the right thing. Your brother will not reach you here, and neither will Lord Ashley."

"They will try to hurt you, Nick. While my brother is powerless, Lord Ashley is not. And I certainly don't believe my brother is here alone."

"And I dare them to try to get to you. You are no man's property and are not obligated to pay for your brother's mistakes in any way. If there is one thing I can promise you, it's that I will end their threat against you."

Looking at him, Amelia believed every word.

Chapter Sixteen

Nick leaned back in his chair, his hands clasped behind his head as he contemplated his next move. They had heard nothing and had not seen her brother again after yesterday's incident. He had just disappeared. The reprieve was temporary, Nick knew. But it gave him time to find a way to eliminate the problem of Amelia's brother. Paying him off wouldn't work; men like him only came back, groveling for more. And if they weren't given further handouts, they retaliated. That wasn't a risk he was willing to take. No, he needed to find a better way; something permanent, because the last thing he wanted was for Amelia to look over her shoulder for the rest of her life.

Publically ruining a man as depraved as her brother had been described would be a simple process, but it would also bring to light the fact that Amelia was living in his house. While that circumstance might be acceptable for his secretary, he doubted many would be as forgiving about an earl's daughter doing the same. And if she wanted anonymity so she could start a new life, he would protect her identity.

There was also the problem of Lord Ashley. But Nick would take care of him once he found a solution for her brother.

Nick scrubbed his hand over his face and rolled his shoulders before pushing away from the desk. It was early yet, but he wanted to find Amelia.

Huxley walked in just as Nick stood.

"I did not think you would return until tomorrow," Nick said.

"Didn't much expect to either. Caught an early train once I had what I needed."

"I assume the trip went as planned?"

Huxley had spent the past few days in Highgate, listening to the rumors of Murray's sale of the estate and surrounding lands. Nick needed to know if anyone was opposed to the deal so he could approach them on his own terms. This was an important purchase for him, one he didn't want to sour before he had a chance to pay back a man who had robbed him and his sister of a decent childhood. But all this seemed secondary to the issues with Amelia.

"Yes," Huxley said. "Have you spoken with Murray since your dinner?"

Nick shook his head as walked over to the sideboard to pour two whiskeys. "I was to dine with him last night but had to reschedule, as something more important came up." And he'd talk to Huxley about that in a moment. "I doubt Murray will ask for more than I have offered. He cannot afford to keep the property without risking it being run down further than it is. The only problem will be his secretary."

Nick intended to fix up the house and turn it into a home for wayward boys and girls. He was going to give it to his sister to run. But that was years down the line, as the house was in a state of disrepair.

"I can confirm that Murray's secretary is the eyes and ears for the vicar," Huxley said.

Which was precisely what Nick thought. He had been hoping for better news. Of course, Nick had an ulterior motive for wanting the Murray estate. There was a bigger plan at play than simply starting a school for his sister; that could be done anywhere in London. There was a man in Highgate Nick owed a debt to, one that would be paid with the other man's blood.

"And how is the old vicar?" Nick asked.

"Up to his old antics, I'm afraid."

Huxley was probably the only other person who knew of the vicar's dark proclivities. Not that Nick had explained it in great detail to his man of affairs, but it wasn't hard to guess how vile the old man was after watching him for a couple of days. By all accounts, the vicar either didn't remember Nick, or he wasn't privy to the particulars of the sale. Either way, his reign over that part of town was fast coming to an end.

"He's neither here nor there until I gain control of the estate," Nick said. Setting his glass down, he leaned against his desk and crossed his arms over his chest. "There are other problems with which I need your assistance—they involve Amelia."

The news didn't seem to surprise Huxley. Then again, he was a man who didn't display a lot of emotion. "I saw Devlin on my way in. Marney told me what she knew, which wasn't much. What kinda trouble she get herself in before coming here?"

"It seems her brother is in town. Goes by the last name of Somerset. He's the Earl of Berwick." He hadn't needed Amelia to tell him that; it had been staring back at him from his catalog of peerages when he'd gone to retrieve her from Vic's shop. Not that he'd told her that.

"I can see where he's staying tomorrow," Huxley offered. Nick had planned on doing that as soon as Huxley was back but hadn't wanted to leave Amelia alone, even for a minute. Huxley's offer meant he could spend his morning with Amelia.

"I must attend to errands around eleven, so I'll need you back before then. I do not want Amelia or the others left here without protection. I won't risk it after the letter she received."

Huxley raised one eyebrow but didn't comment on the worry that inflected Nick's voice. It would soon be clear to everyone in the house that Amelia wasn't merely his secretary. She was so much more, but he'd keep up the charade of secrecy for the time being. At least until she came to terms with the fact that he wasn't ever letting her go.

"What were the contents of the letter?" Huxley asked.

"If you must know, it was a threat, Huxley."

They both turned to the door, neither having heard Amelia enter the study. She walked toward them, a resolute expression drawing her features in a series of grim lines.

Amelia wasn't sure how much she should reveal but not knowing the full contents somehow made the threat of her brother showing up not as terrifying. She sat in the chair next to Huxley and looked between the two men. She wished Nick had called her down to the study for this conversation;

it was something she shouldn't have been excluded from. It made her feel too protected and sheltered. She needed some aspects of control if she wanted to remain vigilant.

She decided the ugly truth was better than brushing the issues under the carpet. "The letter was a reminder of what I owe him."

Nick walked toward her, his hand reaching for her shoulder. "You don't have to do this."

"You're wrong. I do. I have been hiding from him for as long as I can remember. If I pretend what he wrote is not as bad as it really is, then he wins. And if you want Huxley to watch me, he should know what he is up against."

Nick let her go, but he didn't look happy. When he perched himself on the edge of his desk again and looked at her, his stone-gray gaze gave nothing away, and his expression was devoid of emotion. She couldn't tell if he was angry or just irritated.

"My brother is a man greatly indebted to Lord Ashley, the Earl of Kilmore. I was the bargaining chip my brother needed to settle his debts, and my brother promised his lordship my hand in marriage." She folded her hands in her lap as she recalled the harsh words with which her brother had threatened her, and a chill cut her right to the core.

"My first instinct was to run away, which I did. I thought I was free of him, but he found me anyway. He promised to strip me himself"—she left off some of the more gruesome parts about her past—"and watch as my fiancé raped me. He promised if I screamed, he would slit the throats of every woman and child in this house."

What Huxley couldn't know was that the words contained in that letter weren't an empty threat. The most frightening aspect wasn't that Jeremy had written the things he had, but that her brother was true to his word, no matter the depravity he had to sink to accomplish his promises.

She couldn't believe the words left her mouth so calmly. But she'd had two days to think of the contents, and she was past scared. She was so spitting mad that she wanted to stand up to her brother herself and dole out the same cruelty he'd shown her.

Huxley curled his hands into fists. His face was red, and his lips pressed into a thin angry line. "I will fucking gut the bugger myself."

Amelia's attention snapped to Huxley's rapt gaze. She'd never heard him so angry. She omitted the remainder of the letter. That would stay between her and Nick, though Nick's response had been more explicit than Huxley's.

Nick chose that moment to say, "We will rotate our shifts at the house, starting tomorrow."

"Aye, but when I catch the wee bastard I will nail him to the wall meself and cut him from sternum to windpipe." Huxley's accent thickened when he was riled up with anger.

"He has not made an appearance since giving the letter to Devlin. For now, we have no choice but to wait him out," Nick pointed out.

Huxley stood suddenly. "I'll check around the house tonight."

Nick nodded his head and let him leave without another word.

Amelia pressed her hand to her heart when he was gone. "I did not expect to elicit quite that reaction."

"Huxley does not take threats well. We both grew up in St. Giles, not the most loving or kind environment. Threats are often very fatal and if you do not fight for what you believe in, you end up floating in the Thames."

She hadn't known that about him. She'd known about St. Giles. It was one of the worst slums in London, known for its overpopulation of immigrants and criminals, though she doubted the last two went hand in hand. That was part of his past? Her heart ached for both men.

"I know you didn't want me to tell Huxley so much…"

Taking her hands in his, he pulled her to her feet. "Never apologize for needing to do something that helps you move forward from your past."

"You sound as if you speak from experience."

He didn't say anything.

They needed a change of topic. "You have been ignoring all your appointments because of me."

"Just a few errands around town that can be done any time."

"I can take care of myself too, Nick. Both you and Huxley have more important things to do than watch after me, day and night."

"Make no mistake—I want nothing more than to take care of you every single night." His voice dropped an octave.

She swallowed, feeling that familiar ache of need deep inside her. How did a few simple words make her feel this way?

Even the way he looked at her made her want to crawl into his lap and let him do very wicked things to her. She should be worried out of her mind about her brother having found her, but she felt safe—even protected—when she was with Nick. And it looked like he had no intention of letting her escape.

She'd slept alone last night, still feeling the twinge of pain from their first night together, but now that the pain was gone, she wanted him that way again. She tore her gaze away from his, afraid that he would see the hunger flooding her eyes. And what was wrong with that? It was evident he wanted her in the same way.

"Now that Huxley is back, we need to set boundaries during the day. I do not want anyone to think less of me because I'm…we are…"

"Say it." He maneuvered her toward the library. The look in his eyes would undo her if she didn't break this spell over them. She bit her lip.

"Say the word, Amelia." His demand was firm.

"Because we are having an affair," she blurted out, hating how awful that sounded to her own ears. "Everything with my brother complicates things further. We need to be circumspect."

"An affair implies a short attachment." He took another step toward her, pushing her up against the sofa. There was nowhere else for her to go. "Try again."

She swallowed, not sure she wanted to continue whatever game this was he was playing. "What is it you want from me?"

"I have told you want I want. And I won't stop until you are completely mine."

The promise in his words had her heart pounding so hard in her chest that she found herself suddenly breathless.

"In the middle of the afternoon?" It was a sorry excuse, even to her own ears. She hungered for him, but here? Surely they'd be caught.

"Which makes it as good a time as any."

"Anyone could walk in," she said, trying to be the voice of reason, hating that she wanted him anyway.

He left her standing there in a dither, and she breathed a sigh of relief. He trotted back into the room a minute later, his bearing cocky as he grinned at her like the cat that ate the canary.

"The door is now locked."

Of course he had locked it.

"That does not mean they will be blind to what we are up to." Surely they fooled none of the staff. But she didn't want to think of the repercussions associated with that.

"They will think we are discussing a possible solution to our problem." It wasn't her problem but theirs. Why that gave her a thrill of excitement, she didn't know, but it did. It meant he wouldn't abandon her if her brother came on too strong.

He leaned closer…close enough that they could kiss, but he didn't cross that final distance to press his lips to hers. He held back, keeping her in the balance of want and desire. He made her yearn for all the things she shouldn't want and made her lose all sense when he set his focus solely on her. It wasn't right, but she was helpless to push him away, and she couldn't even contemplate stopping him, now that she knew the door was barred to everyone else.

She'd turned into a harlot since leaving her home. The path she'd thought she'd carve for herself once moving to London had turned out far differently than she had imagined.

Wasn't she essentially surrendering to a different kind of enslavement than the one her brother had envisioned for her? Giving herself to Nick had all sorts of implications she didn't want to think about. Essentially, she'd sold herself to one man instead of being forced to marry another. No. That wasn't right. She'd given herself to Nick. Freely. Completely.

She stretched her hand between them, stalling his forward advances. She remembered now that she'd come down to talk to him. Not to be thoroughly seduced.

"How is it that I feel more alive and more like the person I always thought I was when we are together?" she asked. "How is that possible when we have only just met, when we still have not uncovered every facet of each other's personalities?"

Nick settled his hands on her hips and pulled her pelvis tight against his. To be lost in his arms was exactly where she wanted to be.

"Because there are some things that words cannot give you." He pressed harder into her. She could feel the outline of his hardness against her belly. "There is no doubt in my mind that we were made for each other."

"How can you be so certain?" Her hands were between them, curled over her heart and stopping her from being crushed against his larger body.

"I just know. What we have is right," he said. She wished she could be as sure as he was. She wished she knew what compelled her to want this man as thoroughly as she did.

"I feel like I am losing myself in you," she said.

"Are you sure you have not found yourself since coming here?" he countered.

His words gave her pause. He was right, and she wanted to laugh at the realization. Yes, she'd learned more about herself this past week than she had since leaving Berwick more than a month ago. She knew what she wanted—to some extent—from her life, from her job. What she wanted from

Nick in the end, she couldn't say, but she wanted to be with him, to share a part of herself with him to which no one else was privy.

Her hands flattened against Nick's torso, and she pushed up onto the tips of her toes, needing his kiss more than ever.

Before her lips touched his, she gave him one last warning, "My brother is not a problem that will go away. I am afraid of what he will do."

"Do not let him win by being afraid. I will catch you if you need me to."

The promise. The conviction. It felt so right to hear him say it that she wanted to put all her trust in him.

Her breath stilled in her throat. This man was too good to be true, but for how long would that last? She'd been charmed by her brother's friends in the beginning, only to be burned. There was something different about Nick, though. Her heart seemed to have known that all along.

Nick pushed her against the arm of the sofa and started to gather up her skirts. She swallowed hard but didn't utter another protest.

She closed her eyes, wanting to feel every caress of his hands, every flutter of cool air brushing across the skin he would expose.

"Look at me, Amelia."

She opened her eyes only because he took a step away from her. She bit her bottom lip to hold back a sound of protest. The way he looked at her made her feel so many things she couldn't describe. Her body hummed with a new awareness, with a desire and need so forbidden that it made her want him in every way possible.

"Do you trust me?" he asked.

"I do." Her voice was so hoarse. Needy.

"Hold your skirts up and sit on the edge of the sofa." When she did, his hands spread her knees farther apart so the slit in her drawers was open, exposing her naked flesh to his ravenous gaze.

"So wet for me." He ran his thumb over her vagina, through the folds of her sex to spread the dew that had started to flow the moment he'd backed her into the library, his intent clear as he stalked her.

Then, to her surprise, he brought his thumb up to his mouth and sucked it off, watching her while he did this. She thought her heart would beat right out of her chest when a rush of wetness dampened her core with his primal action. She couldn't even formulate a response to what he'd done.

She was still in shock and surprise as he went down to his knees between her spread thighs. His face was level with her sex, and he wasn't hiding the fact that he was staring at it. Dipping his head closer, his breath was hot against her core. "Hold on to the edge of the sofa, Amelia. You're going to need a good, strong grip for what I have in mind."

She didn't question him. She did exactly as he asked. A shiver of pure ecstasy stole her sanity as his eyes ate in the sight of her bare mons. With one hand spreading the lips of her sex, his dark head came close enough that he could lick between the folds of her sex like she was the tastiest treat he'd ever eaten.

Then he kissed her thighs. The brush of his beard over her sensitive skin was a delectable contrast to the slickness of his tongue. She wanted to thrust her body tight against his mouth so she could drown in the forbidden sensation of his licking her in the most private of places again. She tangled one of her hands in his hair, needing to hold him, to feel his movements. This time he kissed the slit of her sex instead of licking it.

"Nick," she cried, her voice thick with unspoken need.

"Tell me what you want, Amelia."

"I want your tongue on me."

A shiver wracked her whole body. Her mouth parted on a sigh as he licked through her folds from the entrance all the way up to the little nub of her clit to circle it. He sucked her wetness in his mouth before thrusting his tongue inside her sheath. The motion was so sudden that she yanked on his hair. He didn't seem to mind, so she spread her legs wider and pulled him closer. She wanted to feel his tongue everywhere all at once and blushed at the thought.

His tongue worked in her like his penis would, until she was clawing at his head, close to her release. And then he stopped. In a guttural voice, he told her, "Undo the buttons of your bodice. I want you to play with your nipples while I suck you to climax."

If there was one thing she was fast learning, it was that she couldn't say no to him. How did anyone say no to him? She wanted him with a fierceness that surprised her and a hunger that only grew instead of abated.

She scrambled to do as he asked but was thrown off balance and teetered right back onto the sofa. He stood between her spread legs like a predator about to devour her. Her cream coated his beard under his bottom lip. He swiped it away with his tongue as he came around the side of the sofa and practically ripped the buttons from the bodice in his haste to have it off her.

He yanked down the front of her low-cut corset enough that her breasts popped free. Her nipples were already hard little points, just begging to be sucked and pulled. And he did take them in his mouth as he moved her farther up on the sofa, biting the sensitive tips before releasing them, only to come at them again with a softer tonguing.

He didn't play with her breasts for long. No, he tossed her skirts above her waist again, settled his hands under her bottom, and lifted her core up to his mouth so he could do as he promised and tongued her like it was his penis moving in her.

She'd never felt anything like it. Could not compare it to any of the wicked things she imagined him doing to her since their first time together. His tongue slicked through her folds over and over again. This was raw. Feral. So deliciously naughty she could no longer mute the sounds of pleasure that slipped past her lips to fill the silence of the room as he closed his mouth around her clit and sucked.

Her arms were braced behind her head, barely keeping her position as he ate her like a man starved. The more frenzied she grew, the more he wanted to take.

Moans fell in tandem past her lips as sensation after sensation swamped her body. His tongue danced to its own tune, flowing through her folds and around the most delicate parts of her.

"Nick," she cried, desperately trying to grasp his hair and anchor herself to the moment. "Please."

He only growled against her like a ravenous wolf, wanting its fill before he let her go.

"Nick," she cried again, feeling her crisis coming, feeling the release sitting at the precipice, at the point where she was going fly right over the edge into pure, unadulterated pleasure.

His tongue thrust hard inside her, his beard scuffed against the skin between her entrance and her anus, but she didn't dare pull away from the odd touch, as it only added to the wicked sensations bombarding her. When he licked his tongue through her folds again, she wrapped her legs around his head and pulled him in tighter, grinding her core against the assault of his tongue and beard, needing him to finish her so badly.

Nick reached up with one hand to cover her mouth and muffle the noises she could no longer hold back. She bit down, her teeth creasing into his skin as he continued his sweet torture with his tongue. Moving higher, he sucked on her clit again and used his free hand to stretch her sheath with his fingers. In and out he thrust them, over and over, never letting up. The slap of his palm against her wet flesh only heightened everything she was feeling.

And that was when she felt it—the moment of perfect calm before her body slammed through the dam of pure pleasure and let go. Her voice stilled in her throat, her thrusts against his tongue paused. And she broke apart under him as the perfect feeling of complete abandon washed through her and made her limbs lax and loose as she rode out her high on his tongue.

Nick kissed her core one last time and came over her body, positioning his legs between her spread ones. She looked between them and could see his hard cock straining against his trousers. When he reached behind him to pull his shirt free—she wasn't sure when he'd lost the waistcoat—the tip of his cock was visible at the edge of his pants. She wanted to touch it, but had lost her nerve to be so bold now that she wasn't lost in desire. He opened his trousers, and his cock sprang free from its confines. She wanted him to fill her, to take her harder than ever before. But first, she had an idea.

With her hands on his arms to stop him from moving, she focused on his eyes. His cock looked impossibly larger than she remembered. She swiped her tongue over her lips. Would he let her do the same as he'd done for her? He must have seen that very question in her eyes, and in answer, he wrapped his hand around his thickness and stroked the length of his manhood. She scrambled up to a sitting position, her breasts jutting out above the hard lines of her corset. She didn't try to hide herself from him.

"I want you to ask for it, Amelia."

She shot a tentative look at him. His desire had mounted so high that his gray irises were eaten up by his pupils. He stood now, the jut of his cock level with her face. All she had to do was lean forward. She'd never seen anything so erotic, so viscerally raw.

While she warred with what she should do, he never stopped stroking his length as he brought the head of his cock closer to her mouth. Did he want her to suck him like he'd sucked her?

"I do not know what to do. Tell me how." The very idea of her sucking his cock right now drew his balls up so tight that it took every ounce of control he had not to come all over her mouth.

"Kiss it." He wasn't sure he could handle much more than that.

She kissed the head of his penis, the touch tentative. She was asking permission; he could see that in her eyes. He didn't stop her as she opened her mouth to pull in the rounded head of his cock. Her wicked little tongue traced the slit on his crown, sucking the bead of semen that had emitted from the tip.

His motions were uneven as he lightly fucked her mouth, not going farther than the head because he didn't want to scare her with his need to take her rougher, to feel his cock bumping the back of her throat. He was going to embarrass himself if he continued this.

A palpable desperation stole over him to take her hard. Instead, he pulled out of her mouth and squeezed the root of his penis hard to stop himself from climaxing. A small shot of semen came out the tip, landing on her bared breasts. With a groan, he squeezed himself harder before stepping back enough that he could rub his seed over her breast. Her blush was adorable.

"I will go off like fireworks if you suck my cock right now." His voice was pained even to his own ears.

Sitting next to her on the sofa, he grabbed her by the waist and positioned her over his lap so she was straddling his thighs. He wished he'd taken the time to strip her naked so he could watch the root of his cock slamming into her tight sheath but settled with the fact that he could suck her pretty little nipples as he taught her how to ride him.

Kissing her deeply, their tongues dueled as he brought the head of his cock to her entrance. She sank slowly down onto him, throwing her head back with a moan. Her sweet hands grasped onto his shoulders as she seated herself to the hilt of his rod.

When she looked at him, the innocence and beauty with which she watched him nearly undid him. Reaching under her skirts, he grabbed the rounded globes of her backside, rocking her body forward. At first she only coated his cock in her wetness, but then he pushed up inside her. A small gasp escaped her lips.

Nick rocked her over the wet slide of his cock. Had anything ever felt so good? When her hips moved without his guidance, he spread one hand over the center of her backside, keeping hold of her so she didn't slow but instead worked herself into a breathless frenzy. His other hand spread the lips of her sex so her clit could slide against his the root of his cock and abdomen with every roll of her hips.

She placed her hands on either side of his face, staring at him without saying a word. A simple look had never been so erotic, and it fired him up, making his balls draw up tight and burn with the need for release.

She lowered her hands again, her hips moving faster as her crisis came to a breaking point again. The harder she rode him, the tighter she gripped his shoulders. He wanted to flip her on her back and take her so hard that neither of them could walk, but she needed to be the one in control of this, so he ceded those desires. He pistoned into the tight clasp of her sheath, his whole body coming off the sofa as he drilled deep. Sucking her pearled nipple into his mouth, his teeth lightly scraped the hard tip with every slam of their bodies.

"I could suck these pretty things all day." He wanted to squeeze her breasts together and bury his face in them—hell, bury his cock there and fuck them like he was fucking her sheath. Another time.

Nails digging into his shoulders, her orgasm came hard and fast. She threw her head back as high-pitched mewls fell from her lips. Her sheath milked him like a fist clamping around him, and he was two seconds behind her release, shooting hard inside her.

"Fuck," he muttered against her breast, kissing, licking, sucking hard on her nipple as she drew out every drop of semen he had. He slowly relaxed his hands where he grasped her bottom tight.

Replete, she collapsed on top of him, her forehead resting against his shoulder. His cock twitched inside her, only temporarily satisfied. He could take her again right now. As tempting as it was to lock themselves away for the rest of the day, they had to be careful. While he didn't care if the house knew they were more than employee and employer, he had a sneaking suspicion she would care.

He kissed her neck, her jaw, and finally her mouth. She didn't object, just flicked her tongue along his as he delved deep into her mouth. When he pulled away to look at her, her eyes were sleepy. He rubbed his thumb across her bottom lip, loving how she felt on him, around him. He hated that they had to fix themselves, to be presentable, even though he wanted to toss her back on the sofa and ravage her all over again.

Amelia didn't know what had come over her. She'd come down to the library only to see Nick, as she'd been contemplating thoughts of her brother all day in private. She wasn't exactly sure how to extricate herself from his lap, so she stayed where she was as he lazily kissed her. Her body felt well used, deliciously sore, and satiated.

He was still hard inside her, as though he could never get enough of her, of what they did. The thought of continuing for a second round had her blushing. She hid her reaction by pushing herself from his lap. As she pulled away from him, a rush of fluid trailed down her leg.

Nick stood, tucking his hard penis back into his trousers, a pained expression on his face.

"Have I hurt you?"

He smiled the smile of the devil. Pure wickedness washed over his features. "Far from it. I will never get enough of you."

She yanked up the front of her dress, trying to cover herself before she lost control and gave herself to him again. Would that really be a bad thing? The back of his knuckles caressed a seductive path along the top curve of her breast. She closed her eyes for the briefest of moments. Just to feel him. Nothing more. He was undoing every bit of control she prided in herself.

There was no denying that this man made her crazy. She wanted him with a fierceness that was so different from every reaction she'd had to other men. *He* was different from them.

Right from the start she'd fallen a little in love with him. She'd never believed in love at first sight, and she supposed it wasn't truly at first sight, but it had been shortly thereafter that she'd wanted to lose herself in him.

Pulling a handkerchief from his pocket, he kneeled in front of her. One of his hands disappeared under her skirts and lightly brushed over her knees and thighs before he wiped away the evidence of their lovemaking. She stood paralyzed by a choking shyness that stole the rest of her thoughts and had her blushing from her temples, all the way down to her chest.

It felt strange, allowing him such liberties. Amelia lightly cleared her throat as she started to button up her bodice. Nick had turned her into a nymphomaniac. She wasn't even sure how she knew such a word. But it perfectly described her.

Nick balled up his handkerchief and shoved it back into the pocket of his trousers as he pulled his shirt over his head and tucked it in place.

A rakish grin set over his features as he watched her poor attempt at doing anything but focus on him. She'd never hide what they'd been doing when a handful of buttons at the front of the bodice were torn or missing. It was stupid, but it made her want to cry.

Nick caressed the side of her face. "Why are you upset?"

She took a steadying breath, giving up on the buttons. Nothing she could do would make her look less disheveled. "Any woman who just did what I did would suffer from…embarrassment." She couldn't even voice her thoughts aloud without blushing. She bit her lip. "In the midst of everything with my brother, I feel ashamed by what we have done."

"I think we should cure you of this *embarrassment*."

Nick leaned close to her and cupped both her breasts, squeezing them together with a groan. She didn't have the strength to stop him, not that she *really* wanted to stop him. Still, a small sense of reason came through, and she forced herself to push him away.

"A shame to cover them at all," Nick said, handing her the shawl she'd been wearing before their interlude. It would have to be enough to cover up the evidence of their frenzied lovemaking.

"Thank you," she mumbled as she turned away from him. "How I feel around you frightens me."

Her voice wavered, but she held her head high as she adjusted her skirts so she was more presentable. It didn't help. She felt as rumpled and disorganized as her dress, as warring thoughts bombarded her mind.

"That's the last thing I want," he said.

"Your appointment book said you were meeting Lord Burley for dinner."

"My appointments can wait." Nick reached out to her, caressing the side of her face with his hand. "We were only going to discuss our approach with Murray. Are you trying to get rid of me?"

"No. I just need to change," she said, which was partly the truth.

Nick grasped her hand before she could make her escape.

"This is all so new to me, Nick. My life has changed completely and in so short a time. My brother, added to everything else, makes it all the more confusing. I just need some time. To think."

He let her go.

She didn't question it, and didn't look back as she left him standing in the middle of the library, his hands tucked in his pockets. She had a feeling he wouldn't leave her alone for too long. She only required enough time to think about what she was doing and what she wanted. Enough time to come up with a plan to deal with her brother and make him leave her alone once and for all. If such a thing were possible. More than anything, she just needed to think clearly, and she couldn't do that when she was around Nick.

CHAPTER SEVENTEEN

The silence was killing her. The inaction from her brother disturbed her. But she didn't know how to find him, especially considering he didn't want to be found. No more letters had come, and waiting for something to happen made her edgy and nervous. Nick had left only twice in the past few days. Huxley was there when Nick was gone. She wasn't sure if she should be thankful or if their constant presence would drive her insane.

In the past few days she wasn't any closer to sorting out her feelings for Nick either. There had been no repeats in the library, but their nights were another story entirely.

Unable to remain idle and wanting to focus on anything to keep her mind from straying back to her brother, Amelia decided to finish responding to a few letters while Nick worked in the study. It was hard to think straight with Nick sitting not ten feet away from her. Every time she closed her eyes, the memories of their nights flashed through her mind. The things that Nick had done to her, the things she imagined doing to him. She pressed her fingers against her mouth, feeling the press of Nick stamped into her very flesh.

She slammed the door on those thoughts as she picked up the silver letter opener and sliced another envelope open. This was not an appropriate place or time for those kinds of thoughts. And despite all they had done, she felt that Nick was holding some of himself back.

Nick's warm hands massaged her shoulders. She'd been so focused on her task that she hadn't heard him come up behind her. She moaned with each rotation of his thumb into a tight knot that tensed up one shoulder. His touch was like heaven. It gave her comfort and offered a sense of security.

Her life truly had been flipped on its head the moment Jeremy had come back into it. But Nick had given her so many new memories to help her forget all the horrible events in her past.

A firm knock came on the study door, startling her. She felt her face flame at the idea of being caught, but Nick was already sitting back at his desk as the door opened.

She needed to learn how to control her blushing if she was going to carry on in the illicit affair with her employer. If she didn't hide her feelings and her reactions to Nick during the day, someone would figure out what was going on with her and the master of the house—though it was possible some already had guessed, not that they had treated her any differently.

Mrs. Coleman entered the study. "A number of packages have arrived for you, Amelia. Would you like to set them up in your dressing room?" Amelia looked at Nick, wondering if she could be pulled away. "Or should Jenny and Josie arrange everything?"

Amelia pushed out her chair. She probably should have let Nick answer for her, but she was feeling restless and needed to occupy her thoughts elsewhere. "I haven't seen what Miss Newgate selected. She surely selected something tremendously awful. I do not mind bringing the packages up to my room."

Glancing at Nick, Amelia saw his smirk. Was his reaction because he suspected the mutual animosity between the two women? Perhaps he had detected the thread of jealousy Amelia couldn't keep from her voice. Either way, she didn't say anything with Mrs. Coleman there to witness their level of comfort with each other. Nick couldn't expect them to carry on as they were indefinitely. Or was this just how men carried on during an affair with their mistresses? She internally cringed at likening herself to such a thing, but that was essentially what she was. She'd have to discuss her future in this household with him soon. The longer she put it off, the worse she felt about every sin-filled night they shared.

As she left the study, she realized the only reason she fretted about the direction of the relationship was because she cared for him. More than she probably should have cared. What if he didn't return that regard?

She focused on the task set before her. Entering the foyer, she pulled her shawl tighter around her shoulders. The front door was open, allowing a rush of cold air to sweep through the room. Boxes of every shape and size littered the entry table. "I do not remember ordering so many things, Mrs. Coleman."

"I wouldn't complain, child. You will need it if you're to attend business meetings with Mr. Riley."

"I suppose so, but I have never owned such extravagance." A frown furrowed her brow. "It feels wasteful." And undeserved. As though the items were payment for something other than her secretarial services.

"Cannot be wasteful when you'll need to be dressed like a lady of means. What should Mr. Riley's clients and business associates think if you showed up to dinner in a ratty old dress you probably stole from another maid?"

"No one cared how I dressed when I was teaching. Or answering correspondence. It's neither here nor there, I suppose. I will see how many more boxes remain." Amelia stepped outside. The cart her boxes were in appeared to be empty. A driver was perched in the high seat, holding the horse's reins. She curled her hands over her arms. "Good day to you, sir," she said with a wave.

He turned to tip his hat forward before she turned away from him.

A hand clamped around her forearm and yanked her forward. She let out a surprised squeal as she tried to get her feet under her. But she was pulled too quickly and tumbled against the tall, thin figure of a man as she half fell down the stairs.

She didn't have a chance to regain her balance until she was on the pavement. Yanking her arm away from the man who had accosted her, she fell on her bottom on the hard cement beneath her. "What in God's name are you doing?" She dusted off her scraped hands before climbing back to her feet and getting a good look at the person who'd dragged her down the stairs. She froze as the man stood tall, lifting the brim of his beaver hat away from his face.

"Jeremy." Her voice was but a whisper as she looked at her brother.

His skin was sallow, his eyes sunken as though he had binged on nothing but alcohol since she had last seen him in Berwick. His eyes were the same blue as hers, though they looked dead inside. He was impeccably dressed, though his suit looked ill fitting to his thin frame. He looked like he was on death's door.

"You look well, Amelia." The venom with which he said her name paralyzed her on the spot.

This can't be happening. "I can't say the same for you." She didn't know where she'd found her daring tongue, but she was glad to show him a braver side of herself. She would not be frightened by him ever again.

"Cheeky, my dear. Watch your tongue before I mind it for you."

She glared back at him, realizing she wasn't so much afraid of him as she was disgusted by who he was. How had he turned into this vile man? Before she could hold back, she asked, "I cannot see an ounce of our father or mother in you, yet you are my own flesh and blood. That alone shames me."

"You always have been too sentimental, my dear. Had you learned your place in life, we would have gotten on a lot better."

"You mean had I gone through with the marriage to Lord Ashley, you could have continued to pretend that life was grand—as long as he was paying you an annual allowance."

Something dark crossed his eyes. Perhaps she had pushed him too far. But she would not be led by fear. She would stand up to him once and for all—and maybe he'd leave her the hell alone.

"It was a decent match, sister. Do not play it for anything less. You would have been a countess. Any young lady would vie for that position. But you had to throw it all away."

"I refuse to marry him. He cannot marry me without my consent."

"Do not be so naïve. There are a hundred vicars who would marry you to Ashley."

This was not a battle she was going to win with her brother. "What do you want?" she asked coldly. "I am expected somewhere right now."

"I am afraid you will not make that appointment," he said, making her feel suddenly uneasy. The door to the townhouse was a stone's throw from where she stood. She could run for the door.

"Leave me the hell alone, Jeremy." Picking up her skirts, she didn't hesitate to make her escape. She was halfway up the stairs before Jeremy hauled her back down, her arms scraping raw along the way as she tried to protect her head as she fell.

Jeremy stood her up roughly, holding on to the shoulder of her gown. His hand hard and firm, he slapped her across her face. "Such language from my own sister."

She licked the blood from the side of her lip where it had split open. She wasn't surprised that he'd raised his hand against her; he'd done it so often before. Instead of retreating from his violence as she previously had done, she didn't temper her voice as she yelled, "Let me go, you bloody devil."

There had to be twenty people milling about on the street, watching the interaction between them. Ladies in finery crossed the street to steer clear of the trouble between them. A few gentlemen stopped to watch, though they did nothing to help her. They didn't know her, and for all they knew, she could be his wife, his charge. His. That thought had her stomach roiling in disgust.

Jeremy dragged her down the street, farther away from the safety of the townhouse. She fought, punched, and tried to pry his hand free from her dress, tearing the material in the process. "Someone. Please. Help me. Nick," she all but screamed. "Nick. Mrs. Coleman." In a smaller voice, she begged, "Please. Jeremy, let me go. You hold no right over me."

"I hold every right, *sister*," he said, loudly emphasizing the last word for those milling about, seeming torn between helping her and turning their backs. They finally did the latter as if she were some wayward sister in need of reprimand.

Her brother laughed. It was never a sound of joy when he laughed; it was too dark to be considered mirthful. He lowered his hand to her wrist, his grasp unrelenting as he pulled her along with him. She tugged back, trying to loosen his hold on her, but he didn't let up. "It is time I took you to see your fiancé, is it not?"

Bile rose in her mouth, and she nearly threw up right there, but she knew she couldn't appear weak. She needed to fight him off. She dug her heels into the ground, but Jeremy only dragged her when she fell over.

She scratched at his hand, desperate to stop him. He turned around and smashed his hand across her temple. Her vision went blurry, and she dropped like a bag of stones to the street. The sudden action forced her brother to release her. She was too disoriented to scramble out of the way, though by all accounts she didn't need to, because that was when she saw him.

Nick.

Nick. Thank God.

He charged directly toward her brother as she pushed herself into a sitting position.

Mrs. Coleman's warm hands came around her shoulders then. "Don't you worry, child. I have you. You are safe." The housekeeper helped Amelia move out of the way.

Nick's bulky frame smashed right into Jeremy's, knocking them both down to the ground. Nick's arm came up and pummeled into her brother's face, over and over again, unrelentingly.

Amelia cried out, "Please, Nick!" *You will kill him*, she wanted to say but not when there were so many spectators. She stood on wobbly feet and wavered as she reached out to a wall to steady herself.

The wet smack of flesh as Nick hit her brother was the only thing she could hear above the roaring in her ears. It made her sick, and she vomited on the pavement, with people closing in on them as Nick never let up. Mrs. Coleman rubbed her back, saying soothing words that Amelia didn't really hear.

While there was no love lost between Amelia and her brother, she didn't want to see him dead; she didn't want to be the cause of that. She didn't want to be the cause of Nick turning into this beast that seemed to have one purpose—destroying her brother.

As Amelia stumbled toward them, Mrs. Coleman tried to hold her up so she didn't topple over again. "Nick," Amelia called out, "you have to stop. You're killing him."

Tears washed down her face. Not for her brother, but for what Nick had done for her. For the beast she'd created because she'd been so stupid as to come outside alone for even a moment. This was her punishment for letting her guard down and thinking no harm would come to her.

"Stop." She took another step, not sure how close she could get as Nick didn't seem to be aware that she was standing there. Would he lash out at her in his rage? She didn't think so, so she dared another step toward him.

"Nick," she pleaded. "Nick, please. You have to stop." She reached for him then, touching his shoulder carefully, not wanting to be caught in the fray. He stilled and released her brother. Jeremy dropped to the ground, his hands flying up covering his head and face as though that alone could ward off Nick from his warpath.

Blood covered Nick's hands, and splatters were all over his face. He reached for her to wipe away the tears that tracked unbidden down her cheeks, but he stopped short when he saw the mess of his hands. It appeared as if Nick was bleeding too, and that thought churned her stomach. She went down to her knees to look at her brother. Thankfully, he was breathing, though his breath was labored. Jeremy rolled to his side and spit a wad of blood out next to her foot.

"You will pay for that, Amelia," he hissed. "Do not think you can hide behind your protector forever." He spit again; this time, a tooth came out with it.

Nick's arm wrapped around her waist, and he hauled her off the ground, away from her brother.

Nick went after him again, only this time he lifted him clear off the ground so they were facing each other. Jeremy's feet dangled a few inches in the air. "Look around you, you piece of shit." When Jeremy didn't comply, Nick shook him hard. "Look around you. There are twenty witnesses to your actions."

"She has vowed to marry another far more powerful than you," Jeremy insisted.

"I don't think I have made myself clear." Nick let go of her brother, and he fell to the ground. "You're the only one in the wrong, Berwick. I suggest you back the fuck off or next time, I will not hold back from delivering the justice you truly deserve."

"Your threats do not scare me."

"Consider it a promise."

Mrs. Coleman wrapped her arms around Amelia, whispering soft words that Amelia didn't hear as she watched Nick. He was forcing her brother away from her, making him walk backward.

"You so much as threaten a hair on any of my employees' heads, and I will have you strung up by the balls before you can say boo. Stay away from my house and away from your sister."

"This isn't over."

Nick took a few steps toward Jeremy, who backed up and fell to the pavement again. He put his hands up in front of his face to protect himself, but Nick didn't strike out again. "Get out of London, or I will send some friends for a long visit to the hovel where you have holed up."

Nick didn't spare her brother another word but gave Jeremy his back and walked carefully toward her, as though afraid she'd take flight.

Nick was one man she would never run from. How could she? She was in love with him.

That thought froze her to the spot.

"Let us get you back inside. We will call the doctor to ensure you're well," he said evenly, as though the rage had fully leeched out of him now that he was focused on her. His arms smoothed over her arms. His touch was so gentle and careful.

"I need a minute with him," Amelia said. He let her go, though he didn't go more than an arm's length away from her.

"Only a minute," Nick agreed. "I don't want him getting any ideas."

She nodded, understanding his hesitancy.

Looking at her brother's bloody and beaten face, she said, "I am sorry, Jeremy." She truly was. She wouldn't want this kind of thing to happen to even her worst enemy. "Just…just stay out of my life. I have never asked you for anything. But no good will come of your being here. I have a life here. A home. Please, leave me alone."

Her brother laughed, the sound sinister and dark. She'd known that would be his response, but she still had to try to get through to him. "Take your platitudes with you. You owe me, Amelia. Make no mistake—you will pay your debts." He ended with a ragged, hacking cough.

"She has no debts to you, Berwick," Nick said.

Amelia knew her brother better than anyone. If he wanted to play dirty, she could expose him for the man he really was—expose his debts to their fullest. Expose him for the terrible things he'd done to good people. She almost wanted to dare him to try but bit her tongue.

Instead, she turned into Nick's arms and looked up at him, searching his eyes, which were still focused on her brother.

"Can we go home?" she asked.

Nick simply lifted her in his arms and carried her back home.

"I am sorry about everything that happened," Amelia said.

Nick cupped the side of Amelia's face with his bloodied hand. He hadn't left her, not even to wash or to look after bandaging his knuckles. When they'd entered the house, every single person of the staff was waiting for them. Nick had instructed Devlin to fetch the doctor and Huxley to follow her brother to see where he went. Marney had promised to bring supplies to them so they could wash any cuts and tend to any other damages. Then Nick had brought her into the parlor and sat next to her on the sofa, as though afraid to let Amelia out of his sight again.

Nick clasped her hand. "You could not have known he was waiting for an opportunity to kidnap you from the steps of your home."

She shook her head. He was wrong. She should have at least guessed at the danger of leaving the house alone. "I cannot make excuses for acting stupid. You and Huxley knew what kind of threat he was. That was why you made sure someone was always home with me." She closed her eyes, hating the trouble she'd caused, hating what Nick had done to defend her.

"I'm not going to let anything happen to you, Amelia. I know my words cannot mean much when I have promised to protect you and failed. I will do everything in my power to keep you safe from this moment forward." He pulled her into his arms, tucking her head between his shoulder and neck.

"You didn't fail me. I failed myself by not being more vigilant. You were there to stop him."

"We will track your brother's movements. He will not catch any of us unaware again."

"Jeremy will not stay away. I know my brother better than anyone. Once he's made up his mind on something, he will pursue it like a rabid animal."

Nick's hand caressed her back, soothing away her stresses. Her head hurt, her lip was sore and tender, and her body felt like it had been used as a punching bag. But she didn't want to be anywhere else but in Nick's arms. When she was with him, she felt safe. She felt loved.

There was that word again. Did he feel for her what she felt for him?

"Everyone saw what you did, how you treated me. How will we carry on?" she asked.

"I don't care what anyone saw, Amelia. The thought of almost losing you today broke something inside me. I have wanted you from the first moment we met. And that might make me a cad of the worst sort, but it's the truth. And since our first kiss, I knew that our finding each other was meant to be. I do not question the insanity of such a statement; I just embrace it. I will fight for you. And if that means hurting your brother for trying to take away what belongs to me, than that is what I will do."

Her breath caught and a thin trail of tears washed down her cheeks. It wasn't a promise of forever, but it was a declaration that for now, she belonged to him. Even after everything that had happened. And she had been afraid he'd ask her to leave after the trouble she'd caused.

"There are so many secrets between us. So many things that seem to continually come at us." She wasn't sure what else to say to him. While she'd been forthcoming about her past, there were details she'd left out, sparing him from the brutality her brother had delivered.

"If there is one thing we have, it is time." Nick traced his hand down the side of her face as he lifted her. "I have been forthcoming with you from the start, Amelia. I don't intend to shut myself off from you now."

A heavy knock came at the parlor door. Amelia hated to share Nick with anyone right now. She wished they could lock themselves in here, but the household was in a bit of a panic after the events of the afternoon.

"Can we not leave it?" she asked, wanting selfishly to spend more time with him.

Nick chuckled and called out, "Come."

Amelia sighed and pulled herself away from Nick.

How had her life changed so drastically in the course of a week? She barely recognized the woman she'd become, barely knew the woman she thought she'd always been. *That* Amelia seemed like some other woman. Someone who was weak and afraid. She was neither of those things now.

Mrs. Coleman came into the room carrying a bowl and pitcher, as well as some linens and ointments. She set up her items on the table in front of Nick.

"Clean up Amelia first," he said when Mrs. Coleman reached for his knuckles. Nick stood up to pour the heated water into the basin.

"Poor child," Mrs. Coleman said, clucking as she dunked a few of the linen strips and then dabbed away at the blood on Amelia's face. She winced when Mrs. Coleman blotted the wet cloth against her lip but held still for her ministrations, just wanting them to be over. "I expect the doctor will be here soon. He will have to look at that goose egg on your temple."

Tentatively, Amelia ran her fingers over the bump at the side of her head where her brother had given her a good wallop. She hissed in a breath when she touched it, not expecting it to hurt as much as it did. "That explains the headache pounding behind my eyes."

Mrs. Coleman studied Amelia carefully. "The dress is ruined, don't think it can be mended much either."

Amelia looked at herself. Blood and dirt covered her. Her dress was torn along both shoulders and down the arms. The front was full of runs and holes. She hadn't realized just how awful she looked, hadn't realized how bad the tumble really was, until she saw the damage of her clothes and the scrapes on her arms where the material was torn away.

"I suppose not," she said as she stood. The motion made her dizzy. Nick grasped her arm and held her steady. "I was not expecting that."

"You took quite a blow. We'll have to watch you for the rest of the night, make sure you really are unharmed." There was a deep thread of worry in Nick's voice.

"Mrs. Coleman, can you see to his hands?" Amelia asked.

The housekeeper pulled Nick down beside her and had him dunk his hands in the bowl of water. It turned pink, and then Mrs. Coleman dried them off and spread an ointment on them.

Amelia walked over to the window and cranked it open to let in some fresh air. She took in a few deep breaths, fearing that she would lose consciousness at any moment. The last thing she needed was to give Nick another fright. She held on to the frame of the window until Mrs. Coleman finished attending to Nick and packed up the supplies she'd brought to the parlor.

The sky had turned a deep scarlet with a lilac line streaked through it. *The light in the darkness,* she thought ironically.

Nick's past was likely as complicated as hers, maybe more so when she thought about the scars that covered his back. If they could get through today without destroying what was between them, then she felt they could conquer anything that stood in the way of their relationship and their future.

If the events of the day had taught her anything, it was that she was thoroughly in love with Nick Riley. Irrevocably, head over heels in love.

Alone again, Nick stood behind her, his arms circling her waist under her arms. His chin rested lightly on top of her head. "What has you deep in contemplation?"

"Us."

"If anyone in the household has guessed what you mean to me, they will not say anything." He thought she was worried about what everyone thought.

A ghost of a smile played on her lips. She wanted to turn in his arms and tell him that was the farthest thing from her mind. "It is a conflict to be both your secretary and your lover."

"I don't give a damn, Amelia." She heard the frustration in his comment and didn't want him to think she doubted what was between them.

She turned in his arms and wrapped her arms around his shoulders. The spattering of blood had been wiped away. "Well, I do not give a damn either."

Nick kissed the side of her mouth, her cheek, her forehead. "Good."

"Nick?"

He pulled away so he could look at her, a question in his eyes.

"I want you to know something."

"What is it?"

"I don't want you to feel obligated to return any sentiments, but I think you should know that I love you. I know it's sudden, that it does not seem possible—"

Nick kissed her full on the mouth. He nibbled at her upper lip, and pressed light kisses on the lower, where it hurt too much for her to reciprocate. Releasing her with a growl, he pulled her tightly into his arms. Her head rested against his chest, and she could hear the heavy pounding of his heart.

"Nick?" She tried to lift her head but he held her close, almost as if he were afraid to let her go.

Very quietly, he said, "You are my world, Amelia. If there is one thing I can promise to prove my devotion to you, it is that we will sort out your brother and make sure you're free of him."

Amelia didn't care about her sore lip anymore. She turned her head and pressed a kiss against his heart. "We will do it together."

For the first time in her life, Amelia felt like she was home. But it wasn't home without Nick. And she would do everything in her power to keep him in her life. Because that was all that mattered to her now.

Keep reading for a sneak peek at

DESIRE ME MORE

available August 2015 from Avon Impulse!

An Excerpt from

DESIRE ME MORE

London, 1881

Amelia Somerset stretched out her arms, only to find the immoveable force that was Nick lying next to her. Stifling a yawn, she spread her hands over his chest, molding every dip and plane of his body. What a deliciously wicked way to wake up in the morning.

Amelia rolled over and grabbed Nick's pocket watch that had been set on her bedside table last night. Flipping it open, she was pleased to see that it was still early enough that she didn't need to get ready for the day, yet late enough to rouse Nick from his slumber. A grin tilted up her lips.

And then she wondered if it was wrong to want to wake up in his arms like this every day.

Fundamentally, she knew that what they did wasn't something polite society would welcome with open arms. It didn't matter how she felt about him, that she was in love with Nick, that the thought of him not in her life would have made the past few weeks unbearable. None of that would matter to anyone looking in from the outside.

The man lying next to her had opened her eyes to an entirely new way of life and love. Shown her things she never thought to see. He'd given her things that she never thought she could have. And made her feel things for which she had never dared to hope.

But when she really looked at the situation they were in, she knew that she was essentially his mistress.

His mistress...and his secretary. Though she hoped no one yet guessed about the former.

She trailed her hand over his warm body, skimming his right bicep with just the tips of her fingers, making sure to trace every line of muscle as she explored him more thoroughly than she'd ever had the chance to do.

She could do this all day and night and rather wished she could. But they only had an hour before he'd have to sneak back into his room and pretend they hadn't spent the night in delicious sin.

As she grew more daring, her hand lowered to his navel, her fingers circling his toned stomach. Should she play this safe? Wake him up and get started on the one hundred and one duties that awaited them, or...

Or trail her fingers lower.

Curiosity decided her next course.

With a quick flick of her hand, she tossed the blanket off his chest and stared in awe at the perfection of his body.

That he was naked shouldn't catch her off guard; there hadn't been a night they'd been together that he hadn't slept *au naturel*. That he crawled into bed next to her last night without a stitch of clothing had wetness slicking between her thighs. She moved her legs, wishing his hand was buried there to ease the need building fast.

She brushed her fingers against his long, firm manhood. She could make out the dark vein running down the center of his shaft. The skin around the head was pulled back and the plum-colored head of his cock pointed right at her. Almost begging her to take it in her mouth.

His cock moved, growing impossibly thicker as a bead of semen formed at the slit. The sight fascinated her. Drew her closer. She had a sudden desire to touch that creamy drop of fluid…feel him like he often felt her. Taste him. She'd had the head of his penis in her mouth before, but she hadn't really known how to pleasure him.

Could she do so now?

Perhaps she could just lick him, as he'd licked through the folds of her sex. Would that draw more fluid out of the tip? Would that give him the same pleasure it had given her?

Glancing up at Nick, she saw that his eyes were closed, his breathing even. She turned her focus back to his penis, lowering her hand enough to touch the wetness that had gathered at the tip. Her breath caught in her throat when it jerked and throbbed. She brushed her fingers against it again. Feeling more daring, she curled her hand around the soft head and squeezed it in her hold. Doing this excited her so much that she thought her heartbeat might be loud enough to wake him.

Nick wrapped his hand around hers before she even processed that he was awake. Her face burned with shame at being caught touching him while he was unaware. But under that shame, there was only desire.

ABOUT THE AUTHOR

Deciding that life had far more to offer than a nine-to-five job, bickering children, and housework of any kind (unless she's on a deadline when everything is magically spotless), **TIFFANY CLARE** opened up her laptop to write stories she could get lost in. Tiffany writes sexy historical romances set in the Victorian era. She lives in Toronto with her husband, two kids, and two dogs. You can find out more about her and her books at www.tiffanyclare.com.

Discover great authors, exclusive offers, and more at hc.com.

Give in to your impulses . . .
Read on for a sneak peek at four brand-new
e-book original tales of romance
from HarperCollins.
Available now wherever e-books are sold.

BAD FOR ME
A ROCK CANYON, IDAHO NOVEL
By Codi Gary

WILD WITH YOU
INDEPENDENCE FALLS BOOK FOUR
By Sara Jane Stone

THE DEVILISH MR. DANVERS
THE RAKES OF FALLOW HALL SERIES
By Vivienne Lorret

NEED ME
A BROKE AND BEAUTIFUL NOVEL
By Tessa Bailey

An Excerpt from

BAD FOR ME
A Rock Canyon, Idaho Novel
by Codi Gary

Not so very long ago, trusting someone changed
Callie Jacobsen's life forever—and not in a fun
way. So when former Marine Everett Silverton
takes an interest in her, Callie's more than a little
wary. No matter how charming he is, men are
a bad idea. In fact, she's got the scars to prove
it. Everett will do whatever it takes to show her
she's safe with him—all she has to do is take
a chance, take a step . . . and take his hand.

Callie was bundled up in jeans and a puffy jacket, but her blonde curls had flown behind her in a mix of gold and crystal, flashing like streaks of lightning in the moonlight. Everett's hands had itched to get tangled up in that mass of curls as he imagined pulling her against him, kissing those sweet lips until she relaxed, breathing in her sweet scent and holding her. Forgetting all about why she was bad for him and why things could never work between them.

But before he could think better of it, he'd opened his mouth and told her she was beautiful.

Only instead of jumping into his arms at his compliment, she was now staring at him like he was a Peeping Tom.

Callie hopped off the swing like it was on fire. "Sorry. I just needed a minute alone."

"You do that a lot," he said, taking a step toward her.

"What?"

"Want to be alone."

"So?" she said irritably. "What's wrong with wanting a little privacy?"

"Nothing. It's just . . . when you spend so much time on your own, you start to get lonely."

"Why do you care if I get lonely? You want nothing to do with me, right?"

He kept getting closer to her. "I did say that, didn't I?"

"Yeah, you did, and I'm sorry to have bothered you—"

"Do you know why I holed up in my house with a book I've read at least a dozen times instead of having fun with my family and the rest of my hometown?" He had her nearly backed up against the tree and wanted to press himself into her and feel her soft curves.

"Because hayrides and haunted mazes creep you out?" she asked quietly.

"Hmm, no, I actually like Halloween," Everett said.

He was a foot away now, close enough to touch her.

"Then what?"

Everett leaned over her, his arm against the tree. He ignored the bark biting into the flesh of his arm and the warmth of her body calling him closer and said, "Because I was afraid if I saw you, I'd forget everything I know and everything I've been telling myself about you."

"Like what?" Her small, pink tongue darted out to lick her lips, and his cock grew heavy with need.

"That you're bad for me. That if I get involved with you it will destroy me."

He saw something flash across her face before her expression shuttered. Hurt? Longing?

"Then leave me alone."

He should. He should turn around and head back into his house, locking the door on her and his desire.

"I can't. I can't stop. You get to me, and I'm not strong enough to walk away."

A soft cry escaped her just before his mouth came down, claiming hers.

God, she tasted like fresh honey. His tongue slipped inside to sweep along hers, delving into her warmth as his hand came up and tangled in her hair. He wanted closer, wanted to surround himself with her scent, her body, and push all of the doubt from his mind.

Everett came out of his fog of desire when Callie shoved at his chest, turning her head away from him. She was breathing hard, panting.

"I am not a plaything. You keep saying that I'm not what you're looking for, but the truth is, I wasn't looking for you either. You popped into my life and sought me out. Then you learned something you don't like about me, and suddenly I'm this toxic thing you have to resist?" She pushed him hard, and he backed off. Every word was true, and it made him feel like an asshole.

Because he was acting like one.

"I've got a newsflash for you. Being self-righteous and judgmental doesn't make you a good person. You don't know me or what I've gone through, and yes, I've made some bad choices, but they were *mine*. I've taken responsibility for my addiction and changed. And that's all anyone can do, but I don't need you telling me you want me or that you're better than me."

In the distance, someone began calling her name, and Callie turned without saying anything else.

He couldn't let her go, not with that statement hanging between them. In three strides he was behind her, his hand on her arm. Callie stopped but didn't turn. Everett moved closer until the top of her head sat just under his chin; then he gently pulled her unruly curls back over her shoulder. She was still as a statue, even when he leaned down to whisper against her ear.

"You're right about everything, and I'm sorry. I'm a self-righteous prick, but I don't think I'm better than you. You just scare the hell out of me." Everett was so tempted to kiss the pulse point below her ear. "I never wanted to make you feel less-than, Callie, and hurting you is the last thing I want to do."

Seconds ticked by, and she said nothing. He was still scared shitless, but he couldn't ignore this thing between them. Distance and avoidance hadn't made his desire for her go away, hadn't lessened his infatuation, and her passionate speech only made him want to keep pushing, peeling back her layers until he could see right into her soul.

And just when he was sure he'd blown it, she shocked the hell out of him.

"What's the first thing?"

An Excerpt from

WILD WITH YOU
Independence Falls Book Four
by Sara Jane Stone

One night with a hero is just what she
needs. But more spells trouble . . .

Dr. Katherine "Kat" Arnold left Oregon and
never looked back at the town that failed
her as a child. But when a new patient from
Independence Falls joins her clinical trial, she
returns determined to show everyone in her
hometown how she has thrived—including
her high school crush, Brody Summers.

Brody parked his willpower in the hall and led the blond doctor through the door marked Pool. If his brothers saw him now they would laugh their asses off. He'd driven up to Portland to save two families—the stranded hikers and his own. Instead, he was taking an emergency room doctor who probably sent the men of New York City racing to the ER with a long list of fake ailments for a swim. But he couldn't walk away.

Beyond her beautiful face, he'd witnessed the relief in her eyes when she'd learned that the kid was safe. One look at her and something inside him had snapped. For the past few months he'd navigated a boatload of stress through choppy waters. And heck, he wanted a break.

His grip on her hand tightened, his mind focused on the here and now. The feel of her soft skin. The sound of her breathing, which quickened as they moved through each door. Every sound she made suggested her desire matched his, poised to spiral out of control.

A few paces into the warm and thankfully empty pool room, he turned to face her. Her breath caught as he stared into her eyes. Hesitation? Heck, maybe she'd read his mind and knew he wanted to bypass the pool, taking her straight to his bed.

"Brody, if you're having second thoughts, we can head back into the hall and call it a night. But if you want to stay and, um, celebrate, I promise I won't take advantage of you in your underwear." She spoke in a low tone that left part of his body hoping he could convince Little Miss Perfect to break her word.

"And if I can't make the same promise?" he challenged. The past twenty-four hours—heck, the past few months— had chipped away at his calm logic and left him emotionally rung out. He felt as if he was standing on the edge of wild.

"That won't be a problem."

The way she said those words—she might as well have wrapped her hand around his dick.

But instead of reaching for the part of his body threatening to wage a war against what remained of his common sense, she released his hand. "Wait here."

Brody watched her move toward a metal closet, taking in the pool room's layout. A line of lounge chairs filled the space to their left. Along the wall to the right stood a table stacked with towels. Next to the pile, a shower and a sign that clearly stated all guests swam at their own risk. Brody glanced at the long narrow pool that ran the length of the room. The stairs leading to the shallow end stood directly in front of him. And in the corner opposite the entrance sat a hot tub, steam rising from the swirling water.

He bit back a low growl as images filled his mind. Kat stripping off her clothes and joining him in the steaming water . . .

"Where are you going?" he asked, returning his attention to the present as she opened the door. She rummaged for a moment and turned around, triumphant.

"To find this." She held up a sign that read POOL CLOSED.

Her heels clicked against the cement pool deck as she headed to the door. Poking her head out, she scanned the hall and then slipped the sign into place.

"Just in case someone else wants to celebrate," she said.

"You know all the tricks," he murmured. "Have you done this before?"

"When I was a teenager, I occasionally snuck into places I wasn't supposed to be. I got caught once and learned my lesson. Most people obey a Closed sign."

She settled onto a lounge chair. Planting her palms on the cushion, she leaned back and crossed the long legs he'd admired earlier while lying at her feet. Her skirt slid up her thighs, stopping short of offering a peekaboo glance underneath.

"You're just going to sit there and watch?"

"I can close my eyes while you undress if you're feeling shy. But I can't promise I won't peek."

He tried to remember the last time a woman had toyed with him and came up blank. Back home, he might as well have had the word "serious" tattooed on his forehead. Women looked at him and saw long-term. And yeah, he liked being that guy, the one people knew they could count on. When it came to his family, he wouldn't have it any other way. But sometimes—like when he wanted a chance to explore a beautiful blonde's long legs without worrying about the long-term picture—it was just plain lonely.

"I'm not shy," he said.

"Then lose the clothes, Brody."

He pulled his Moore Timber T-shirt over his head and

tossed it aside. Stealing a glance at his audience, he saw her green eyes widen. She uncrossed her legs, drawing his attention to the smooth skin of her thighs. His gaze traveled up her body, leaving him wondering what lie beneath her silky shirt.

"I hope you're not shy," he said, his voice low and wanting, a solid reflection of how he felt. "Because I want to watch."

An Excerpt from

THE DEVILISH MR. DANVERS
The Rakes of Fallow Hall Series
by Vivienne Lorret

When Hedley Sinclair inherits Greyson Park, she finally has a chance at a real life. The only person standing in her way is Rafe Danvers— her handsome neighbor who also claims ownership over the crumbling estate. Rafe is determined to take back what's his—even if it means being a bit devilish. Knowing the stipulations of her inheritance, he decides to find her a husband. The only problem is, he can't seem to stop seducing her. In fact, he can't seem to stop falling in love with her.

"A young woman in society usually flirts when given the opportunity."

How was she supposed to flirt when she could barely think? He stood close enough that she could feel the alluring heat rising from his body. She drew in a breath in an effort to think of a response. When she did, however, her nostrils filled with a pleasant scent that only made her want to draw in another breath. It was *his* fragrance. From their previous encounter, she recognized the woodsy essence and a trace of sweet smoke.

Hedley caught herself rocking onto the balls of her feet to get closer, but then quickly fell back onto her heels. She swallowed, her throat suddenly dry. "I am not in society. Nor am I likely to be. Therefore, I have no reason to flirt."

"You don't need a reason." He leaned in, his voice low. The angular cut of his side-whiskers seemed to direct her gaze toward his mouth. "Flirting is a skill. You use it to get what you want."

Hedley forgot why she'd come here . . . *to get what you want. . .*

The more she stared at Rafe's mouth, the heavier her eyelids seemed to weigh. Why was she suddenly so tired? Perhaps it *was* too early to pay a call. Or perhaps it was because he stood so close that his warmth blanketed her. It would take only a single step to rest her head against his shoulder. "Like a type of currency used in society?"

"An astute observation." He grinned.

She was definitely out of her element. The least she could do was *try* to keep her wits about her. "Then, I should assume that you want something from me."

He moved closer, but she dared not imagine that he was under the same trance. No, he was far too skilled in the ways of society for that.

Even so, the curve of his knuckles brushed her cheek. "What shade of pink do you suppose this is?"

"And that was a terrible change of topic." Believing that he was speaking of one of the colored-glass vases in the cabinet, she looked them over. She found deep red, the color of merlot, a blue vase, bright and clear as a summer sky, and daffodil yellow, among other hues. "Besides, I see no pink."

"No, this color. Here." His thumb caressed her cheek, his fingers settling beneath her jaw.

Was it possible for a man to have eyelashes that looked as if they were smudged with soot, all soft and curled up at the ends? It didn't seem possible to her. Yet, that's exactly what she saw as he studied her. Knowing that her skin had betrayed her thoughts in a blush should make her want to shy away. Yet, she'd gone too long without being noticed to feel an ounce of shame. Instead, she reveled in the attentiveness of his gaze, the nearness and warmth of his body, and the contact of his flesh on hers—even if it was a false show for him.

While not entirely certain that he expected her to answer, she indulged him. "Some roses are pink."

"True." He tilted her chin. Four thin, horizontal lines appeared above the bridge of his nose as if he truly were studying her. "Though when I think of rosy pink, it is darker, redder, than this."

She tasted his breath on her lips. Other than their clumsy spill on the ice, this was the closest she'd ever been to a man. Heat poured from his body, sweeping over her, compelling her to draw nearer to the source. She couldn't help it.

"Berries are sometimes pink," she whispered, wondering if he could feel her breath as well.

He licked his lips. "Only *unripe* berries are pink, and you are a most decidedly ripe fruit, sweeting."

The tone of his voice changed ever so slightly. The silky timbre turned deeper, indulgent, like slipping into a pair of warm velvet slippers.

She wanted to sink into that sound. "Pink carnations."

"Yes. That's it." His hand slipped away. "A carnation pink blush, and berry-stained lips."

Missing the contact, her chin tilted of its own accord. His gaze slowly dipped to her mouth. Whatever this game was, she wanted it to continue. "Is this a lesson in flirting or is the color of actual importance?"

Abruptly, he turned from her and headed toward a tasseled bell-pull on the far wall. It was almost as if he suddenly wanted to put as much distance between them as possible.

She had her answer. He was only flirting in order to gain something. The only thing she possessed that Rafe Danvers wanted, however, was not for sale. No matter how tempting the currency, she would not give him Greyson Park.

An Excerpt from

NEED ME
A Broke and Beautiful Novel
by *Tessa Bailey*

In the second *Broke and Beautiful* novel,
college student Honey Perribow can't
stop fantasizing about her sexy, young
English professor, Ben Dawson . . . and
forbidden love has never been so hot.

When choosing the perfect panties for a seduction, one couldn't be too selective. Careful consideration had to be given to the cut, the style, and, most importantly, the almighty color. Honey Perribow rifled through her underwear drawer from her position on the rug, picking up and discarding undies with the efficiency required of premed students the world over. Red silk was a little too on the nose. It didn't give the guy any credit. Blue? Hinted at mood swings. Yellow with a strawberry pattern . . . *what am I, five?*

There was no help for her. She had to call in the big guns. "Roxy!"

Her roommate of one month propped a hip on the inside of Honey's door a moment later, biting into a piece of toast. "Did you lose your indoor voice in that pile of underpants?"

"What color would you wear if you wanted to seduce your English teacher?"

The toast paused halfway to Roxy's mouth. "Aw, shit. Today is the day?"

Honey took a deep breath and nodded. "I've finally worked up the nerve. No more hiding under my hoodie in the back row. Professor Dawson is going down to Honey town."

"How long have you been waiting to say that?"

"A while. How was my delivery?"

"Not too shabby." Roxy shoved the remainder of the toast in her mouth and plopped down onto the floor, cross-legged, eyeballing the mountain of panties. In the month since they'd become roommates in one of the oddest interview processes of all time, they'd formed a friendship that sometimes seemed as if they were feeling their way in the dark. Honey could still sense some hesitancy on Roxy's part to open up completely, but Roxy's new boyfriend, Louis, seemed to be unlocking a new part of her. Considering Roxy had hidden out in her room at the outset, commiserating over panties was a vast improvement. "All right. So, we know he's studious. He teaches Intro to Literary Theory. How does he dress?"

Honey hid her swoon by turning and pressing her face into the rug. "He has this tweed jacket. It's like a greenish-brown, which should be ugly, but it looks so dang *amazing* on him. If I got up close, I bet it would smell like honest-to-goodness man mixed up with old book leather. He keeps candy in the pockets, too. I can't tell from the back of the room which kind of candy he always pops into his mouth, but if I had to guess, I'd say butterscotch. So the jacket might have a hint of butterscotch smell going on, too."

"Are you telling me *tweed* inspired all that?"

"It's crazy, right? I know it. I can hear myself." Honey rolled back over and stared up at the ceiling. In the few weeks since she'd started courses at Columbia University, Professor Dawson had wiggled his way under her skin like a splinter from a yellow poplar tree. No one back home in Bloomfield, Kentucky, would ever have accused her of being shy. In fact, they would have laughed over the very suggestion. But the day